THE HALLOWED FORSAKEN

FIRST BOOK OF THE ARADIAN

J.A. PETTINGALE

AD LUCEM

FANTASY PUBLISHING

British Library Cataloguing in Publication Data
A catalogue record for this book is available from the British Library.

ISBN: 978-1-8383054-0-6

Printed in the UK

DEDICATION

To Emilie and Leah, without whom this story would not exist.

"But man, proud man,
Drest in a little brief authority,
Most ignorant of what he's most assured,
His glassy essence, like an angry ape,
Plays such fantastic tricks before high heaven
As make the angels weep."

William Shakespeare, *Measure for Measure*

1 - The Perfect Image

───~~~───

Patience had never been Sophie's strong suit. So much to do and so little time to do it. She had books to read, TV to watch, and it had never once occurred to her that things should take more than a couple of seconds to get going. *The plague of an on-demand culture*, she mused, a complex notion for a girl of sixteen, reflecting on the impatient whims of the modern teen.

Her bedroom perfectly reflected the house to which it belonged. Affluence and grandeur took pride of place. Beyond her queen-sized bed and walk-in wardrobe, an imposing bookcase housed endless novels; pages filled with stories that reflected her refusal to be that *common cheerleader*, or so she liked to think. Lovecraft and Kantian ethics dominated the dark oak encasement and created the perfect image of an intellectual that she so desired. Although, it had been some time since she'd actually read one of them.

A timid tap at the door echoed around the room, and Sophie sat up on her bed, grumpy to have been disturbed from her reflection. She quelled her displeasure and spoke lightly.

"Enter."

The door opened cautiously and a young maidservant poked her head and half a shoulder into the room. She made to speak, then hesitated and took a short breath. Sophie's gracious demeanour cracked slightly.

"Well, go on then, what is it?"

The maid leaned in a little more and the door made the creaking sound that always caused Sophie to grate her teeth.

"I... was just coming to ask if you're ready for church, Miss Sophie?"

"Of course I'm ready!" Sophie snapped, the pretence of patience gone. She glowered at the maid. "You should know I'm always prepared and on time. It is only proper."

The poor girl's eyes grew wide and she gripped the door a little tighter.

"Yes, of course, *I know that,* Miss Sophie... your mother... was asking."

"Well, tell her yes, I'm ready."

The maid nodded and hastily retreated.

These servants, Sophie thought, *always so timid.*

Despite her curt response, Sophie checked her appearance in the full-length mirror that stood as proudly as herself in the corner of the room. *All seems to be in order,* she thought, adjusting the waistband of her light green summer dress. The colour complimented her emerald eyes, and the polka dot pattern accentuated the raven locks that hung just past her shoulders. She slipped her bare feet into some matching green ballet flats and did a little jump and tap to check that nothing was loose.

She was no stranger to going to church, her family attended every Sunday, but for some inexplicable reason, today her mother was taking extra precautions to check that she was prompt and presentable. She had no qualms with this, she always loved to attract some eyes, but sending the maid to check on her... why the sudden attention?

As if echoing the thought, her bedroom door swung open – this time with a graceful ferocity. A woman entered with a long stride, her heels clicking on the wooden boards. Sophie spun to face her.

"Good morning, Mother."

"Good morning, my dear."

Cecilia Lockwood had an immense presence, a naturally ostentatious air that followed wherever she went.

"Dear, we're leaving soon. You had better be ready by the time I call you to the car."

"Oh, don't worry Mother, I'm ready now!" Sophie smiled

"Don't be silly – not in that pitiful servant's gown. Put on something proper; you'll embarrass us."

With one simple remark and the slight wave of a dismissive hand, Sophie's heart sank. Her eyes flickered downward for a moment before returning to her mother's gaze.

"Yes, Mother... I'll be ready."

Cecilia gave a curt upward nod, jutting her chin forward before turning to leave. Sophie dared to ask… "Mother?"

She turned her head slightly to look back.

"Yes?"

"Will Father be joining us?" Sophie's confidence wilted even as she spoke.

"Your father will meet us there. Now get changed."

Without another word, she left before Sophie could think about prolonging the encounter – not that she wanted to.

Glad for the respite from her mother's severe expectations, she let her shoulders slump and quickly closed the door.

Maybe one day I'll manage to impress her? she thought gloomily, kicking off the wretched shoes and returning to her wardrobe.

The dark oak sliding door revealed an array of extravagant dresses – outfits for any occasion or weather, and then some. It was a sight that always pleased her.

Carefully, she removed a fashionable black knee-length dress, with layers of fabric overlapping to give it texture. She changed into it and stepped back in front of the mirror. She truly hoped that this would pass under the captious eye of her mother.

Satisfied, she went to the window and knelt on the generous sill to look outside. She let her feet hang behind her and pressed her palms flat on the cool glass. It was something she'd done ever since she was a child – to survey the acres of land she was heir to; to watch the little people work and till the land that would be hers. From her lofty vantage point the estate workers seemed so modest and feeble, perspective creating the illusion that she could hold them in her upturned hand. She had always liked that thought.

Sophie brought up a hand to shield her eyes from the Georgian sun that assailed her bedroom so intrusively in these early mornings. As blinding as it was, she enjoyed the effect it had on her room – making it even more visually striking. The light flooded through the great window and seemed to be absorbed by the black wooden floor, frames and wall paint. At the same time, it was reflected back by the blindingly white crisp linen of her bed and from the spines of her book collection. Sophie liked to fantasise that anyone entering the room to be greeted by this dazzling assault on the senses would attribute it to her radiant beauty. But it was just the contrast between light and dark, even she had to admit that.

She gazed out of the window for quite some time before seeing "him" again. Sophie couldn't remember the actual name of the chauffeur and general groundsman, but he always unsettled her. His complexion was of a sickly pallor and when he walked, he moved with such grace that it almost seemed unnatural. He was standing beside her mother's Mercedes-Benz S-Class, a fine piece of modern engineering with an extravagant price tag.

The car and the aberrant man waited patiently on the gravel driveway. Sophie watched him standing idly, looking down the estate road. What was that line her parents always said about him? She couldn't quite drag it from the cloud of thoughts that occupied the recesses of her mind. The thought was almost in reach when she spied her mother parading out of the pristine, tinted glass doorway of the house, her usual snide smile in place. Before Sophie could react, her mother turned on the spot with the refined movement of an experienced dancer and set her eyes upon the window of Sophie's bedroom on the third floor. Piercing cerulean eyes burrowed deep, critical fissures into Sophie's chest and her body automatically lurched as she noted a single beckoning finger.

Sophie leaped across her bedroom floor and forced her feet into some black mid heels, before almost staggering out of the room – a travesty if any servant saw her – but she didn't have time to concern herself with such vexations.

Hurriedly, she made her way across the balcony landing, moving quickly while attempting to retain as much dignity as possible. She passed the doors to the second living space and her parents' bedroom that she knew so well, and descended the two-way marble staircase, her hand gently sliding down the burnished banister.

Reaching the ground floor, her head automatically inclined downwards. She caught sight of her mother's reflection in the polished marble, illuminated by light pouring in from the open front door. She quickly flicked her head upwards and corrected her hurried step, strutting up to Cecilia, now standing in the doorway, watching her daughter approach with a probing stare.

"It's time to go dear. You seem more suitably prepared for the occasion I see."

Respectful confirmation was given as Cecilia took her daughter's hand, guiding her to the prepared car which growled to life when mother and daughter neared. Sophie heard the front door click shut behind her and allowed herself to be led around to the left-hand side of the vehicle. The chauffeur opened the leaden rear passenger door of the Mercedes and in a single fluid gesture, motioned for her to settle herself comfortably inside.

Sophie slid the seatbelt into the lock and lay her head against the rest behind her. Her mother mirrored the movement effortlessly. Glancing in her direction, Sophie's hunger to mirror her mother's flawless demeanour only grew each time she watched Cecilia Lockwood perform any action. Each movement was purposeful, all of them equally vital pieces in an intricate mosaic of perception, designed for the eyes of others.

The car doors closed with a heavy thud and it began its crawl down the driveway, the familiar crunch of tyres over gravel eradicating the birdsong in the grounds. Minutes passed before the gate to the Lockwood estate loomed in the distance. The substantial black bars of the gate shifted and turned inwards as the car approached and passed through them. Like flicking a switch, the car gained a sudden momentum, with an immediacy that seemed somewhat unnecessary. Sophie always revelled in the sheer speed at which she was driven down the long country roads of north Georgia state.

Twenty minutes into their silent journey, Sophie watched as their local Evangelical church vanished behind them, out of sight within seconds of passing it. She arched a perplexed eyebrow before turning to her mother.

"We missed the turning Mother! Where are we going?" Her tone was urgent, but respectful.

Nonchalantly, her mother turned to look out of the back window.

"Oh yes, we aren't visiting our usual church today." She turned back around, failing to elaborate.

Sophie looked from side to side, unsatisfied.

"Where are we going instead?"

"A more *exclusive* church. You're old enough to join me and your father there now."

"Exclusive?" Sophie persisted, still seeking clarity.

Cecilia gave a curt nod.

"Indeed. Attendance is only permissible by direct reference or relation. Melissa and Devon are members. You know them. Everyone is eager to meet and welcome you."

All the while, her mother kept her eyes on the road ahead, but Sophie sat a little straighter with newfound alacrity.

People are practically dying to meet me, she exaggerated in her mind, then surmised, *Maybe I really am finally getting her approval if I can join her new church club.*

The car purred on as Sophie observed the hills and trees roll by. A smile spread across her face as she reflected upon the situation. The chauffeur drove silently and turned the car with minimal inflections of his wrists and fingers. Truthfully, the car seemed to possess more personality than the man who operated it, and the thought amused her greatly.

They had been travelling for close to an hour when a deafening, inexplicable pop filled the air, jerking Sophie from her soothing reverie. She instinctively sought her mother's hand and gripped it tightly. After the initial shock of the sound, her mother composed herself swiftly and gestured for the chauffeur to pull over to the side of the road. With his preternatural poise, he glided smoothly to a halt and exited the vehicle. Sophie watched him kneel down to inspect the right-hand rear wheel of their transport.

Cecilia exited the vehicle and ushered her daughter out, bidding her stand at a respectably safe distance from the road. She turned to accost her driver.

"You mindless simpleton! How have you managed this?" Cecilia seethed at him.

He seemed entirely indifferent to his employer's harsh words.

Sophie looked at the tyre he was now removing. A segment of it had somehow fulminated under some considerable heat. Parts of the rubber dripped and solidified on the road. She couldn't believe that such grievous and profound damage had been caused by unsteady driving.

Her mother rolled her eyes, muttered more displeased comments, then turned on her heels, clutching Sophie's hand tightly

"No matter... it isn't too far from here. Come dear, let us leave this working buffoon to his toils and we shall walk the rest of the way."

Sophie sighed inwardly and fell in alongside her mother's imperious stride.

These shoes were made to look good on me, they're not for walking down the side of a road! she lamented.

After ten minutes of walking along the path her legs began to protest. Just as she was opening her mouth to raise the classic childish query, she noticed a small, dispersed collection of exorbitant cars ahead. They were gathered around a focal point that seemed to be a clearing in the trees, with a dirt track shepherding away from them.

"Ah, we're here. Excellent," Cecilia chimed.

Her mother adjusted her hold on Sophie's hand and continued to traverse the road which moved from tarmac to simple dirt and hard packed soil.

At the head of the track lay a large but visually uninspiring – even ramshackle – church building. Sophie was exquisitely, unimpressed.

2 - The Cult of the Deorum

Traversing the dirt track, Sophie frowned at the repugnant structure alleged to be the "exclusive" church her mother had spoken of. Its single short steeple was a little lopsided and crumbling from weather corrosion. The traditional stained-glass windows were no less dispirited, thickset mire lathering their surface, successfully obscuring the images suffocating beneath.

The entire building appeared to be practically derelict, except for one feature. Standing at what looked to be twice Sophie's height, the main door to the church seemed fortified and rejuvenated compared to its surroundings. Its wooden surface was polished and adorned with riveted semicircles, connected by darkened iron braces.

Mother and daughter approached the edifice via the surrounding cemetery in the glade. Headstones of a bygone age were arranged in no particular fashion within the low, fragmented curtain wall. Sophie took to reading the epitaphs with a mixture of disquietude and curiosity. She noted that all the dates on the graves she'd seen were from the 19th Century or earlier. *Whatever is this place?* she wondered.

Then she stopped.

She was almost at the door, but was halted by a sudden deep misgiving about continuing onward. The door itself seemed to exude trepidation. Was it her imagination, or did it groan and warp as if taking a breath? Telling herself that this was impossible and not to be stupid, she was nevertheless struck by the impression that the door was drawing her in, threatening to engulf her. A bedevilling anxiety forced its way through her body, and she noticed her palm become clammy in her mother's hand. A sharp urge to take flight besieged her, assaulting her good sense. Natural psychological processes at their most primitive begged her to flee, but her mother's grip was like iron.

Then, a distraction across the glade. Sophie glimpsed movement in the tree line and turned her head a fraction. *What was that?* Some kind of animal prowling in the woods? This new potential threat further assaulted her primeval intuition and her inner conflict reached a peak. Pupils dilated and cheeks flushed, she forced out a deep breath and willed her gaze to return to the door. The timbers now seemed to have been restored to their regular structure and the feeling of foreboding in Sophie's gut was muted as she fought to batter it down.

Keenly aware of the consequences of vexing her mother, either through hesitation or disobedience, Sophie steeled herself.

No, she thought, *I'm better than this fear. I'm a Lockwood. I command a room with presence, just like Mother.*

Sophie closed her eyes for what felt to her like eons, then took a step forward. She glanced at her mother and was surprised to see her looking proud, gratified, as if she knew what had just occurred.

Vacillation conquered, Sophie allowed her mother to guide her up the steps to the door. Cecilia took hold of the iron knocker and gave two short, light raps. These were followed by a further two, slower, more substantial blows. A code? The sound echoed for a second before being replaced by a wounded cry from the door's hinges, their true age emphasised.

The door opened partially and the upper body of a man appeared. He was squat and stout, his posture hunched and craven. Or perhaps it merely reflected his desire to prove just how low he could stoop before Cecilia.

"Mrs Lockwood, it's most wonderful to have you return for today's service. A true honour as always."

"Certainly," Cecilia waved dismissively. "Has my husband arrived?"

The man looked exhilarated to be addressed with more than a curt greeting.

"Oh yes, he arrived most prudently early Mrs Lockwood. He always is…"

"Yes, yes, thank you." Cecilia brushed past the man, sending him staggering backward a step, instantly obscured from view.

Sophie always marvelled at her mother's adeptness at disregarding those she considered below her. Seeking to emulate her, it was an art she was in the process of refining herself, but had not entirely mastered. She was often intimidated by those taller and more imposing than herself.

With a final suspicious glance at the glade, Sophie stepped over the threshold of the door that had inspired such distress in her. Inside, as her eyes adjusted to the change of light, pure astonishment was the only reaction she could ascribe to her new surroundings. Compared to the dilapidated exterior of the church, the interior had a sleek, lavish feel to it. Extensive dark oak pews were positioned in two rows down the large open space, bisected by an aisle that ran between them. An opulent wine-coloured carpet with gold edging traversed its length, and smooth, high-reaching pillars punctuated the centre aisle; three on each side, all evenly spaced for structural support.

Drawing the majority of her attention, however, were the windows that presided over the contents of the church, positioned above tenebrous doors that presumably led to other rooms. The intricately designed stained glass panes cast themselves over the nave, their sheer magnitude presumably designed to suppress and humble any worshipper who found themselves within the church walls. In contrast to the usual vivid, varied colours of a Christian church, however, each panel reflected a similar shade of purple, be it a light violet or deep indigo. The effect was to infuse every inch of the nave with a purple haze. Even the air itself seemed to possess an amaranthine hue.

She walked on, incredulous at her surroundings. Never had she seen such petrifying elegance and beauty in one room. Its aura banished any semblance of fear left within her, leaving only wonder. As she took in its impressive vista, she realised her pace had slowed and her mother was now markedly ahead, lowering herself softly onto a front row pew with her usual refined grace. Sophie hastened to her side and, after meandering around two worshippers locked in heated debate, she sat down.

"I'd forgotten what a staggering sight this must be for your first time dear," her mother intoned as she sat calmly, her hands in her lap.

"Yes, it's… it's amazing!" Sophie replied, the words slothful in leaving her mouth. "When do I get to meet everyone?"

"Keep to yourself for now dear. Your moment will come once proceedings begin."

Cecilia cast a knowing glance to the pulpit at the head of the immense structure. It was dark oak with gold plating decorating its edges, similar to the other wooden structures of the room. Sophie caught the glance and matched it, wondering if it meant what she thought it did.

Am I expected to introduce myself in front of everyone? To say a few words? I wouldn't even know what to say!

Silently she panicked a little, yet the thought of the attention she would garner intoxicated her.

Heeding her mother's words, Sophie sat patiently, her hands neatly nested in her lap. The low murmurings of the worshippers echoed in the rafters and she couldn't help but observe the people she would soon become acquainted with. At the far end of the nave she spied the Dinwoods, the wealthy descendants of southern plantation slavers. They were engaged in what appeared to be a riveting discussion with Melissa and Devon Perristone, present as her mother had confirmed they would be. The two families were the influential, *almost as prosperous*, neighbours of the Lockwoods. She thoroughly enjoyed being slightly more well-to-do than the children next door.

Sophie continued her inspection of the other wealthy families, all pristinely dressed. She recognised faces from various social gatherings and country club meetings over the years. *I have really made it into the big time now*, she glowed, easing back around to face forward.

Now her attention fell upon the large stone altar situated alongside the pulpit. Intricately carved patterns edged its smooth surface and atop were placed three boxes in a systemised fashion. Before she could ponder what they might contain, the triptych that dominated the back wall purloined her attention entirely. Sophie gazed again at the blending shades of purple stained glass, but this pivotal piece was different to the others. The two side segments used a lighter grey palette and presented a scene of featureless worshippers supplicating before the central glass frame, which itself depicted three towering figures. They were equally featureless apart from their magnificently petrifying wings that spread out to encompass all, created from a mosaic of intense white glass that dominated the surrounding images with its glare.

For the first time Sophie wondered how the light pierced the glass so keenly, given the sheer defilement of their appearance on the outside. She chastised herself for not thinking of it sooner, but the thought came and went like a wave breaking on the shore.

Half an hour passed and Sophie was growing increasingly bored. The pride that drove her mother to ruthlessly maintain their image at all times denied her the privilege of playing on her phone while she waited, sat neglected at the bottom of her mother's Birkin bag.

A moment later, however, conversations around the building began to cease. Families took seats scattered around the nave and left ample space between each grouping. It gave the impression of a plutocratic gathering of noble families, preparing to determine the proceeding steps of a grand republic, and Sophie shuffled closer to her mother as the lights seemed to dim automatically, allowing the mauve air to consume the room.

"I thought Father was going to be joining us?" Sophie whispered in her mother's ear.

"Hush, dear." Cecilia kept her eyes focused forward on the pulpit, dismissing her daughter. Sophie knew better than to protest.

The same doorman who had greeted them ambled down the centre aisle and Sophie watched as he crossed in front of the altar and moved to open a side door. Before he had opportunity, the door was vigorously forced open from the other side. The poor man was propelled backwards as Vincent Lockwood strode into the body of the church.

Every eye in the room tracked his movement past the altar to ascend the pulpit, attention unwavering. The entire gathering seemed held in a single moment of tension. Lockwood reached the top and took in a heavy breath. As he exhaled, the tension in the room dissipated as easily as the air from his lungs. He began to address the worshipers in the soothing voice Sophie knew so well. The voice that could walk across water and mollify any resentment, no matter how grave.

"Friends! Family, brothers and sisters… welcome to this *very* special occasion."

His cadence was skilfully honed by years of oration. He held the room with a well-practised pace – tempered yet deliberate, frequent inflections emphasising carefully selected words.

"Today, is a *very* special day," he continued, his hands resting on the railing before him. "For today is the anniversary of the day those *vermin*, the traitorous lesser gods, *banished* our lords, oh, so long ago."

Sophie listened intently. The subject of the speech was entirely lost on her, but the manner in which it was given captured her attention regardless.

"We *dedicate* our hearts, our very *souls* to our most unspeakable champions. But *today*…" – his hand gestures became more impassioned – "…my beautiful wife and I are willing to truly present our *devotion*. Devotion manifest in the most imperious of ways."

The worshippers murmured amongst themselves. Was it confusion or anticipation? Sophie couldn't tell.

Vincent made his way down the pulpit steps and stood before the altar as the obsequious doorman hurriedly transferred the three small boxes to a side table, keeping his head bowed. Sophie could do nothing but stare openly as her father's gaze swept across the crowd and ended, firmly meeting hers.

"Sophie, my darling, come on up."

He gestured for her to come forward with a twinkle in his eye, a sharp grin across his clean-shaven face. Sophie's heart pounded irregular rhythms in her chest. Her moment had come. Her mother gently encouraged her and Sophie slid out of the pew, rushing forward with a mixture of pride and trepidation. Her father wrapped an encompassing arm around her shoulder as she took her place beside him.

"My *very own* daughter, before you all, will present her undying commitment to the Deorum, our masters. She is *willing* to take the passage! To unite with an untethered entity of our lords!"

At this declaration, the worshippers rose to their feet and cheered. Even Cecilia elegantly clapped her fingers into the opposite palm with a smile of admiration and pride, directed towards Sophie.

The glory, the pure gratification of the attention of these people overwhelmed Sophie. They represented everything she desired to become. Focusing her mind once more, her eyes darted up at her father who loomed over her, hand still firmly on her shoulder.

"What happens now, Father?"

Her voice was almost lost in the bellows of the worshippers.

"Follow my instructions and soon you'll feel the embrace of our lord's warmth *forevermore.*"

Vincent gently stroked his hand through Sophie's hair and she gave him a wide grin.

"Father... I don't understand the history of our lords, or who they are. Will... will that be a problem?"

"*Of course* not, my darling. You will know everything soon enough."

Sophie nodded.

Overwhelmed by the moment, and of her own volition, she then found herself obeying her father's directive to lie down on the stone altar. Her mind raced, awash with a surge of confusion.

What happens now? she wondered. *Now comes, what… my… my baptising? Do they do that here? Do their… my gods baptise? I suppose it's time to find out.*

She felt lost. Reassured by her father's presence, she smiled up at him as he stood beside the altar. But he returned her look with a laconic grin – all teeth and no warmth now. He grasped her left wrist and guided her arm upward to an intricately carved sigil in the top left corner of the altar. As her skin made contact with the marking, she felt an attraction – an invisible pressure on her wrist that restricted its movement to naught, fixing her hand in place.

Before she could express her surprise, her father had repeated the process with her free arm, and the toxicant of proud confidence left her. Sophie struggled a little, attempting to lift her wrists from the table, only to be met with an increase of pressure. A twang of pain ran up her arm.

"Father, what's happening? Why can't I move my hands?"

Fear sought to overwhelm her. In an insistent, higher pitched voice she pleaded,

"Father! What are you doing?"

The worshippers continued their ballyhooing and her protests were swallowed in the roar. Sophie could only watch in abject terror as her father removed her shoes and fixed her ankles, uncomfortably flat, in the two remaining corners. Her breath became short and fast. Her emerald eyes flitted from focus to focus – her father, the strange building, the enraptured congregation spun by.

Discomposure and anxiety clashed, and adrenaline flooded her body. Sophie attempted to thrash from side to side to free herself, but to no avail. Vincent Lockwood looked down upon her with a vexation in his eye. In a final treacherous act, he used one finger pressed firmly to her forehead and Sophie's head was pinned to the altar, imprisoned, her freedom entirely curtailed.

Restricted, deceived and without a hope, she could do nothing but stare at the ceiling. A painting covered the entirety of its surface. It was one of the *Deorum* her father had mentioned in his speech. Its skin had an awful pallor and wings grew from its back at unnatural angles, curling around towards its face – or simply its head, for it had no real face. It was featureless apart from closed slits for eyes and a small open mouth that resembled the soulless mouth of a cave.

Sophie heard the sound of a latch being flicked open. An attempt to look around was in vain, but presently her father appeared into view, a glinting ceremonial dagger in his grasp, the handle black and hilt golden. Her voice was merely a whisper in the air when Sophie begged.

"Daddy... *please*..."

She sniffled up at an unmoved, uncaring face.

"It's time to embrace your saviours, darling. This is what you've been *waiting for.*"

An agonised scream burst from Sophie's lips as the tip of the blade pierced the skin of her left forearm. She felt the blade trace upwards and her scream peaked at new heights. White hot pain struck like lightning and Sophie frantically wiggled her fingers and toes. She could do nothing more to resist.

The image of the god peering down at her seemed to shift. Sophie blinked away tears of disbelief as the creature's clawed fingers seemed to transform into three dimensions and flex. The throbbing in her arm grew increasingly tortuous, and through bared teeth she was compelled to gaze at the aberration as her father continued his grim carving. The claw was indeed lifting away from the surface of the painting, followed by the creature's head, then shoulders. Harrowingly, it wrenched itself out of the curved ceiling inch by inch. The great strain of the creature's movements was evident as it screeched and clawed at the surrounding beams, splintering a few with its talons in a single slash.

Sophie's psychological processes were overloaded by the sheer magnitude of the beast, writhing its way towards her. Coupled with the inconceivability of her situation, her sanity seemed to turn in on itself and she forgot how to function. The pain spiked and she screamed, but her own voice sounded far away, as if it belonged to someone else. The creature's illogical wings spread out as its torso fully clawed itself out of the painting. Now those talons reached ravenously for her, but even this action seemed far away as her vision blackened.

Sophie felt betrayed, hurt, lost.

No more.

Blackness.

Welcoming darkness was all she felt.

Her thoughts were a distant echo, along with the world.

The only impression her broken mind could form was an acceptance that this was how she died…

Then…

As if charged by a defibrillator, Sophie was electrified back to conscious reality as a calamitous explosion blew the church doors off their hinges. The creature screeched once more before being frozen in place; trapped and unable to make further progress towards her. Her father was still beside her, the knife lying on the altar, slick with blood, but a young voice rang out.

"I OBJECT!"

All eyes were fixed on a new figure in the devastated entrance. At last, Sophie managed to turn her head weakly to the side. There she saw a young woman with multiple figures behind her. The woman spoke.

"Oh… this is definitely *not* a wedding!"

3 – Officer Pierce Reporting

———✦———

An incredible groan filled the bedroom and blended with the shrill ringing of a phone alarm. Sariyah sat up in bed, cursed loudly at no one in particular, and swiftly silenced the alarm with the tap of a finger. It was Sunday morning and only her second week back working in the Adytum, after what felt like a lifetime away. She let out a long exhale and attempted to quiet her frantic mind, just as she had been taught. She let her anxieties rush out with the air from her lungs and pictured them doing so.

"You're an officer now, protecting mortals and innocents from the magical world, one bad guy at a time. You're doing pretty good for yourself, so don't you forget it."

She slipped out of bed and began to carefully brush her hair in an undersized mirror, straining and hunching unnaturally to suitably view her work. The tug of the brush through her hair was the only sound in the room, so her mind began to wander.

The title of official Adytum Officer, with all of its perks, didn't come without a degree of stress and responsibility. Yes, it commanded respect from her peers – and that pleased her significantly – but the respect was afforded begrudgingly. Most of her fellow Sorcerers had not taken to her prolonged "vacation" with any form of grace or leniency. However, she had proven her natural aptitude for, and connection to magic time again. Enough to be reinstated by the Consuls, only one of which held any degree of sympathy for her case.

"I *deserve* to be here," she told herself. "I've worked harder than those other indolent goldbricks."

Unsuccessfully, Sariyah attempted to quell her frustration at her colleagues' contempt for her. Her mind brimmed with memories and emotion. Quiet voices echoed inside, disrupting the steady rhythm of the brush – voices that would soon turn to cries of anguish and a harrowing silence to follow. A veteran of her affliction, Sariyah recognised the impending, overwhelming distress and unlocked her phone without hesitation. Beginning to sing along to *Somethin' Stupid*, she suppressed the unwanted intrusion before it could take hold.

As the song went into the second chorus, Sariyah twirled on the spot and began to use her brush as a microphone, eyes closed, just her and the music. This brought a welcome smile. She tittered to herself thinking how a smile a day could keep the doctor away… or was it an apple? Now she was hungry.

She dressed briskly before heading downstairs to her cramped, darkened kitchen, still winsomely accompanying the artist playing out of the phone in her back pocket. The house she was renting while stationed in Atlanta possessed a reassuring inadequacy. She much preferred a home that was explicitly average for the area. Not opulent enough to entice a passer-by, but not so decrepit as to attract disdainful attention. While rifling through the cupboards hunting for a light breakfast, the music was interrupted as her phone rang sharply. Sariyah let out a sigh and answered the call.

"I thought I had until 8:00am before I had to meet you?" she chimed before the caller had a chance to speak. A pause was followed by a man's unimpressed response.

"Yes, and now it's 8:15am. Hurry up or we're going to miss our opportunity." He ended his reprove with a short chuckle.

"Oh… OH! Dammit. Sorry, give me fifteen minutes."

"Formidable fighter, lousy timekeeper… fifteen minutes."

The caller hung up and Sariyah abandoned her search, grabbing a breakfast bar and making haste towards the front door.

"Cursed daylight-saving," she cavilled to herself snatching her light grey jacket from the bottom of the stair banister. Pulling it on awkwardly while exiting the house, she stepped onto the garden path with bare feet and headed towards her 1967 Ford Shelby Mustang on the driveway. Engine roaring into life, she pulled into the road and away from her semidetached suburban home.

Fifteen minutes later she pulled into a layby on the very outskirts of the city and espied her partner, Coltish Hollow, apathetically leaning against his own car. He seemed to be gazing at a country lane, far in the distance. It was so far away she was only just able to make it out over a low meadow, dotted by trees. She gave him a light pat on the shoulder, having to reach up to do so.

"So, what are we doing all the way out here? I thought we were assigned to search for the Cult of the Deorum *within* Atlanta?"

He didn't move his eyes from the object of his scrutiny, despite her arrival.

"I'm aware of that," he intoned, sweeping long brown hair out of his eyes. "There's some kind of event or gathering in an old church outside the city. All the top hitters are there, even Vincent Lockwood."

"Jeez!" Sariyah let out a prolonged exhale. "Don't think I was ready to hear *that* first thing in the morning. What kind of event?"

"I don't know, an evil wedding maybe. Do evil cultists get married in their churches?" Colt chuckled at his own remark.

Sariyah laughed with him and steered the conversation back on track.

"So, what are we waiting for here?"

Colt gestured to the front seat of his car. Sariyah took the hint and retrieved a small pair of binoculars which she proceeded to use.

"I did some reconnaissance about an hour ago," he informed her. "Everyone we know should be, *is* present, including our own support. Everyone apart from Cecilia Lockwood that is. This is the only road to the church that I could make out. It would be nice to pick her off, maybe use her as leverage of some kind."

"Good idea," Sariyah remarked, studying the road that ran alongside a treeline through the field glasses. It was relatively well maintained, apart from the occasional dip due to environmental corrosion and tyre wear. As she gazed through the slightly dirty but still effective lens, she felt jealous of her partner. *Smug by-blow can see this perfectly without any assistance! Enhanced vision – the faculty of the perfect scout.* She lowered her arms, blinked to readjust her focus and raised a query.

"What do we do if she shows?"

"Tunnel us over there, blow a tyre, and kidnap the poor lady of leisure," he returned casually.

Sariyah nodded a curt confirmation. She let out a sigh and began to encourage herself internally to inspire confidence in her abilities. Shortly, her actions would need to be expeditious and immediate if they were going to help Colt's plan succeed. The ambience of the countryside grew mute in her ears...

I can do this. I haven't done it for a while, but it's just like riding a bike... I hope.

She became dimly aware of a shaking; a slight pain in her shoulder. Snapping back to reality, Sariyah's eyes fluttered open and she could just discern the outline of a car emerging on the road, traversing her view with great speed. The shaking? Colt was responsible.

"Pierce, *now*! Tunnel us!" he commanded, his voice saturated with urgency.

Sariyah vaulted into action.

She knelt on the ground, palms and soles flat to the earth. Magic flowed through her, as it does all things. Simply being aware of this fact, Sariyah could sense and detect that very magic within her, nestled in her stomach. She grasped onto the feeling, harnessed its incredible power, and channelled it into the earth via her limbs. A rumbling grew deep below the surface, which began to crack and split, forming a tight shaft that Sariyah began to sink into, Colt clinging onto her.

The two continued to sink until the ground had almost entirely swallowed them and a void of darkness consumed them. Sariyah shifted position, the magic flowing through her like a boiling liquid, and pushed forward. Her velocity increased, rock and earth parted in her wake, then reformed behind her. The sheer volume of the clangour was overwhelming. Her ears rang, but the blissful pandemonium actually quieted her mind, giving her focus and purpose.

Whenever she made use of it, magic was one of the true joys of her life, and reaching out with magical energy, she felt a different surface ahead – the familiar grit of tarmac. Reacting accordingly, she pitched her angle and began to rise out of the earth, upward, until an explosive burst of sunlight temporarily blinded her. In an instant, the deafening thunder of the earth was cut off as it re-sealed itself, leaving Sariyah kneeling beside the road without a mark of defacement other than a single bead of sweat on her forehead. Colt, however, staggered backwards beside her, his clothes wreathed in layers of earth and splintered stone.

Sariyah shrugged off the residual shock of her first successful tunnelling after prolonged inaction and scurried forward, glimpsing the vehicle steadily disappearing into the distance. Without losing focus, she took a purposeful step forward and planted herself in a balanced, grounded position.

With a careful celerity she drew her right arm in and splayed her fingers, fixing her mind on the gentle breeze that flowed through them. She concentrated on how the particles of air that rested against her fingertips were just one small part of a greater series, interlinked by magic. What happened to one would have a knock-on-effect on the rest in the series. Equipped with this training she harnessed her magic once more and funnelled it out through her fingertips. As she did so, she focused on the heat released by the energy transfer and, repeating the process, fired a blindingly fast column of air.

It caught the fleeing vehicle within seconds and Sariyah felt the heat of the impact-induced explosion of the rear tyre from where she stood. Far ahead the car began to coast into the side of the road and Sariyah darted into the treeline to avoid detection. Colt mimicked her movements.

Traversing the roadside in as clandestine a manner possible, the two approached the car, a Mercedes S-class. *Fancy*, thought Sariyah, *but not like my baby blue*. Colt made a silent gesture towards the vehicle. The driver was already inspecting the burst tyre. He had a sickeningly pale complexion and an unnatural disposition and grace to his movements. Sariyah recognised it all too well. *Vampire*.

She kept low as she watched with abject loathing, her fingers gripping the dirt where she crouched. She began to prepare the magic that swelled within, fuelled by the emotions boiling inside her. Colt silently drew a revolver from his belt and slipped bullets into the chamber one by one. Gently, Sariyah rubbed her right thumb and middle finger together, focusing on the friction it created, letting the heat swell and grow into a steady burn within her. The car door opened and Cecilia Lockwood stepped out, cerulean eyes mercilessly penetrating her surroundings.

Colt clicked the drum into place and thumbed back the hammer, aiming directly for Cecilia. Sariyah let the heat consume her entire hand and forearm, preparing to let burst a flame. But then, following Cecilia, gripping her hand tightly, came a young teenage girl. Sariyah hesitated. Her state of pure aggression and adrenaline was momentarily disrupted, torn by the realisation that a young girl's life would be irreversibly changed by a split-second decision to attack. Taking Lockwood down would be a change for the good of all who practised magic, but not for an innocent mortal girl. Sariyah couldn't ruin her innocence; she knew what that was like.

Colt's finger tightened on the trigger and Sariyah made a split-second decision for the good of the innocent. She twisted her body and a quick but powerful shot of air with the element of surprise ensured that Colt was pinned down, Sariyah on top of him, her hand over his mouth and the gun scattered into the trees.

Silence ensued. Sariyah dared not breathe as she stared into Colt's glare – a mix of confusion and rage. After an agonising minute, the sound of clicking heels on tarmac was heard – two sets, moving away from the car and down the road, accompanied by the sound of faint conversation. Satisfied the girl was now safe with her mother, Sariyah released Colt and moved to the side, remaining silent. The vampire was still a mere stone's throw away up on the road. Colt glowered at her and spoke in a whisper that was almost lost to the breeze as he righted himself and recovered his weapon.

"What was *that?*"

"I won't harm a kid," Sariyah replied in an equally hushed voice, "It's not her fault her parents are killers." She displaced the air around her with subtle hand movements, escorting the sound to Colt's ear and no further.

"And how do you know she isn't brainwashed and knows exactly what's happening?" Colt retorted contemptuously.

"I… had a feeling."

Her confidence in her decision was unwavering. She knew it was the right thing to do, even if it was the *wrong* thing as far as her duty was concerned. Her partner was about to form a reply when his face contorted with horror. Whipping up his revolver, he fired multiple shots over Sariyah's head. Instinctively, she dropped to the ground and caught sight of the vampire tearing over her, tackling Colt to the ground. The two became locked in combat, a scramble for dominance over each other.

Regaining her wits, Sariyah jerked back, rapidly splaying her fingers and snapping her palm forward. The column of air impacted the fighters and separated them with ease. Colt sprawled onto the road, but the vampire was launched through the air to impact on a nearby tree with a harsh snap. Sariyah scrambled to her feet and sprinted to Colt, kneeling to turn him onto his back. His neck had been ravaged by the rabid animal and his head was hanging by a thread. Blood spoiled the side of the road where he lay and his eyes were open, staring with agony and terror, but no life. Sariyah let out a grieving sigh and took a moment to concede another friend, lost to the scourge of the vampires. It was a moment too long and she felt an acute pain. She was forced head over heels from the impact of the vampire's claws in her back. Rolling to a stop, her hand quickly reached back. No puncture in the jacket. *Thank God for reinforced clothing.* The vampire loomed over Colt's lifeless corpse, bloody fangs bared and short claws extending out of its fingers.

She took a deep breath and pre-empted the attack, swiftly dodging to the left as the vampire leapt, carving its claws into empty space. Eager to keep a step ahead, Sariyah clicked her fingers, harnessing heated friction and coupling it with her magic. She summoned a flame in the palm of her hand and launched it before the vampire could react. The flame dispersed itself over his clothing and set alight, causing him to screech in agony. The sound emitted was animalistic and barbarous, unlike any sound a human can make. The creature stumbled towards her, attempting to make a swipe before the flames consumed it, but Sariyah was in her prime now that she had settled into the fight.

She twisted sideways, dodging the attack, and lashed a kick to its shin, partially disabling its movement. She fired a column of air in the same direction, so powerful it extinguished the flames, but brought the creature fully to its knees.

She rose onto the toes of her left foot, channelling magic into the ground, causing it to crack and isolate a large section of tarmac. To end the fight, Sariyah slammed down her heel, causing the chunk of tarmac to burst free from the road and slam down with terrifying impact upon the vampire's head, as it crouched on all fours.

Her shoulders slumped and she breathed a sigh of relief as she watched the vampire fall to the side. Unconscious or dead, it was impossible to tell with a being that had no pulse. She made a mental note to inform the Magical-Mortal Relations Department of the location, so they could perform the necessary clean-up. Then she took to her heels, running with a sprinter's pace down the road with the remains of her fight adrenaline.

Thank God it's morning and not night, or that fight would have gone very differently, she told herself as she ran.

She arrived close to a dense outcrop of trees that provided a vantage point a safe distance away from the church. Ahead she could see several plain transit vans discretely parked, the favoured inconspicuous transport of Adytum militia personnel. Sariyah stopped and planted a foot into the ground, firmly connecting with the surface. She closed her eyes and concentrated, attempting to detect any irregular pressure exerted on the earth in the nearby area before she moved to rendezvous with the militia. As she did, she brought her mind to a state of composure once more. Now was the time to focus on the mission – *her* mission now – to save the girl before she could be corrupted by her parent's influence, or worse. There would be time to mourn for Colt later.

Sariyah detected significant footfall ahead and made her way into the treeline where she found a band of Mage soldiers, around twenty-five in total. Each was dressed head to toe in the customary black armour plating, much like a mortal SWAT officer, with a visored helmet and large black boots and gloves. Each was also equipped with a yellow band, one on each arm to signify their magical discipline. Sariyah motioned to the two Adytum officers who were leading the group, Sorcerers like herself, and they set off. Light footsteps became the only sound as positions were taken up around the decaying church. Sariyah took an eight-man escort with her as they crept to the front door.

The door was large, significantly taller than her, and Sariyah noted that it created deep-seated misgivings within her. The very timbers of the building seemed to exhale and conure up feelings of perturbation, but Sariyah recognised this for what it was – a warding charm designed to terrify; to convince any who approached that entering would be a grave error. Effective on mortals, less so on Sorcerers. She smirked and applauded the cultists' cunning ingenuity before taking a deep breath. As she did, the Mages raised their hands in preparation and Sariyah felt pressure build in her chest. She took a final moment to prepare herself for the coming fight.

You can do this…

She paused to think of something witty to say. Primed, with adrenaline coursing through her veins, she transferred the pressure through her body and to her palms by means of her magic. She snapped her palms forward once more and ruptured the charm. Then she blew out the hinges and decimated the door, exploding it inwards into the church.

4 – LIFE AND DEATH

W orshippers bellowed their outrage at the intrusion. The Mages promptly engaged them in armed confrontation and Sophie watched it transpire through rapidly failing vision. The black spots in her eyes grew increasingly large, consuming the world around her. All her body's efforts were focused on simply remaining conscious, let alone making an effort to move, but she clung on and somehow resisted passing out.

She was aware of her dress billowing uncontrollably as a miraculous gust of cool air thundered over her. It was followed by the sound of splintering wood as Vincent Lockwood was blasted backwards into a collection of plinths.

Sophie found it difficult to draw breath, each one arriving with a tormented croak. The grotesque creature remained above her, locked in time, entirely motionless. But she could still feel its magnetic attraction, its energy reaching and grasping for her, groping for something physical to bind onto. She continued to stare at its distorted features until another face, human in appearance, came into focus. It was a woman, youthful, with a Middle Eastern complexion, deep brown hair plastered in parts to her cheeks. Sophie felt warm hands on her wrists, then ankles, each touch leaving an odd sensation she couldn't place. The binding pressure on each limb diminished.

Sophie felt the woeful attraction to the creature lessen, but no sooner had her final appendage been freed than the inconceivable brute above her reanimated and shrieked in frenzied anguish. Its wings began to burn and shrivel, swiftly followed by the rest of its contorted figure. The animalistic scream rang in her ears as the beast perished and fragmented into ash. She raised her hands above her head, curling reactively into foetal position.

The sounds of savage combat continued to overwhelm her senses. Try as she might to make sense of her situation, she was only aware of the chaos surrounding her and a constant, agonising throb in her arm. She could feel a numbness beginning to take hold of the entry wound, but dare not open her eyes to look at it.

The cries of fallen worshippers in the building petrified her, then came the unexpected contact of hands, startling her again, wrapping around and lifting her into the air. Instinctively, she kicked and writhed, the energy to do so coming from deep reserves of adrenaline, as her bodily functions managed to react in the face of some new external threat.

The cold church floor rushed up to meet her and fresh pain shot down her shoulder as she impacted with stone slabs. Sophie sobbed, instantly regretting her decision. Her vision returned to pinpricks of light, bursting through an all-encompassing darkness. Through it, she was just able to distinguish the elegant form of her mother, cowering behind a shattered pew to one side of the church hall. Gradually, through sobs and gritted teeth, Sophie crawled to her mother and desperately reached for her hand.

"M… mom, help… me…" Her voice left her lips as an unintelligible drawl. Cecilia cast her eyes down at her daughter's broken body. With a single dismissive shove and a snarl, she forever shattered Sophie's heart.

"You?! You rejected a god; you are no daughter of mine!"

Sophie felt the dark wood smack against her head as her mother pushed her away. Now the light left her eyes entirely, the world darkened, and at last she fell into unconsciousness, eyes brimming with tears.

Sariyah hurtled backward, sprawling across the floor, finally coming to a stop next to the fallen body of a Mage. The Consuls had informed her that Vincent Lockwood was merely a priest, influential, but with no real magical power. *That was a tremendous lie*, she thought, as she rose onto one leg, staring at her enemy. Lockwood held two spheres of crackling yellow energy in his upturned palms and his eyes glowed with the same light.

Narrowly dodging a sizzling blast of energy, and losing a few hairs in the process, Sariyah observed the ongoing struggle around her. The two Sorcerers that accompanied her lay deceased at one end of the hall, having been caught in Lockwood's deadly shockwaves. Multiple Mages had fallen alongside many worshippers and were in the process of being forced into a retreat, blinding yellow energy leaving their palms, eyes shining with lethal grace. Blood and corpses stained the once opulent purples and luxury fabrics of the nave. Then Sariyah finally caught sight of the young girl she had freed from the altar moments before.

Without a second's hesitation she made haste towards the girl, slumped against a pew, dress stained with gore, the open knife wound on her arm still seeping blood. Sariyah knew she would die of blood loss if she wasn't provided medical attention and soon. Lockwood predicted this manoeuvre and fired a sustained scorching beam of energy in her path. Sariyah made a quick response with a slight inflection of her wrist, whipping the air towards him. She disrupted his attack, knocking it off balance by precisely the right amount to allow her to slip under the beam and reach the girl.

Sariyah scooped her up in a single swift movement, cradling her unconscious body close. Catching an encroaching energy blast in the corner of her eye, she twisted, letting the crackling energy disperse on her jacket. The reinforced clothing took the majority of the damage, but nevertheless the blunt force of the shock caused her to stumble, almost tripping over fallen debris. Looking up, she could see the battle was approaching defeat. If she didn't make her own fast escape within the next minute, she would be alone and entirely overrun. "Just need to get outside" she repeated to herself multiple times while bounding towards the ruined entrance. The militia forces holding the point were rapidly thinning in number, due to the onslaught of worshippers, sending columns of air and shafts of sizzling energy alike.

Wood splintered and a chair leg snapped over Sariyah's back – a worshipper attempting to intercept her escape. Despite the pain, the force propelled her on. She slipped past two Mages and called for a retreat. Like ants to their queen, the remaining Mages instantly disengaged from the battle and fell back to the treeline with startling pace. Sariyah, feet on natural earth once more, channelled her magic down and sank into the ground taking the girl with her. As the earth resealed over her, so the cries of the skirmish ceased.

Sophie became dimly aware of an incredible rumbling of stone, like that of a quarry or workmen drilling in the roadway, and the bitter taste of dirt. But the sound felt far away and she was unable to tell if her eyes were open or closed. Darkness consumed all and she felt as though her life was slipping through her fingers.

5 – The World You Didn't Know

⁓

The bedroom was cramped and rectangular, filled with box upon box of unsorted clothes and various belongings. Sophie had never seen the room before in her life and couldn't begin to fathom how she had come to be there. Yet, she couldn't help but feel a sense of equanimity as she lay, cosy and sheltered in the comfortable bed. She noted that she didn't seem to be able to focus properly, as if she were drifting through time, half asleep, entirely indifferent and detached from the world and any concerns it might bring.

Blissful though this mental quietude was, she tried to constrain her thoughts, angling them towards the previous day. She had been betrayed, desecrated by her own parents – those who should have sworn and held a duty to protect her! She thought of the creature that had almost devoured her soul; its hideous appearance and abhorrent voice. Had these thoughts encroached on any other day, the notion of these horrific truths would have brought Sophie to tears. But not this day. At this precise moment she felt simply *fine*.

Other questions drifted across her consciousness. There was the quandary of what species that creature was. And how, by any understanding of natural science, were the people in that church able to perform the feats they did?

Finally, who was the woman who had saved her? All these questions could be dealt with another day, Sophie thought dreamily. For the present, all she wished was to savour this moment of serenity.

The bedroom door opened, shattering the silence with an appalling creek, disturbing Sophie's tranquillity and provoking a sigh. She turned her head a fraction to see who was entering. It was the woman with the dark brown hair. She appeared tired to Sophie; perhaps in desperate need of a full night's sleep.

"Hey, you're awake," the woman said. "I hope you don't mind my intruding. I was just coming to check on you."

Her voice… it was like satin to Sophie's ears. Soft, gentle, delicate in cadence. Sophie couldn't seem to bring herself to reply, despite trying hard.

"Oh… oh, yes!" The woman remembered something and skipped towards Sophie to kneel beside her. Cautiously, she reached for her arm. Sophie now noticed that it had been carefully and securely bandaged. The bandages were steadily unwrapped and the woman removed a micro-thin sheet of warm metal from underneath. Sophie craned her neck to view her wounded arm, but the woman replaced the bandages as swiftly and skilfully as she'd undone them before she could see.

With the metal sheet removed, Sophie could feel her senses reactivating, righting themselves. Her thoughts unscrambled and began to arrange themselves in a logical flow once more. Most importantly, she found herself able to form a coherent sentence.

"What… what was that? I couldn't think clearly."

Her words were slothful as her tongue reacquainted itself with the art of articulation.

The woman looked down at the metal plate in her hand before placing it in a first aid box to one side of the bed.

"Ah, it's a hormonic regulation plate."

Sophie gave no reply.

"It calms people down and keeps them happy after a traumatic experience… while they heal," she added, noting Sophie's puzzlement. "They're addictive, so must only be used when necessary after a serious event. I figured your situation counted."

The woman sounded nervous, but had a very kindly demeanour.

Sophie stared in utter perplexity at her rescuer. She owed this woman a debt; she'd just saved her life.

"Thank you… for saving me," she managed.

"Aww, it's okay. It's my job after all. I'm Sariyah by the way. Sariyah Pierce."

She gave a reassuring smile that Sophie appreciated.

"I'm Sophie Lockwood, heir to the Lockwood estate, franchise and patent. Although… I'm not so sure I am *now*."

The realisation of her lost status dawned on her.

"Where am I? What happened? How did my father summon that creature?" Now the questions tumbled out.

Sariyah made a motion to rest her hand reassuringly on the girl, but Sophie rejected it and tucked her hand back under the covers. *I may owe her my life, but I can still preserve my dignity,* she decided as she did so.

Sariyah retracted her hand, slightly embarrassed by her presumption that compassion would be welcomed. Instead, she pulled over one of the many boxes in the room to use for a seat.

"What I can tell you is that you're in my home right now – my guest bedroom."

"Well, it looks like you've barely moved in with all these boxes," Sophie retorted. "Not much room for guests!"

Feeling increasingly more like herself, Sophie's natural inclination to command and marshal any conversation she thought she could had quickly returned.

"Ah, well… I haven't had much chance to unpack," Sariyah explained defensively. "I've been working every day since I got here. This is my first day off, actually."

The poor woman seemed acutely aware of the comparative squalor in which she lived. However, working daily without some form of repose was a conviction Sophie could respect.

"I'm sorry, that was a little rude of me. I only meant that it seems a little busy to have many people visit." Apology made, Sophie returned to her queries. "But what happened? How did you all do what you did? I have never seen anything like it before. It was like magic in a film."

Sariyah let out a short laugh.

"Well, you're not so far off there. I'm not sure I should explain until I have approval."

She seemed to backtrack. Sophie frowned.

"No, please… I must have an explanation. I *need* one. You owe me that much!"

Sophie watched the woman hesitate. She could see the internal argument taking place.

"Okay…" Sariyah paused, searching for the best approach in which to shatter this girl's beliefs and perspective on reality. "You've seen movies and read books where people use magic to do amazing things, right? Well, some of those acts aren't fiction."

Sophie raised a sceptical eyebrow. "So, you're telling me you're *magic* then?"

"I am. Just like the stories." Sariyah smiled as she said it, seemingly proud of the fact.

"Where's your wand?"

"My what?"

"Your wand. You know, *expelliarmus!*" Sophie retained her composure, despite wanting to chuckle at the madness of the conversation.

Sariyah let out the chuckle Sophie wished to.

"We don't use wands – it doesn't work like that."

Sophie frowned at Sariyah's ineptitude at explaining the topic to her.

"You said it was like the magic *in books*?"

Sariyah sat back a little and revaluated her explanation.

"Magic is the lifeblood of the earth. Every person has a connection from their being to what we call *the source*. Some have a stronger connection than others. Those people can harness that connection and… sort of… *channel* magic and use it to do amazing things."

Slowly nodding, Sophie attempted to rationally decipher the explanation to no avail.

"Like the force in Star Wars?"

"Uhm, a little bit I guess," Sariyah replied. "But magic – pure magical energy – is far too unstable and powerful to be wielded in its natural state. Doing so is impossible. But if someone ever did manage it, most agree that it would be catastrophic for the balance of the world. Instead, Sorcerers like me use it to accentuate or augment natural processes. For instance, the slight heat created from friction can be converted and channelled into a roaring flame. Or a trickle of a breeze made by waving your hand quickly can be turned into a gust of wind."

Each utterance from Sariyah continued to astound Sophie, yet multiplied her doubts.

It can't be true, I'd have seen it. Then again, after yesterday maybe I already have?

The last dregs of the effect of the special metal Sariyah had removed were ebbing away and Sophie began to feel an uneasy tightening in her chest. In response, she quickly distracted herself with a demand, surmising that if all her doubts were expelled, her nerves might quell.

"Show me some," she said.

Sariyah shrugged and muttered to herself. "I've come this far…"

She raised her hand for Sophie to clearly see. Pressing her middle finger to her thumb, Sariyah began to rub them together, gently but intently. For a few seconds nothing extraordinary happened, then Sariyah let her fingers snap in the traditional way with a loud click. In its wake was left a burning flame, seemingly sparked from nowhere, now burning tamely in her palm. Sophie could feel the heat from where she lay, a metre back, supported by her elbows.

"How did you do that?!"

"Magic!" Sariyah laughed and extinguished the flame with the flex and curling of her fingers. "You said show me."

Scratching her head, Sophie's nervous tightening waned to be replaced with a mix of pure astonishment, exhilaration and curiosity.

"So I did."

The situation she found herself in was bittersweet. She felt that somehow a new reality lay before her. *The ability to create fire, with a click of the fingers?* What other avenues were there to explore that had previously lain shrouded in mystery? Sophie could only guess. But with those such as her father in the world, summoning malevolent creatures to consume his own daughter in a wicked sacrifice, no doubt external threats would likely become a prominent feature of her life from now on.

"Why didn't I know about this until now?"

This query was met with hesitation, before a delayed and truncated response.

"The majority of people don't have a strong enough connection to the *source* to harness magic. Some people with magic think that is pure evolution, the survival of the fittest, and that we should rule that majority. Others, like me, think that is an outdated concept. Ruling by fear and domination would only cause more troubles, as well as being morally corrupt."

The concept resonated with Sophie. It was straightforward to determine which of the two categories her parents fit into. Perhaps even herself, until this recent dissolution. The notion that she could be elevated higher than others by birth right had always pleased her greatly. The thought of the masses, cowering before her might, brought a smile also. However, there was one thing within this series of uncertainties and revelations she was sure of. Without a shadow of a doubt, Sophie refused to find herself on the same side or within the same ideology as her mother and father. The very thought of their acts sickened her, not only with disgust, but also sorrow. Furthermore, she did not want to see *all* those of a "lower class" trampled underfoot. She was beginning to take to Sariyah rather fondly. Her timorous sensibilities coupled with a clear competence in ability (even if she would not state that herself) was attractive to Sophie. She could get along with this person.

As her mind wandered, Sariyah addressed her once more.

"We need to get to the Adytum as soon as possible, if you feel well enough to travel a little."

The mention of being led to another unknown location rapidly welcomed the return of the tightened chest.

"No. The last time I was led somewhere new, my parents…" Sophie faltered, greatly resisting the urge to let tears fall, the calming effects of the magical device now entirely diminished.

Sariyah took Sophie's hand successfully this time. There was an incredible physical warmth to the touch. Emotional warmth too. It alleviated the pressure.

"I know, it's horrible Sophie, but I promise you, the Adytum is a good place. It's where other people like me work. We fight the wrongdoers and protect people like you – not like your father."

Gazing into her saviour's eyes Sophie felt a deep-seated trust growing within. Her subconscious confirmed the truth and the good in Sariyah's intentions. After a full minute of deliberation she found the strength to reply.

"Okay, I trust you."

"Alright. I'll give you some time to steady yourself and freshen up. Call if you need help and I'll be downstairs when you're ready to go. Okay?"

Sariyah gave her that comforting smile once more.

"Thank you," Sophie nodded.

Sariyah swiftly rose up and exited the room, closing the door behind her.

"This is… I have no words to describe it!" Sophie whispered. She lay back for a moment, dumbfounded, her eyes closed.

The ramifications of this new knowledge of the world began to take hold of her. Gradually, it grew inside, at first exciting and enticing, but soon intimidating her. It was foreign, unknown. Commandeering her train of thought, Sophie let out a deep breath through pursed lips. She listened to the faint whistle that escaped with it, aiding the final resolution of her thoughts.

"Magic… *it exists*! People can use it to harm me. Others can use it to protect me. If I learn more about it, then perhaps *I* may be able to protect and elevate myself? Prove I'm worth more than to be chastised, to be sacrificed. Yes, I can do this. I will never be powerless again!"

A second extended breath escaped her lips and Sophie opened her eyes. She sat up and swung her legs off the bed. Two minutes passed before she stood, legs trembling but secure. The pain in her arm was now reduced to a negligible amount, but she dare not peel back the bandages to inspect her injury. Inspecting herself as a whole, she found she was dressed in a simple plain T-shirt, some blue jeans that were marginally too large for her, and some fluffy white socks. Sariyah's no doubt. Lifting the shirt collar to her face she caught the vague scent of Sariyah locked in the fabric, confirming her suspicion.

Evaluating the strength of her legs, she stepped outside the room onto a small landing. Two other doors led to further rooms. Each door was made of a dark wood, similar to the floorboards, and somewhat battered and distressed. The walls were painted an off-shade of red. While traversing the landing to try a handle, Sophie ran her fingers along the perhaps more red-brown walls, collecting a significant amount of dust as she did so. She retracted her hand and rubbed it on the waistband of the jeans.

She discovered that the first door led to a simple bathroom. Sophie tried the handle of the remaining door. It rattled loosely in her hand but opened inwards with a creak onto a bedroom that defied the neglected impression of the other aspects of the home. Sariyah's bedroom.

Inside there were gleaming, vivid red walls. Shining white bedsheets adorned a king-sized bed in the centre of the room. A set of stygian drawers sat against the wall underneath a window and there was a small neat wardrobe to one side. The juxtaposition between this room and the others she'd seen only intensified its impact and Sophie took an involuntary step back to admire her surroundings. The window looked out onto gardens and houses on the outskirts of the city that Sophie could never fail to recognise as Atlanta.

Further investigating the wardrobe, Sophie found a pair of relatively antiquated trainers and slipped them on. They fit adequately, and she tied the blackened laces tightly. Moving to leave, Sophie noticed the door. Upon entering, the door had appeared the same as its siblings – dark, dusty, and dented in the centre and around the handle from years of use. The reverse of this door, however, was polished to a gleam, the true deep brown of the wood permeating through. The entire room, especially the door, reminded her of the saying *two sides of the same coin*. One side's grandeur and the other's blemishes, viewed together, created a jarring effect. It highlighted the rift – the fundamental difference – between two states of being. Sophie appreciated the symbolism greatly. With this final thought she exited the bedroom, paying her silent respects to the designer.

Sariyah waited patiently at the foot of the stairs for Sophie to come down. She had earnestly considered the decisions and actions she'd taken during their recent conversation, analysing and fixating on every mistake and thought how to create a better impression.

Thankfully she likes me a bit. At least, I think she does, she told herself. *Gesture will know how to handle things going forward. I'm doing good, I just need to keep her safe and get to the Adytum. Everything will be okay…*

Her self-reassurances were disrupted by the sound of shoes on the hollow wood of the steps. Sariyah looked up to see Sophie approaching, a gentle smile on her face. It was good to see, considering what she'd been through.

"Ready to go? It'll be a bit of a drive, sorry to say."

Sophie nodded.

"I like long drives… as long as we can get food on the way." She allowed a soft chuckle to drift into the air.

Sariyah gave an approving hand gesture and opened the front door to step out onto the path.

"Oh, there is no doubt about that!"

Sophie followed, then raised an eyebrow.

"Aren't your forgetting your shoes?"

"I'll explain in the car. Come on."

"Where actually is the Adytum?" Sophie raised a final inquiry.

Sariyah smiled, the way she always did when heading home after time away.

"New Orleans, of course."

6 – INFLUENTIAL BENEFACTORS

⌁

They had been travelling down Interstate 85 toward Alabama for roughly thirty minutes before Sophie was finally able to raise the question that had occupied her mind since the journey began.

"So, how old are you? You're already going on proper missions, but you look like my cousin Casandra and she's twenty."

Sophie had been barraged by seemingly never-ending inquiries from Sariyah since they had left the city. She appeared to be gathering all the information she possibly could on her, but for what purpose Sophie couldn't begin to fathom. She trusted Sariyah, however, and that was enough to suppress any anxieties for the time being.

"Ah, well that's a tricky one," Sariyah hesitated to answer, eyes still on the road. Sophie had to admit she was an impeccably swift yet careful driver.

"What's so tricky about it? It's just a number."

Sariyah removed a hand from the wheel to impulsively scratch a phoney itch on the back of her neck.

"Okay, don't be alarmed, but I'm in my forties."

"What?!"

"I said don't be alarmed!"

"But you look like you've just left school, not like someone who could have grandkids!" Sophie protested.

"I know. Those who are able tap into their magic and harness it – well, it brings rejuvenating qualities with it. Sorcerers and Mages age much slower after magic floods them for the first time. I was nineteen when it happened to me."

Sophie sagged back in her chair and observed the other vehicles being overtaken by Sariyah's Mustang.

"Does that mean that *I* can't learn magic until then?" she mumbled dejectedly.

Sariyah touched her shoulder reassuringly.

"You can learn magic at any age, it's just that I only truly began to practise the art when I was that age. You can start as soon as you want."

Revitalised by these words, Sophie sat up again.

What a strange world I've found myself in, she thought, revelling in the bizarre brilliance of a reality she had never known existed. She also found herself pondering the true ages of her parents. Fifty? Five-hundred? Does age mean anything to those who live for multiple lifetimes? A jumble of thoughts flooded her mind for the remainder of their six-hour journey.

Sophie continued her musings during the significant stretches spent in the car. The pair stopped to rest in both Montgomery and Mobile. It was only now on their travels that she realised, as affluent and indulgent as her life had been, she had seen precious little of her country. She had visited San Francisco with her father when she was an infant, but besides that, very few trips had ever been taken outside of Georgia that included her.

The Frank Davis Memorial Bridge loomed into view and Sophie felt a flush of satisfaction at the promise of their journey's end. While she was well aware that patience was not amongst her finer qualities, she was fine with long car trips. The aforementioned vacation to California was driven, not flown. She had always wondered why that was.

"Here we are," Sariyah beamed as they crossed the boundaries of the city. She seemed elated to be home. Sophie gazed at the buildings flying by until they pulled into the side of the Nike Community Store in midtown. Sariyah cut the engine and gathered her essential belongings.

"Why are we stopping here?" Sophie asked. She glared at the visually uninspiring sportswear vendor before them.

Sariyah seemed equally perplexed by the question.

"Because we've *arrived* at the Adytum."

"A Nike store? What are we going to do, fight my father with tennis shorts?!"

Turning her eye back to the building, Sariyah gave a short but cheerful laugh, as if she found Sophie's ignorance amusing.

"Come on!"

If this is a secret community, I suppose their headquarters wouldn't be obvious, Sophie mused. *And the church wasn't all it appeared either. It was dazzling inside those drab walls.*

The deep purples and golds of the church returned to flood her mind's eye, and she decided to give the store the benefit of the doubt… for now.

With a small satchel tucked under her arm, Sariyah guided her toward the front entrance, but halted abruptly a few feet before it.

"I almost forgot."

She addressed Sophie sternly for the first time since they had met. The contrast in tone was staggering.

"If anyone asks you for information, *do not tell them*. No one, under any circumstances, should know your name or identity. *Do you understand?*"

"Yes, I understand!" Intimidated by Sariyah's sudden coldness, Sophie's response was curt and high-pitched. Her eyes locked with Sariyah's, but she daren't ask why.

As swiftly as she had changed, Sariyah returned to her usual kindly demeanour.

"Sorry… it's just vital you don't tell anyone, okay?"

"Okay."

They walked on in silence, leaving the tension of the moment outside as they stepped into the store. If Sophie expected to encounter a wondrous splendour similar to the church, she was disappointed. She was confronted by the mundane regularity of… a sportswear store.

The ceiling was high, creating space for walls of trainers, shirts and swimwear in a variety of colours. Cashier desks ran down the left-hand side of the immense open space, and expansive changing rooms were tucked into the back right-hand corner, beyond the miscellaneous accessories section.

Oh, Sophie thought, despondent, *it's literally just a massive shop. Why do the bad guys always have better style?* she lamented as they made their way toward the changing rooms.

A calculated nod was exchanged between Sariyah and a man who was sorting through a clothesline at the entry. Sophie was escorted directly into the changing room area without so much as a questioning eyebrow. She followed Sariyah into a compact changing cubicle and the gust of air created by a blue curtain being pulled vigorously across behind her briefly disrupted her hair.

Regarding herself in the mirror, Sophie admired the way the overhead light caught her eyes, shimmering like two virescent stars in a night's sky. Her clothes were mundane, though comfortable, but she still held the blessing of her beauty to attract attention away from them. Sariyah interrupted the flow of her thoughts.

"Sophie, you coming?"

Sariyah stood with one hand gripping the curtain, ready to pull it open. She looked at Sophie with a slight smile.

"Coming where? All we've done is stand in this cubicle for a few seconds."

Sariyah rolled her eyes with a chuckle and pulled the curtain across. They exited down the same corridor they'd used to enter. Puzzled, Sophie followed and initially all appeared the same: dull grey walls, blue curtains. What differed was the hushed murmurs emanating from the direction of the store proper; multiple voices travelling in a multitude of directions as far as she could make out.

She caught up with Sariyah and her suspicions were confirmed. She stood in reverence at the sight before her. In place of the lacklustre store, Sophie was greeted with what she could only describe as a palatial reception of some kind. Every feature of the open space seemed grandiose, from the vermillion carpets partially covering marble floor, to the chalk white desk that spanned the immense space between two curving staircases in the back corners of the hall. These stairs, also marble, led onto an offset balcony that overlooked the desk below. A door at least four times Sophie's height stood fixed and secure in the centre of the balcony. It was entirely golden, covered in skilful engravings of floral patterns and figures, though she wasn't close enough to make out its features in detail.

She followed Sariyah into the reception along a path seemingly marked out by the red carpets, tracing from the entrance to the front desk, before splitting and leading up both stairwells toward the remarkable doorway on the balcony where they joined seamlessly. Before arriving at the desk, the two passed under a central chandelier, a maze of crystals so bright it was impossible to make out the actual bulbs that emitted the light.

Now within touching distance of the desk, Sophie stroked a hand across it and recognised the unmistakable texture of ivory. Consumed with the awe of her surroundings, she still managed to hear the exchange Sariyah shared with a man who looked to be an administrator of some description, formally dressed in a light grey suit jacket and waistcoat.

"Officer Pierce for an update on the Lockwood case."

"Yes…" he said without looking up. While his cadence remained utterly professional, he managed to embellish it with a condescending veneer. "Consul Gesture has been waiting, but he is currently indisposed. If you have a seat I will call when he is available."

"Right," Sariyah gave a short sigh. "I have the daughter of Vincent Lockwood with me. She poses no threat to us and shares no allegiance to the Deorum. I would like to take her through also, for the approval of her temporary presence in the Adytum."

"I'm afraid I can't provide such an approval and neither can you," the man snapped, looking up. He maintained his outwardly calm demeanour, but had forsaken his professional etiquette. "Especially for one so closely linked with malicious people such as her father!"

Sophie caught his glare as he spoke. His manner provoked deep indignation.

"Hey, I'm not…" she began to protest, but Sariyah cut her off.

"Whether she is approved or not is for Consul Gesture to decide. I didn't ask you to *do* anything – only to let us *both* pass when he's free." Her brow furrowed.

"Yes, of course," he replied, irritated. "But you will have to fill out this form to do so."

He thrust a sheet of paper in Sariyah's direction, containing multiple questions and formalities, and provided a pen to write with. Sophie would have chuckled at the thought that bureaucracy existed even in a magical world had she not been fuming. She watched Sariyah snatch the paper and pen out of the man's hand and move to one side where she began to scribble on it. Unsure what to do, Sophie moved to her side.

"What do I do now?"

The whisper that escaped Sophie's lips surprised her. Perhaps she was subconsciously afraid of revealing her *naïveté* to the few people milling around the hall. Sariyah replied kindly:

"Oh, uhm, just have a seat. I'm sure Gesture won't be too long. Could you take my bag too?" She held out the brown leather satchel with a smile.

Sophie took it and held it close to her chest.

"Okay, sure."

She moved away, leaving Sariyah to complete the form. She couldn't help but feel some trepidation at meeting this "Consul Gesture". People seemed to refer to him with great reverence. She was confident that yet another imposing figure would soon loom before her.

Sophie explored the open space, religiously following the carpet path, examining the walls of the reception as she did. An artistically unlevel surface, engaged ionic columns like those of ancient Roman temples were evenly spaced along the walls, stretching from floor to ceiling. They were marble, like the floor, surrounded on both sides by gleaming golden walls. She was doubtful that the material was really gold until she let a hand rest on the surface and her doubts were dispelled. They were indeed solid gold as far as she could tell.

The feeling of wonder and disbelief she was becoming so accustomed to fell upon her once more as she regarded the windows of the building. A window stretching toward the ceiling with a sill as high as Sophie's shoulder stood between every column, apart from the back wall by the stairs and behind the desk. The glass panes were crisscrossed with diagonal metal strips that formed a lattice of diamonds, each one of the same white, radiating a brilliant light while simultaneously appearing opaque to the eye, providing no view of the world beyond.

Taking a seat on one of the many thin benches that encircled the hall, placed directly under each window, Sophie let out a long exhale and attempted to compose her disoriented mind.

You're in the most amazing reception hall you've ever seen. Take it in and revel in it.

She followed her own instructions.

And this is only the reception! What's the rest of this place like?

As her thoughts slowly reorganised themselves, she spent time observing the other people sitting in wait nearby. She counted three men and two women in three groups. Two of the men were dressed in all black, with visored helmets and what looked like an insignia of some kind of the most vibrant yellow. One woman wore similar clothing, but without a helmet. Her black reinforced jacket held medals on the lapel. Next was a lone man, dressed similarly to Sariyah in smart-casual attire. His feet, however, were clad in a pair of leather boots, unlike Sariyah. The boots seemed to have an unnatural grounding to them, as if they were rooted to the floor when stationary, forming a bond.

Finally, sat on the same bench as Sophie was an albino woman, with hair white as snow and eyes a dull grey with a flair of pink close to the pupils. She seemed to be staring at nothing in particular, deep in thought. She wore an almost entirely black outfit and her boots, capped just below the knee, clicked as she rhythmically tapped one heel against the hard flooring. Her dark grey trousers were smooth in texture and skin-tight, but most notable was the trench coat that hung around her shoulders and flowed down to her thighs. It was black as pitch and had embroidery of the deepest grey across the breast. As Sophie looked, the coat seemed to bubble with a life of its own. Despite being open at the sides, all she could see that lay within was a soulless void of darkness that threatened to consume anything that might dare to venture closer.

Drawing her attention away from the room, her anxieties subdued and curiosity satiated, Sophie sat back, hands in her lap, and waited with as much patience as she could muster. After about ten minutes her resolve caved and she searched for some new form of entertainment. At first, she attempted to determine who the others waiting alongside her were, and what fantastical abilities they might have. After a short burst of imagination, she realised that the truth would most likely be far more astounding than she could fantasise about.

Sophie took the satchel that had been resting in her arms and opened the top flap. Inside were a few belongings, initially of no aid to Sophie's plight, but through dedicated searching she withdrew Sariyah's phone – an old model but useable. Sophie racked her brain until she had a sweet epiphany and remembered the passcode. She had spied the combination after watching Sariyah use it at a service station.

Joy of joys! Surely she has a game on here somewhere? If not, maybe I could download one. Do magic headquarters have Wi-Fi?

After a minute of browsing Sophie found that Sariyah had *Angry Birds* installed and began to play, boredom quelled.

She had been playing for less than five minutes when a voice like silk gave her goosebumps up both arms.

"I always get stuck on that level."

The address was casual, the accent English, but the tone had a coldness to it that bit into the room's warmth.

"I suppose I've never been one for games, but I dabble occasionally," the voice continued.

Sophie looked up to discover the albino woman had moved closer. Her lips were blood red and eyeliner encased grey irises that stared right into Sophie's soul. She did her best not to sound terrified in response, but her voice retained a quiver.

"Yes, it's not so hard once you know how to do it."

"I'm sure. Never had such luck myself, it seems."

The woman drew back slightly and proffered a slender hand.

"Apathy Crypt. Sorry if I made you jump, but you certainly caught my eye."

"I did?" Sophie replied with a mixture of perplexity and fear. "Why?"

"Oh, I shouldn't get into that now, but you seem like an interesting one. Why don't you tell me about yourself?"

Sophie caught her breath at the inquiry and remembered Sariyah's insistent warning.

"I'm… not sure I should," she blustered, "although I'm also not sure why."

Apathy smiled at this and adjusted her posture. Her coat swayed gently as she did, and the void within seemed to shift somehow.

"Very good! You see, your identity holds great power. If a person knows your name, how you look, and perhaps some basic information about you, they can control you if they know what they're doing," Apathy informed her. "It's merely a tradition now, an insurance policy. Voodooists are in decline nowadays you see, but you never can be too careful."

Sophie frowned.

"But I know *your* name, and my friend Sariyah's name. Plus, I'm looking at you right now!"

"You know the names we have decided to make our own," Apathy informed her. "The names we gave ourselves to protect us from such charms. I assure you, my mother didn't spend hours birthing a child just to call her Apathy!" She chuckled at her own quip and Sophie couldn't help but chuckle too.

"I see," Sophie replied, unsure how to handle this stranger who'd begun talking to her. Her gut told her that Apathy was clearly knowledgeable, and despite her slightly disconcerting appearance, the fact that she could inspire such uncertainty in Sophie merely by her presence was something she could respect. The contrasting emotions were rather disorientating.

"So, do I just make up a name for myself and then I'm protected?"

"Not quite, but you'll know when you have taken your new name, I assure you."

Apathy leant back a little, one knee hooked over the other. She held up one hand. Sophie stared as a sliver of what seemed like a deep black liquid, impossibly dark with no consistency or shape, began twisting through and around Apathy's fingers, with a life of its own. The sight alarmed yet fascinated her.

"What in the world is that?" Sophie exclaimed.

Apathy looked at her fingers and tutted, seemingly shooing the black substance away. It retracted into her coat, into that deep void.

"Naughty little things, they're always coming out to play when they aren't needed."

Eyes fixed on Apathy's coat, Sophie found herself speaking without considering the words that came out.

"Show me more!"

A smirk spread across Apathy's face and the black substance flowed out of her coat in a thin stream and danced with startling alacrity between her hands, twisting and turning in response to minor flicks and movements from Apathy's fingers. It followed her lead like a well-trained pet.

Sophie found herself infatuated by the movement, mesmerised by the texture.

"What is it?"

"The shadows of Necromancy, our most vital and practical tool," Apathy replied. She flicked her fingers suddenly toward Sophie, and a small snake of shadow curled in Sophie's palm. It held a form of solidity and felt physical in her hand, yet its movement reflected that of a liquid that didn't wet. Then again, its energy and the irregularity of its movement paralleled a gaseous substance. These shadows seemed to simultaneously comprise aspects of all three states of matter.

"Necromancy? That's stuff I've only heard about in books – zombies and things – but never this!" Sophie rambled in wonder, eyes fixed on the so-called shadows in her hand.

After another minute of admiration, the shadows retracted into Apathy's coat.

"It is very real, I assure you, though most artistic representations of us Necromancers are wildly inaccurate."

"They got the Goth part right," Sophie commented, to which she received an arched eyebrow in response.

"Dabbling with the magic of death has certain physical side effects. They can be avoided, but I embrace them," Apathy said.

Sophie felt herself longing for the feeling of holding the shadows again. They almost *called* to her, she thought. Apathy seemed to notice.

"It seems I was right. You truly are an intriguing one."

"What was 'interesting'?" Sophie asked. "You didn't tell me the first time."

"There's something different about you," Apathy said. "I can't be certain what, but my shadows call to you. I can tell you would make a fine Necromancer."

Out of the corner of her eye Sophie spotted Sariyah handing back the form and making her way over to where they sat.

"Yes… I think so," she responded, without really understanding.

With a casual turn, Apathy regarded Sariyah and nodded before returning her gaze to Sophie.

"I will assume you haven't decided upon what magical discipline you would like to begin learning – if you will learn at all?"

Sophie shook her head.

"I would advise you to read up on what is available to you. If you feel so inclined, the Necromancers of America gather in Las Vegas to study. I'm sure your friend here could provide some transport."

Sariyah lightly stroked Sophie's shoulder.

"Making friends? Not taking advantage of her I hope, Miss Crypt?" Her tone was serious but friendly.

"Oh, just giving the sales pitch. You needn't worry."

"Good," Sariyah nodded. "If you'll excuse us, we have a meeting to attend."

She motioned for Sophie to follow her. She gathered up the satchel and stood at Sariyah's side.

"Thank you for the information, Apathy. It was nice to meet you."

A concluding nod was given in return and Sariyah began to lead her away, down the crimson carpets towards the stairwell.

I'm liking this magic business more and more by the hour. Sophie shivered with delight, knowing exactly what type of magic would be the first she would read about.

7 – DONOVAN GESTURE

"He escaped?" Imperator Orotund raved, arms flailing wildly. "We had Vincent Lockwood in our sights and your agent let him *escape*? A disgrace!"

"I assure you, Officer Pierce did all she could to apprehend him. She was severely outnumbered and frankly outmatched."

Orotund's cherry cheeks grew redder as he continued his scathing address.

"Then send her reinforcements! I will not have my reputation marred by your poor delegation skills, Consul Gesture. I appointed you to your position and I can remove you just as easily!"

Donovan looked down upon the Imperator who stood before him, entirely unphased. Ever since he had known Orotund, he had considered him a bombastic man who made a significant number of ludicrous claims and achieved extraordinarily little in light of them. A personal opinion, of course, but he had always been a good judge of character.

"My apologies, Imperator. Next time we have contact with Lockwood, I will personally see to his capture."

"You do that!"

Orotund made a motion to prod Donovan's chest but seemed to immediately reconsider, realising the extent to which he would have to raise his arm to do so. Instead he simply ambled out of the chamber. Without so much as a backward glance, Donovan sat back down at the central table and continued an interrupted conversation with his second, Consul Montanaro.

"Apologies. Where were we?"

Montanaro drew his eyes back from over Donovan's shoulder and rekindled his focus.

"Yes… the Adytum in Chicago has issued another statement in conjunction with Los Angeles. They've declared their offer of 'support', should we require it against the cult of the Deorum."

A grave sigh preceded Donovan's reply.

"We both know that's just a veiled threat of intervention if we cannot control the situation soon. The north and west have always been quick to jump to our 'aid'. At least we have the east coast on our side."

"For now, but I wouldn't count on their support should Chicago take control. They've been at our heels ever since that idiot Orotund took up as Imperator."

Montanaro finished his address with the look Donovan so profoundly despised.

"Don't even try."

Montanaro's tone became one of despondent frustration.

"Oh, come on, Donovan. You could topple that fat bastard without breaking a sweat, everyone knows it. Weak leadership gives rise to insurrection and unrest is rife. Sorcerers and Mages alike are looking to you for an example!"

The second sigh of the encounter.

"I don't want the job. Find someone more suited."

"There isn't anyone more suited!" Montanaro flared. "You may not want the job – hell, I understand why – but when the time comes, you'll be forced to take it for the sake of our liberty. It's better to act while we still have a choice in the matter."

Silence engulfed the room. Montanaro's final words resonated around the perfectly curved surfaces of the walls. Donovan felt the weight of responsibility momentarily bear down upon his shoulders, but shook it off with a dimissory shrug.

"I'm sorry my friend, I confess that if circumstances force it upon me, I will act accordingly, but until that day I'll keep my independence."

His partner gave a curt nod and rose to leave the chamber, briefly resting an assuring hand on Donovan's shoulder before exiting. Donovan had known Montanaro for long enough to understand its meaning. They'd had their fair share of disagreements, but such differences would never bring hostility to the relationship.

Donovan remained still for a moment, contemplating the words spoken. The four Adyta of America had been divided into two clear factions for the majority of their coexistence, only truly uniting during times of global crisis. Chicago and Los Angeles held the north and western Adyta, while New Orleans and New York contained the southern and eastern. Each had their own Imperator or Imperatrix and a council of Consuls to take responsibility for the protection of mortals and the regulation of magic in their respective areas. Despite this responsibility, the majority of each Adytum's time was dedicated to hoodwinking the others and pursuing their own interests.

After a moment's repose, Donovan exited the meeting chamber and made his way toward his personal office. He passed directly through the Hall of Consuls as he did. It was a mistake that could easily have been avoided, but ever since the "incident" he found that the compulsion to walk the corridor overpowered him every time.

He surveyed the Adytum's semi-engaged columns, each precisely placed and designed, lining both sides of the corridor, the wall space between them suffocating under hubristic gold plating – one of Orotund's revolutionary interior design concepts. Each time he left his office, Donovan did his best to disregard the new façade and sought to retain the memory of the modest, smooth granite that had preceded the new flair.

Between the columns, thankfully obscuring large areas of gold, were multiple portraits arranged in pyramids. The portrait of each previous Adytum leader hung proudly at the peak of the pyramid, while the two Consuls who served as their second and third made up the base. This pattern was repeated between columns for the full length of the central corridor and Donovan knew each one and their history of servitude to the southern Adytum in detail. This was no obligation of his duties, he just preferred to be informed of the errors of his predecessors.

Donovan held his mind in deep reflection as he walked the corridor – a futile attempt to distract himself from the oncoming threat to his composure: the most recent addition to the Hall of Consuls. The endmost collection of paintings, despite being the most contemporary in material and art style, lay neglected in comparison to its neighbours. He was looking for one particular piece.

Multiple layers of dust coated the painting's surface and the frame was tarnished, still partially retaining the fingerprints of those who had mounted it. Donovan let his pace decrease until he stood before the forgotten depiction. He knew better than to attempt to correct the imperfections of its facia, sparing himself another rebuke from Orotund, but there was one thing he always found the time to do.

Carefully, he extended his hand and wiped away the grime that obscured the name plate of the revered Imperatrix Emmaline Gesture, allowing a burdened sigh to escape as he did so. Even gazing at him from a painting, her piercing blue eyes burrowed deep hollows of guilt within him. Her youthful complexion reinforced the truth that death waits for no one. Upon each viewing of her elegant features, blemished by an uncaring warden, Donovan made the promise that he would someday provide her with the respect she deserved. He would certainly ensure that Scarlett would never have to view her mother in this state.

Footsteps echoed, approaching the hall, and Donovan briskly turned on his heels, rounding the corner to continue on his journey. While the on-comer may well be a supporter of his, he preferred not to be caught languishing.

Entering his office and closing the door behind him, Donovan exhaled as if for the first time, pouring out pent-up anger and anxiety. Stilling his mind, he vowed to continue the day with his usual aplomb. Seated behind his desk, resting on his elbows with fingers steepled, he reread the report Officer Pierce had handed in the night before, focusing on the details of Lockwood's daughter.

It was a curious case: a practitioner of magic purposely barring the reality of the world from his child – one with a bloodline so rooted in magic, she would be an invaluable asset to the Adytum. Donovan was sure that was how most would see her. However, he would prefer the girl made the decision to join their ranks on her own terms. Enlisting a forced soldier invariably created an unreliable one, but it was also a morally ambiguous action, even in the current circumstances. As he mused, his office phone rang shrilly into the warm air. With a swift hand movement, he answered.

"Consul Gesture?" the voice said. "I hope your meeting was a productive one. Officer Pierce has arrived with the child of Vincent Lockwood. They're here to see you."

"Send them in."

"Certainly, sir."

The handset rattled as it was returned to its stand and Donovan leant back in his chair, organising his thoughts and clearing his desk. He was the first of the Consuls to meet the girl everyone was beginning to talk about. He smiled at the thought that it wouldn't be the Imperator.

8 – First Impressions

T he lustrous resplendence of the Adytum didn't dwindle as Sophie moved through the grand reception door into a central corridor, all the while sticking close to Sariyah's side like a nervous but inquisitive child, led by their parent. She was truly impressed by the sheer quantity of gold these magic people had acquired, while achieving strict isolation from the regular world.

The corridor held an identical design to the reception: endless columns, golden plates, exquisite flooring, and a smell like it had just been cleaned. However, instead of windows to occupy the space between the columns, here there was either full sheet gold in all its egoistical glory, further corridors branching deeper into the compound or, more interestingly, paintings depicting apparently important events and people. It was dazzling to behold.

Prying eyes seemed to follow the two as they walked, and Sophie became increasingly self-conscious of her appearance and manner with each passer-by. She noted that some were dressed in casual clothes, similar to Sariyah, while others wore a formal black uniform. The piping of the jackets was finished in a trio of colours, blue, vivid red or bright yellow, perhaps indicating some sort of classification – though the blue piping was proving exceedingly rare among them.

She opened her mouth to quietly request Sariyah's support, as yet another figure cast his eyes over her, but stopped herself. Then she realised, much to her surprise, that it wasn't *her* attracting all this attention. Each person who passed them was directing a disparaging glance towards Sariyah. *Why?* she wondered. Despite this, Sariyah seemed to reveal no outward concern for it and Sophie stayed silent.

To distract herself, Sophie turned her attention to the paintings that adorned the walls. They were clearly intended to represent certain historic events, and the majority depicted three central characters that were recognisable across them. The central and most commonly seen figure was a lean man in robes of the most striking yellow, which obscured his notable features but retained the shape of his body. Then there was another man, shorter but steadfastly built, sporting a more practical, robust attire, not dissimilar to an adapted Roman legionnaire's armour. The third figure was a woman with flowing ginger-red hair, pale blue lightning crackling between her fingertips in every depiction.

Ensuring her voice was hushed Sophie asked, "Sariyah, who are those people in all the pictures around here? They were on the door in reception as well."

"Ah, they're the first people who discovered that humans could harness magic and use it to our advantage," Sariyah returned.

"Oh, really? The first people *that* long ago? One of them looks Roman," Sophie noted.

"Well, we don't know if they were the *very* first to discover magic, but they were the first people to utilise it in the way we know today."

As they walked on, Sophie devoured all the information Sariyah could offer on the subject. The fantastical nature of what she learnt, and the fact that she may one day be able to see and perform these feats herself, filled her with an excitement she had never felt before at any time.

"Guy in the robes... that's the first ever Mage, Velthur Tarquin. He pioneered casting magic into concentrated energy beams, among other things," Sariyah continued, while Sophie nodded along, entirely entranced.

"Aulus Sextus Deucenius – you were right about him being Roman – was the first Sorcerer, like I am. He wasn't satisfied with his friend Velthur's more elegant magic and wanted something a bit more practical, so he used his magic to enhance natural pre-existing aspects of the world, like manipulating the earth or creating fire."

To no avail, Sophie tried to dismiss the wide grin that encapsulated her mood. She had the countenance of a delighted child.

"What about the redhead? She has some kind of lightning powers?"

Her jovial attitude clearly pleased Sariyah as she replied.

"She did – an ability only seen in her and her direct descendants. Caoimhe Birdsong, the Celtic ally that the Sorcerer and Mage met on their travels in the known world. She was the world's first recorded *Pura natus* in fact."

"What's that?" Sophie asked intrigued.

"A *Pure born* they called it. It means someone who doesn't have to learn magic from scratch like you and me, they're just born with it. They have incredibly powerful abilities like nothing anyone has ever been able to replicate. Only catch is, they're exceedingly rare." She sighed with satisfaction as she finished her lesson.

Sophie laughed to herself. *This is incredible. I can barely wrap my head around it. So much to learn, so much to accomplish!*

Before long Sariyah brought Sophie to a stop outside a small depression in the wall that held a grand white and gold door. It had similar engravings to the rest of the building's décor, except for a central protruding emblem above its two handles: two equilateral triangles, one smaller and set inside the other. The edges were straight, but the corners rounded and bulging out slightly.

"Cool door knocker," Sophie observed.

Sariyah chortled in response.

"It's the mark of the Consul, we've arrived. But yes, it is a cool knocker!"

With that she lifted it from its rest and gave three gentle taps against the door.

A few seconds passed before a click sounded and the doors opened inward to reveal an office dramatically different to the rest of the Adytum Sophie had seen so far. The first aspect of the room that struck her was its warmth.

A roaring but controlled fire burned within a grand, open fireplace on the back wall. The surrounding walls were made of two split elements. The lower half of the walls on all four sides were rendered in a dark wood panelling of different elevations, and a dado rail separated this from the upper segment – a smooth, featureless Prussian blue rising into darkness above. The only light in the entire grand office was emitted from the fireplace and a small selection of standing lamps. Warm, yes, but also rather gloomy.

She followed Sariyah into the room apprehensively, glancing back to see the double doors shut gently behind them. Looking around, she noticed the back wall was comprised of towering bookshelves that reached high into the blackness above, fading out of sight. She wondered how it could ever be practical to retrieve books from shelves so high.

Sariyah pulled out a lavish wooden chair with dark blue upholstery and sat before the simple but intricately carved desk. Sophie followed suit. Behind the desk sat a man in a tall, handcrafted, highbacked chair. His face was weathered but handsome, dark stubble aging him to a degree, but accentuating the obvious maturity and experience of his character. His hair was a shade of brown so dark as to appear almost black in the murky interior of his office, and the apparent blackness continued with the exquisite charcoal suit he wore. Sophie's impression was of a professional man, well kempt and with a hint of arrogance that was not unfounded. He looked up and a gentle, but slightly gruff voice echoed into the room as he spoke.

"I trust your journey here was a pleasant one, Sariyah. And our new guest – I don't think we have been acquainted."

Sariyah nodded and exchanged the expected social pleasantries. Sophie stared at the man before her with fascination. *He looks very important and Sariyah seems to trust him.* She couldn't seem to help feeling at peace and guarded in his presence. Furthermore, his relaxed but confidently professional countenance provoked an urge to respect and believe whatever he told her.

"I'm Consul Donovan Gesture." He directed his words toward Sophie in a kindly but serious manner. "I'll be overseeing your protection while you're staying with us."

"Protection? You mean I'm still in danger?" Sophie exclaimed.

Sariyah seemed to wince and made a motion to apologise for her tone, but Gesture held up a diffusing hand.

"It's quite alright, Sariyah. I much prefer to do away with needless formalities, as you know – even for those who are new." Continuing to address Sophie he said, "Yes, I'm afraid that you are in significant danger for the time being, but don't worry you're in very capable hands."

"Does that mean I'm going to be staying here then… sir?"

"It may be the safest option until my officers can determine where your father and his followers are based."

"Respectfully," Sariyah proposed, "I'm sure there are many in the Adytum who will be a little irked that the daughter of the man we've all been after is staying here on a semi-permanent basis. I trust her completely, of course, but most around here are prone to snap judgements." She rested a supportive hand on Sophie's back.

Gesture leant back in his chair steepling his fingers in contemplation.

"What would you propose as an alternative?"

The warm embrace she received from Sariyah alleviated the pressure Sophie had been feeling. She now felt that nothing could go wrong as long as she was with her.

"My friend has an apartment in Dallas, a mortal too," Sariyah divulged. "Nobody would suspect us of hiding out there."

The thought of further hours of travelling didn't fill Sophie with any amount of joy, but she decided that if she could be safe and in a more comfortable private setting, the journey was worth it.

With a confirming nod Gesture sat forward.

"It's decided then. The girl will be taken to your undisclosed location and after this has blown over, I'll send a psychic to set her up with a new family."

Despite her lack of experience in this new world, the thought of a psychic and a new family flustered Sophie, even if she didn't exactly know why.

"Hold on," she interrupted. "Psychic? New family? What do you mean?"

Sariyah winced again. Not at Sophie's tone this time, but at the answer she knew she had to give.

"Ahh… it's just so that you won't remember all the pain this has caused you. You can live happily with a new family and have the normal life you deserve." She squirmed in her seat. "It's sort of like a… memory wipe."

Sophie gasped in horror and leapt to her feet, her chair skidding noisily across the floorboards.

"No!" she exclaimed angrily. "Please don't make me forget. I can't just unsee and forget all of this like it was a bad dream!"

Her voice broke at the end of her plea and she moved to stand behind her discarded chair as though shielding herself. She trembled, expecting a harsh rebuke for her outburst, but to her surprise Sariyah stood and wrapped her arms around her in a soothing embrace. She guided her gently back to the desk so that Gesture could address her.

"I'm sorry," he said. "Let me assure you that we only want what is best for you and your safety. Nothing will be done without your strict consent, unless it be a matter of emergency."

Sophie nodded. Internally she noted that though her outburst would have been deplorable on any regular occasion, she was beginning to find that she didn't object to those she trusted witnessing her more indelicate emotions. Especially those who did not display the same despotic expectations and intolerance of her mother. In spite of the obvious danger of her situation, she felt safer from harm than she ever had. Somewhat emboldened by this, she voiced the timid request that had occupied her mind since she had first learnt of magic.

"Thank you. I don't ever want to be defenceless again, like I was before. Can one of you teach me to use magic, so I'm safer?"

"I cannot, but I'm sure Sariyah would be happy to teach you some basic forms. She is an incredible woman." Gesture reassured her. "Since you will be in Dallas, I recommend a visit to the T.G.L.I.R.M.A."

"The what in what?"

"The Great Library of Informat…" Gesture began, but Sariyah interjected.

"A big magical library – the biggest in America."

Gesture sat back with a smile. "More or less," he conceded.

Once more, Sophie marvelled at the complexity of the world she now found herself a part of. It didn't fail to yield more surprises at every turn. *They have magical libraries too? Incredible!* The wonder of magic would soon be at her fingertips and she had always considered herself a fast learner.

"Unfortunately, our time is spent," Gesture said, checking his watch. "I have quite a busy schedule, but our plan is decided. I wish you a safe journey to Dallas. Don't hesitate to call on support, should you need an escort, Sariyah."

Sariyah stood and exchanged a handshake and pleasant farewell with Gesture, lingering a little longer than one would expect, before stepping back to allow Sophie to do the same. Gesture handed her a small card before extending his hand in the usual manner.

"My card. Feel free to call me if you have any concerns or questions. If I don't answer immediately, don't worry, I will call back when I'm free."

"Thank you, sir," Sophie returned his smile. Taking his hand, she felt an unexpected static shock streak up her arm and flinched. He seemed to notice and gave her a knowing wink before they parted. Sophie hurried back to Sariyah's side.

Exiting the office back into the glittering corridor, Sariyah began to lead the way back to the reception.

"Hope you don't mind another long journey?"

Sophie shrugged. Her mind was still focused on the small shock she'd received moments before.

"It's okay. Can we get something to eat first though? And a change of clothes would be much appreciated."

Sariyah chuckled.

"Sounds good to me. In fact, I know just the place."

They made their way out the same way they had entered, through the sports store and into the open air of the afternoon.

9 – ONE OF THE FAMILY

Wow, I was expecting some store-bought clothes, not a tailored set!" Sophie beamed as she stood before *Harding's Modiste and Haberdashery*, Sariyah at her side. "You don't look like the sort of person who has that kind of money."

Sariyah scoffed and shrugged away the disparaging comment.

"You'd be surprised how well the Adytum pays."

A traditional bell rang out in the sultry air as Sariyah opened the door and guided Sophie inside the deceptively large shop. While clearly seeking to cater for a more stately class of customer, the shop premises appeared rather slim and quaint. Inside, however, the interior stretched back for what felt to Sophie an unreasonably long distance. Archway upon archway led to various rooms for storing, sewing, testing and presenting clothes of a variety of styles and material. The first of these held a few showpiece items, each seemingly from a different decade in style, and a simple wooden counter, attended by an aged but kindly looking man dressed in his own peculiar but exquisite suit.

Sariyah approached the desk and greeted the man in her casual but tender manner. Sophie followed behind, running her hand along the textured green wallpaper as she took in her surroundings. When she caught up to the counter the man addressed her.

"Well, hello there. You're looking for some new clothes. Took you long enough, I've been expecting you for weeks!" His tone was sarcastically frustrated, but overall rather jovial.

Sophie arched an eyebrow.

"Weeks? I only found out about all this the other day."

She was met with a chortle in response, which pricked her temper slightly. She was still new to this and figured the least he could do was be clear about his apparent clairvoyance. Sariyah noticed the frustration and informed her.

"Neurrira, here, is a psychic. The future-telling kind. Notoriously difficult to sneak up on."

"That's right," he asserted. "I've known you were going to come striding through my door for quite some time now. I know... it's quite shocking."

It was only after he'd finished speaking that Sophie realised her mouth was gaping in mixed fascination and confusion. She quickly closed it.

The deep green suit jacket the man was wearing drew her attention. Matched with a plain white shirt and beige trousers, it was crafted to seamlessly fit his body, holding incredible shape. It had clearly been put together with some of the finest tailoring skill and experience money could buy.

Hmm, if he made that himself, then I really am in for a treat! Even if he is a little... strange, Sophie thought.

"So, have you got time to fit her in?" Sariyah asked.

Neurrira nodded.

"Of course. New customers are quite the priority! Come on through, come on through."

With a graceful hand he brushed aside the curtains, the same green as his suit, which covered an archway into the next room, and gestured for them to follow. There was no obvious way to get from one side of the desk to the other, so using one hand for support, Sariyah swung her legs and swiftly vaulted across it. Sophie followed awkwardly, clambering and crawling over it, reminding herself she would have to take lessons in becoming nimbler at some point.

With Neurrira in the lead, the three made their way through a series of open plan rooms linked by further archways until they came to a halt in what seemed to be the largest room in the shop. It boasted a similar dated-but-regimented décor to the rest of the shop and contained table upon table of fabrics from a variety of locations and styles, as well as what appeared to be an oversized sewing machine with a figure seated behind it.

The contraption was of prodigious proportions. Sophie noticed that it had a needle, but no thread was to be seen anywhere. A plate with small triangular spikes ornamenting its surface sat underneath the needle. Its operator was a woman of similar age to Neurrira. Her hair had recently gone grey and lined features revealed both age and experience, while preserving a bygone beauty, still evident, but diminished. She rose to meet them.

"Sariyah dear, back so soon, and with a companion?"

Her voice rang so softly into the air that Sophie felt as though it might break if it was raised above a whisper.

After a greeting kiss, Sariyah directed Sophie to join her, addressing the woman as one would their grandmother.

"Amona, this is Sophie. I rescued her after my last mission. I think I told you."

Amona nodded and smiled.

Sophie took a step back in alarm.

"You said nobody should know my name!" she gasped, her voice piqued with exasperation. "Now you're blurting it out whenever we meet someone new?!"

The room fell silent, Sariyah caught off guard by Sophie's irate eruption. Amona quickly intervened to alleviate the tension.

"It's quite alright, dear girl. Do sit down and leave poor Sariyah alone. I'm not magic in the way that one would traditionally expect. I can't use your identity against you even if I wanted to, most can't in fact. It's strangers you should be wary of."

Even when delivering a reprimand, Amona seemed kindly and explained things in a way that made Sophie immediately feel guilty for her outburst – the second of the day no less.

"Oh," she conceded and sat on a simple wooden chair to the side of Amona. "I see."

Sariyah took a seat next to Sophie while Amona continued, gently rubbing her shoulder as if to apologise.

"I'm just a seamstress. I was never interested in any of the fighting disciplines. That's why I married a glorified fortune teller!"

She snickered at her own comment and Neurrira huffed quietly in protest as he passed her a pile of black and ash coloured fabrics he had bundled in his arms.

"I've never had such a strong connection to magic in the traditional sense, like Sariyah or my husband there. I practice a more… unorthodox kind."

Absorbing the information while she sat attentively, Sophie tried to engage with what she knew of this new world.

"I'm not sure how connected *I am* to magic yet, but I know I want to be able to control shadows, like that lady I met, Apathy."

"Ah, Miss Crypt. One of our pleasant but more boring customers," Amona commented. "Always black upon black upon black," she tutted with a smile.

Sariyah interrupted the conversation before things got side-tracked.

"Want to pick out some colours and tell Neurrira and Amona what you'd like your outfit to look like?"

Excitement bubbled within and Sophie gave a little clap.

"Yes please!"

She made her way over to a large table on one side of the room where Neurrira had presented fabrics of multiple shades of red, grey and some blacks.

"Are we just making an outfit for me?" she enquired. "Sariyah's outfit is nice and all, but wearing some footwear wouldn't hurt." She glanced at her friend. "You look a bit lost and poor without any shoes."

Sariyah blushed a little and tucked her feet under her chair.

"I can't practise earth magic properly through shoes. It's much easier without."

Neurrira chuckled.

"Let the woman be strange if she'd like to be. Now come on, take your pick."

Sophie inspected the offerings and scratched her head. "Why only three colours?"

"Ah, well I knew that you would pick these colours irrelevant of what I displayed here," Neurrira smiled.

"But if you knew I would be here and what colours I would choose, then why ask?" Sophie questioned. "Surely you even knew in advance what I'd want my outfit to look like?"

"That's not how being psychic works," he replied. "I can accurately *guess* at the future. Sometimes I see it clearly, but precise details are tricky. I'm sure you don't want your clothes to be *generally right,* but with several key features missing?"

Sophie shrugged, unable to disagree with this statement. Neurrira continued.

"Now, take those materials and throw them in the mirror."

Sophie should have been surprised at the casual manner in which he issued this instruction, but by now she had trained her mind to expect anything and question nothing with regard to its possibility. Carefully taking the bundles of fabric in her arms she approached a classical, full body mirror at the far end of the room. Hesitantly, she threw the pile of fabrics she held towards the glass.

Much to her wonderment, every item disappeared into the mirror and reappeared scattered on the floor the other side. It was as if the mirror's surface was simply a constricted doorway into an identical room. Except it wasn't identical. Upon closer examination, Sophie realised certain aspects of the room were different to its reflection. Small, subtle things, like a table that rested at a different angle, or a painting missing from a wall. It was remarkably similar, retaining the overall feel and dimensions of the room it was supposed to reflect, but it was a poorly constructed counterfeit of the original image.

Inquisitively, Sophie let her hand reach forward to rest against the glass. She discovered not a solid surface but a vibrating, impressionable film. It almost sent her fingers numb while they were pressed against it.

"I wouldn't try that if I were you."

Amona's voice drifted past Sophie's ears. All she could focus on was her inexorable attraction to this impossible conception before her. With more force she pushed against the vibrations, feeling the film depress inwards. The sensation was not dissimilar to attempting to force together the identical poles of two magnets. It seemed to slide and attempted to escape her advances. She was sure that if she persisted, she might be able to break through. However, her investigation was disrupted. Sophie was snapped out of the trance by Amona's gentle pull on her shoulder, guiding her to step back from the mirror.

"It's fascinating, I know, but entering my mirror dimension would be impossible for anyone but me. I'm surprised you were able to touch it without it firing back at you."

Sophie practically giggled with excitement. "Mirror dimension?!"

By way of demonstration, Amona approached the mirror, stepped into it, and passed right through to the other side with no difficulty whatsoever. As she did so, Sariyah explained.

"Amona is a Mirror Mage. A *Pura natus,* like I explained earlier. They can put a sort of charm on a reflective surface and step into it to store items there, or to have access to more power within the mirror."

"And a great deal many more things too!" Amona chirped. The vibrating texture had stilled and Amona smiled at them through the now solid glass. Her image was reflected to be standing just to the side of Sophie and Sariyah. When she brushed past them in the mirror image, Sophie felt the breeze on her shoulder, yet no physical manifestation of the woman was present beside her where she stood.

Returning to the issue of Sophie's clothing, Amona said, "Do look in the catalogue and dictate a style, texture and accessories for me." She nodded towards a large book resting on a nearby table.

Sophie eagerly consulted the catalogue, streaming through its pages, gazing at the extravagant and stylish outfits contained within. Presently, Sariyah and Neurrira could only stand back and admire the way in which

Sophie described and presented her ideas to Amona with an alarming preciseness of detail. Amona seemed to greatly appreciate the specificity of Sophie's requests. When it came to design, ambiguity only hampered the process of crafting the perfect outfit to the customer's satisfaction.

Sophie sat back with a sigh, as if she had completed a draining and complex task, while Amona began work on the outfit. She laboured at various stations within the mirror, as opposed to the identical ones outside it.

"So, dear Sophie," she commented as she worked, "Sariyah rescued you from the church?"

Sophie nodded solemnly.

"Yes… from my own father. He tried to sacrifice me to a dark creature."

Having divulged this information, Sophie felt a trust begin to grow between herself and Amona, possibly in a similar way to the nurturing relationship she and Sariyah shared.

"That's just awful, I'm so sorry. Your father is a cultist of some kind?"

Before she could process this question and wrestle with a reply, Sariyah came to her aid. She spoke in a hushed tone, as if informing a loved one of tragic news.

"Her father is Vincent Lockwood."

Amona paused her sewing for but a moment before continuing her work, now progressing at a startling, almost worrying pace.

"I see. That is… unfortunate."

"You know of my father?" Sophie was eager to learn the truth and penetrate the fog surrounding her lineage, but she received a curt confirmatory gesture.

"Yes, I knew him a long time ago, before he fell so far into depravity."

The topic of her father seemed to provoke deep seated emotion, long since buried within Amona, but Sophie felt her curiosity preside over sympathy.

"What was he like, before he went bad?"

Amona gave a brief sigh and considered the question for a moment before satisfying Sophie's interest.

"Strong, driven, willing to go to any length for his goals, unless it jeopardised those close to him, or those innocent in the Adytum's eyes. It was a different time. A few centuries ago."

Sophie listened on, absorbed, waiting for Amona to continue.

"But what happened?"

"I suppose at heart he was a true fanatic – a zealot of his religion – him and his siblings. For a time, the Adytum left him and his dark followers alone, until it was discovered he and his wicked mistress were sacrificing their own children in an attempt to provide the Deorum with vessels to possess and rule over our world once more. I'm sure that is what he was attempting to do with you dear."

Courage and curiosity soured, Sophie gulped, goosebumps riddling her arms.

"Oh… and, what happened?"

Amona hesitated and Neurrira interjected.

"The Adytum acted and put a stop to his actions, destroying his churches and placing him under house arrest for many years before releasing him with frequent check-ups."

Sophie's temper flared once more.

"House arrest? After he murdered his children? What idiot makes that conviction?!"

Sariyah gave her a tight hug from behind before Amona continued, unphased by the sudden anger.

"I know. Everyone was conflicted on the matter, but if we imprisoned or executed him as was suggested, his followers would have sparked an outright civil war – a conflict the leaders of each Adyta were not prepared to fight alongside their own squabbles."

Amona breathed a sigh of relief, attempting to dismiss the shivers that overtook her. Sophie felt slight shame at the distress her forceful curiosity had provoked. Sariyah leant in further and shared the concluding words.

"And lately he had been reorganising his followers in secret, until he officially struck out and broke the terms of his parole a couple of months ago. That's why I was stationed in Atlanta – to try and take out some of his cells and capture him. Though he never showed the true power he held, even when he was first captured."

Confusion, shame and anxiety washed over Sophie as she sat in the now silent room. Her parents: harbingers of darkness, sacrificing their own offspring; brothers and sisters she would never know. Her Aunts and Uncles equally as wicked.

Is my whole family evil? What does that make me?

She began to breathe in short bursts. Tears formed at the corners of her eyes and her heart pounded. Then Sariyah's hand on her shoulder quelled the overwhelming tide of emotion. Once more, she imparted to Sophie her optimistic warmth and comfort – more than she'd ever felt from her flagitious mother. Sophie immediately felt the feelings begin to wash away under her protection. Her tears were no longer of despair, but gratitude.

Presently, she felt another presence: Amona. Kindly eyes peered down at her and the neatly folded pile of black and red leather garments in her outstretched arms were offered to Sophie.

"All done," she smiled.

Sophie slowly rose to her feet and tried a smile. Setting down the clothes on the table behind her she searched for the exquisite jacket she'd requested. Finding it, she swung it proudly over her shoulders, donning the leather like a cape.

She looked at herself in the mirror, but was bitterly dissatisfied. She had specified a pristine, tight-fitting black leather jacket, but this garment hung halfway down her thighs and the sleeves fell limp over her hands. Significant bags of material clumped under the arms.

"But, but… this jacket is huge!" Sophie complained with a pout, having regained her usual demeanour. "I'm not that big!"

Amona gave a short chortle.

"Dear, dear. No need to be la-di-da or uppity about it. Just give it a good soak in some warm water and I'm sure it will shrink down very nicely."

Removing the jacket, Sophie refolded the clothes incorrectly. Neurrira corrected them and neatly transferred them to a paper carry bag for her.

"Right. Okay," Sophie conceded. Despite her annoyance, she decided to give Amona the benefit of the doubt.

"Thank you for everything as always, Amona. I'll visit when I get a chance," Sariyah promised, wrapping the seamstress in a tight hug.

"Of course, take your time. I may be old but I'm not going anywhere."

She brushed back her greying hair and turned to Sophie who stared up with a half-smile.

"And goodbye, dear Sophie. It was wonderful meeting you. I do hope we meet again. Let me know how that outfit does for you."

All semblance of the distress Amona had exhibited before had vanished. Sophie couldn't tell whether she had genuinely recovered or was a very good actress. If it was the latter, she was significantly more accomplished at it than herself, with her half-hearted attempt to appear cheerful.

"Nice to meet you both too, and I will," Sophie said. Minutes later, the duo were on the road westward once more.

The Louisianan countryside flickered past the window, and Sophie stared out at the fields and marshy planes by the river, with its many tributaries. She was brought out of her thoughts by Sariyah's address.

"Hey, everything is okay. We'll be in Dallas before you know it. You might want to get some sleep in the car too – it'll make the time fly by quicker."

Sophie gave a despondent response. "Yeah, probably."

"Aw, c'mon. How about a little music? A proper American road trip, the Sariyah way!"

Without waiting for a reply Sariyah fiddled with the stereo until the sweet sounds of a familiar country tune brightened the car.

Sariyah began to sing the lyrics to *Jambalaya*, refusing to accept Sophie's stubbornness. She paused at the end of the verse with a grin and looked for Sophie to fill in the following line.

She had to admit Sariyah's voice had a beautiful cadence to it. After a hesitation, she allowed herself to succumb to her infectious joviality and did so with a chuckle and a voice pitched one octave above the original, but perfectly in tune.

"Son of a gun we'll have big fun on the bayou!"

The two continued in this fashion as the hours ticked down to the promised safety in Dallas.

10 – Heaven Under the Sun

The journey to Dallas was tediously long and the last thing Sophie remembered was gazing at the setting sun spreading its ocherous hue across the sky, while passing through Alexandria. She woke briefly on the outskirts of Shreveport to Sariyah's gentle serenade, in a car lit only by streetlamps and the full moon shimmering above them.

When she awoke fully, she was no longer in the car. Instead, she was greeted by the harsh, intrusive rays of Texan sunlight, penetrating the small parting in a pair of curtains, and doing a good job of blinding her. Grumbling, she twisted and sat up.

She found herself in a red-sheeted double bed within a striking carmine bedroom. Sophie rubbed her eyes, pulled back the covers and swung her feet onto the cream carpet. It was incredibly soft; evidently recently installed. There was no sign of Sariyah, so she moved silently to the curtains, which were velvet and thin, allowing a partial haze of light through the translucent material. Pulling them back, the room was illuminated by the warm morning sun – no longer an aggressive irritation, but rather a welcome guest.

Magic Sorcerer or not, we all live under the same sun, she thought, and this gave her a degree of comfort.

Eyes fully adjusted, Sophie took in her new surroundings. One wall comprised an extensive mirror-doored wardrobe. An ornate chest of drawers rested against the opposite wall, perpendicular to the window. Catching her reflection in the mirror, she noticed she was wearing a blue t-shirt, much too big for her and hanging well below her hips, and relatively well-fitting pyjama shorts. She was unsure exactly how she came to be in these clothes, since her recollection of arriving at the apartment the previous night consisted of hazy, lopsided visions of corridors and the sound of bangs, followed by Sariyah's curses.

She shrugged off the confused stupor of these memories and returned to the present. Sophie decided that due to her new, mostly independent life, she ought to make her own bed. This only resulted in her doing so for an embarrassing amount of time, despite the fact that nobody would witness her attempt. When she had finished, the covers remained skewed and lay against pressed down pillows and crinkled sheets. She stood back to view her work.

Whatever! Not too shabby for a first attempt.

Unperturbed by her everyday incompetence, she smiled to herself, an unexpectedly optimistic mood growing. She regarded the new outfit she owned, handcrafted by Amona in a staggeringly short amount of time, neatly folded and resting on an armchair next to the chest of drawers, equally as red as the rest of the room.

Hmm, I guess I'll try the warm water trick Amona told me about. She seemed to know what she was talking about. Now, where's the bathroom?

She carefully scooped up the garments and exited the bedroom into a short corridor that linked each space of the apartment. She took a lucky guess and tried the door closest to the bedroom, entering a surprisingly spacious bathroom. There was a wide bath with an overhead shower. Sophie turned the taps, adjusting hot and cold until the water was pleasantly hot but not scalding. She considered the various soaps and gels that lined a shelf on the blue tiled wall, but decided against them and placed her clothes next to them on a shelf spanning the wall.

She ventured out to explore each room in the apartment, searching for Sariyah while the water ran. Eventually, she came upon the open plan lounge-cum-dining room, the front door situated between the two spaces. Sariyah was asleep on one of two sofas, a blanket draped over her lower half.

Tiptoeing so as not to disturb her with the sound of creaking floorboards, Sophie gently pulled the blanket up to Sariyah's shoulders, and silently appreciated Sariyah's sacrifice of the bed in favour of her comfort. She was still wearing the same outfit from yesterday, apart from her grey jacket, hanging on a peg by the door. Her hair looked a little greasy, but Sophie refrained from too harsh a judgement. She was beginning to learn of the impact of such things.1

Best leave her be for now. She had a long night of driving and slept on the couch for me.

But Sariyah stirred to Sophie's comforting touch on her shoulder. Her eyelids cracked open a smidgen, the pupils beneath shrinking in the light as she attempted to focus.

"Ugh," she groaned, stretching out her limbs and neck in one long aching movement. "Morning. Didn't expect to wake up to this."

"Thank you for leaving me the bed… it was nice of you."

"Huh? Oh, right. That's okay."

A slow smile preceded her slightly croaky voice. She was evidently not a morning person – a fact that made Sophie snicker.

"You stay here, I'll go make us some breakfast!"

Sophie smiled, confident she could do a good deed for Sariyah. It satisfied the guilt of indebtedness she felt so strongly within, but she also wanted to do it simply because she liked her.

As Sophie entered the kitchen area, Sariyah called back, "Thanks, I think there's some bread in one of the cupboards!"

Just time to get some toast on before I check on the bath.

The kitchen was thin, but long. White topped counters over modern grey drawers and cupboards lined one wall, with overheads for the regularly used cups, plates and bowls, and a fridge freezer built into an alcove to one side. After a moment of diligent searching, Sophie found the bread bin containing the remainders of a simple white loaf and dropped three slices into the toaster next to it, taking an educated guess at the appropriate setting. She got out two plates and discovered half empty pots of jam and marmalade in the fridge.

Satisfied with her work so far, she scurried back to the bathroom to check on the water. It was at a good level for submerging the clothes, per Amona's instructions, so she turned off the taps and carefully, one by one, placed the jacket, oversized boots, premade undershirt and jeans into the water. She did her best to separate each garment and provide it with ample space in the tub, finding this activity incredibly strange – as were most things in this new world she'd been thrown into.

She returned to the kitchen as she heard the sudden ka-chunk of the toaster popping up newly browned bread. She picked out the toast and lay two slices on Sariyah's plate and one on her own, disappointed that it had turned out more of a deep brown than the golden colour she was aiming for.

She gathered the plates, condiments, a small knife, a carton of milk, orange juice and a glass on a large tray. Breakfast prepared, she made her way back into the lounge, eyes focused on the tray, taking short steps.

"Aw, thank you," Sariyah beamed. Then her face contorted, "Oh, watch out for the rug!"

Her warning was to no avail. Sophie caught her foot on the surprisingly firm rug and stumbled, the tray slipping forward and hurtling toward the floor. Sariyah reacted with lightning reflexes, lurching forward, extending her arm down, flexing her fingers and holding her palm upward toward the ceiling, as if holding an invisible globe. Sophie could feel the new energy in the room turn to slight whispers of heat. She felt the currents of air being manipulated to hold the tray aloft, its contents intact. Carefully, Sariyah pivoted her extended arm across and let the tray settle atop the coffee table.

"Watch out for the rug, it's quite heavy," she commented as Sophie corrected herself with a blush.

"Thanks for saving breakfast, you have to teach me how to do that sometime."

"You've been busy, and it looks lovely, I'm glad I saved it."

Sophie handed her the plate with two slices of toast and moved the tray of condiments closer.

"I don't know what you have on toast, so I brought some options; the same with drinks."

With a smile Sariyah began to spread her toast with marmalade and poured herself a glass of milk.

"Well, you brought my favourites, so all is well. It's a little on the burnt side, but all in all a good job!"

"Good," Sophie sighed, beginning to munch on her own slice with added jam.

Sariyah moved the conversation on to casual small talk while she sat on the edge of the sofa, Sophie cross legged on the floor. Despite the unimportance of the topics they conversed about, they each found the other's perspectives and experiences fascinating and both fiercely approved of the situation, now that the important matters were settled.

After a while, Sophie found the courage to ask, "So... what is your real name?"

"My *real* name?" Sariyah raised an eyebrow.

"Yes, I haven't got a second name yet to protect me – and you know my real name – so it's only fair I know yours, isn't it?"

A shrug, followed by silent contemplation, then an answer.

"Alright, since we trust each other, and you don't tell *anyone*."

"Promise!" Sophie crossed her heart for good measure.

"My real name is Jessica. Sariyah was the name of my great grandmother back in Azerbaijan."

Sophie smiled. Knowing Sariyah's true name, while a trivial fact to many, meant a great deal in terms of trust in their relationship.

"Nice name. I don't know what my second name will be. I'm not sure I know what my great grandmother's name was."

Sariyah smiled slightly in response.

"The name you choose can be anything, but you'll know it when you know... I realise that sounds a little unhelpful, but believe me you'll understand what I mean soon."

"Right…" Sophie muttered, wrestling with the irritating abstract nature of this theory and custom.

"Don't worry," Sariyah reassured, "you're on your own little vastation. Nothing better than a cleansing trip to realise some deeper truths about yourself – like your name."

Listening on, Sophie dispelled her anxiety over the topic in favour of her previously optimistic mood.

"Yeah, and can I ask for a favour?"

Sariyah sat forward a little.

"Sure, what can I do?"

"Can you teach me some magic? A lot of it, like… everything you know." She smiled as cutely as she could in a childish attempt to influence Sariyah's answer.

"Okay, okay," Sariyah laughed, "I'll show you a couple of forms before we go to the library tomorrow. That is, if you teach me how to drink tea like a posh person. Deal?"

Sariyah's cheeky counteroffer made Sophie pout sarcastically and fold her arms.

"Deal!"

An hour passed before Sariyah returned to the lounge, having changed and freshened herself up. Sophie had so far managed to hold the intense boredom at bay, kept keen by the potent excitement coursing through her veins.

This is it! I'm going to learn how to perform some amazing acts. Try to hurt me now, I dare you!

She goaded her demons while observing Sariyah. She was arranging the collection of paper and plastic drinks cups they had gathered during their road trip, placing each one with an equal spacing across the dining table. Finishing her set up, Sariyah stepped back and sat at Sophie's side on the sofa, which they had moved to the face the table.

"I'm a Sorcerer, and we use our magic to enhance everyday interactions and phenomena. We're going to start with the easiest of these – to enhance air and manipulate currents."

Sophie nodded, devoting her full concentration to the lesson.

"I'm ready."

"Good, I'll start with a demonstration."

Sariyah rose and planted her feet firmly and securely on the wooden floorboards. She brought her arms around in a wide arc. It began ascending behind her and transitioned to descending forward, where she extended her arms in front of her and finally splayed her fingers, bending the tips slightly. Sophie felt raw energy being released. The air rippled in a straight trajectory and one of the plastic cups exploded off the table and flew across the room.

The wonder of what she'd just witnessed, coupled with eagerness and anticipation for her turn, moved Sophie to involuntarily applause. Sariyah turned back with a smile.

"Glad you liked it. When you get more experienced you won't need such dramatic movements, but they help for beginners."

Sophie quickly got to her feet and copied the sideward, grounded stance of Sariyah.

"Air magic is all in the fingers," Sariyah advised. Then she began to repeat her movement slowly, bringing her arms into the peak of the arc.

"You gather the particles of air, keeping a natural flow in your body before… pushing out!"

The grin on Sophie's face grew more gratified as she watched another cup shoot off the table.

"Let your magic gather around the air you collected and channel it away from your fingers and toward your target. All the while you need to stay well-grounded and in touch with the Earth."

Sariyah broke her stance to guide Sophie's arms in the correct motion, allowing her to practise the finer, more subtle accents of the form.

"Staying in touch with the Earth is the most important part. While the technique is in your movement, we Sorcerers draw our magic from the Earth up. That's why I don't really own any shoes. Keeping the connection is vital, and having materials between you and the ground tends to hamper your abilities."

Sophie nodded and adjusted her stance a little, attempting to give herself the best possible chance of success.

"Alright…ready to try for real?" Sariyah proposed.

"More ready than I've ever been for anything."

"Good, I'm sure you've felt it already – the energy in the air, in the walls, in *you*. Harness it, use it. Allow it to flow through you and out of your fingertips. The magic will do the work, you simply have to guide it."

Sariyah's words reverberated around Sophie's head. She let them sink deep within her and focused on a cup ahead of her. She searched her body for the energy she had begun to feel. It lay in wait at the base of her stomach and, she sensed, inside the very building she was connected to – crackling, throbbing with power like a crazed animal begging to be released from its cage. The words continued their frenzied dance in Sophie's head as she began twisting to the side, bringing her arms around in the same arc. She felt the magic shoot up through her legs, combining at her stomach and splitting once more as it reached her shoulders. Wildly scintillating sparks of magic travelled down each arm, the sheer ferocity causing her to buckle slightly, and each spark dissipated at her fingertips, transferring the energy into the air, rippling it outwards. Each particle of air, linked in an invisible interlocking chain, was being forced forward until…

The cup wobbled.

Sophie stared in utter disbelief. After overcoming the initial shock, she was filled with conflicted feelings. She had used magic! She had felt it boiling within her. She could still feel it now, resting, prepared in her stomach, waiting until it was called again. But she was greatly disappointed that she had only managed to cause a wobble, compared to Sariyah's exhilarating explosion of air. The latter feeling dominated.

"Aww, dammit! I barely did anything," Sophie moaned, shoulders slumping.

Sariyah beamed and wrapped her in a tight embrace lifting her off the ground.

"Yes! I knew you could do it. Well done, that's a great start. Practise some more and you'll be shooting things left right and centre."

The encouragement alleviated her disappointment slightly, but not entirely.

"I suppose so," she said, with a slight smile.

Consistently, Sophie became able to wobble and very occasionally gently knock over the cups Sariyah had arranged, as she practised for around an hour. The magic within her was bubbling and she was beginning to get accustomed with how to conduct it.

"I think that's enough for now," Sariyah instructed, "don't want you exhausting yourself. We can try some more after lunch." She lowered Sophie's arms as she spoke and pushed her legs together, relaxing her stance.

"Okay, but straight after lunch!" Sophie laughed. The anticipation made her dizzy.

"Great job, my new apprentice," Sariyah said approvingly. "Oh, that felt good – never had one before!"

"You're a great teacher," Sophie smiled as her mind began to wander.

She thought of what had transpired in her lesson and the possible future paths for her in magic. What secrets would she unlock? What power? The possibilities enticed and thrilled her more than any flashy show of status ever had.

My outfit! With all this excitement I nearly forgot.

Hurriedly, she made her way to the bathroom to discover her clothes immersed in the now tepid water. She quickly saw to her hair with a brush and prepared herself for the showcase to come. After this, she carefully removed each item of clothing from the bath and carried them back to her bedroom. To her astonishment, each garment appeared to be waterproof and was completely dry to the touch, despite having spent the best part of the morning completely submerged.

Unable to wait any longer, she dressed in the outfit she had designed – zealously yearned for – ever since the idea had arrived in her head. The oversized jacket, now delightfully snug, clung to her like an extension of her own skin, wrapping around her in a perfect fit, along with the rest of the outfit. With eyes screwed shut, she made her way over to the mirrored wardrobes, took a deep breath, and opened her eyes to view the finished product.

The majority of the jacket she wore comprised red and black leather. Two clear sections made up the body piece. Black leather with an off-centre silver zip favouring the left ran up the body, before splitting to form a large parted collar just below the neck. Each section of black held pockets that, upon inspection, appeared far deeper than they should naturally be – two horizontal ones at the sides above the hip, and on the right side a vertical pocket down the chest. Complementing and contrasting the black body and collar, was a seamless transition to a deep red covering the shoulders and making up the sleeves. These were segmented into equal bands via creases, indented between each one.

Alongside the visually striking and stylistically dominant jacket, her plain white undervest held almost skin-tight around her. Deep blue jeans were tucked carefully into her boots. It was the jacket and boots that Sophie admired the most. The boots were the same deep black as the jacket body and rose a little up her shins. They made an incredibly satisfying click as she walked.

She found herself praising the incredible talent Amona had shown in putting together this masterpiece, and was pleased that the shrinking technique had proven fruitful. She grinned to herself, elated at seeing the way the clothes highlighted her natural beauty, not to mention the way it brought out the intense green of her eyes.

"Well, you certainly look striking."

Sariyah's voice from the doorway startled Sophie a little, but failed to phase her enough to wake her from her hypnotic state.

"Oh…" she finally managed, "I like this a lot!"

11 – THE GREAT LIBRARY OF INFORMATION IN RELATION TO THE MAGICAL ARTS

T he following morning gave rise to the intrusive Texan sun once more, beaming down over Dallas to disturb the rest of any who had foolishly allowed space for the light to make its unwelcome entry. But the bedroom of bright crimson remained undisturbed. Sophie woke naturally in the slight darkness, curled up on the left side of the bed. A yawn, a stretch, and she sat up to find Sariyah still fast asleep tucked into the right-hand side, her hair frantic but otherwise sleeping peacefully.

Sophie spent the morning as she had the previous afternoon, evening and night – practising her magic. She repeated the form again and again, the cups wobbling and occasionally toppling on the dining table. She found herself becoming increasingly frustrated at her inability to create more than a gentle breeze.

"It'll come, don't worry. It just takes time."

Sariyah entered the lounge dressed and revitalised, her olive skin glowing. Sophie shrugged.

"I know, but the more I practise the sooner that time will come to pass."

"Perhaps. Ready for our trip today?"

An eager nod.

"Definitely, I can't wait!"

Sariyah slung her satchel over her shoulder and headed for the door, gesturing for Sophie to follow.

"You won't have to, it opens at nine, we can grab some breakfast on the way."

Breakfast was welcome and fulfilling and before long the two were stood side by side before a warehouse on the outskirts of the city. As Sophie inspected the exterior of the premises, she could see cars from a multitude of decades dotted about the area surrounding the building, which had ample space for more.

"There's got to be a lot of books in there." Sophie stared. She loved books and almost licked her lips from the delirium of it all.

"There are thousands, so please don't try and read them all or we'll be here for weeks," Sariyah noted dryly, as they made their way toward the double doors at the bottom left corner of the warehouse. The letters T.G.L.I.R.M.A were engraved above the frame.

A slight ramp led the way to the entry, where Sariyah placed her hands on the two central door handles. Miraculously they began to glow a gentle red colour. The light seemed to emit from the very centre of the handle's composition. Silence ensued for a second before the glowing stopped and Sariyah turned the handle to enter the building. A step away from the threshold she glanced back.

"Don't worry, just do the same as me. It's a security lock and only those with magic can enter. It's to stop mortals from nosing in our business."

With a smile she disappeared, the doors fixing shut behind her.

Sophie quickly approached and repeated Sariyah's actions. The handles began to vibrate gently and lit up with a pale luminescent blue before permitting her entry.

Joining Sariyah, she now found herself inside a small reception area. The décor reflected that of a stereotypical office building – simple sofas arranged around a low coffee table and a drinks machine under a low ceiling made up of removable square panels.

A door at the far side of the room had a flat-screened device nestled into the wall beside it. Sariyah approached the device, raised her index and middle fingers, then pressed and swiped them from right to left across the lower section of the screen. The device burst into life and displayed words on screen that an audible voice confirmed.

"Officer Sariyah Pierce, authorised."

The voice, emanating from nowhere in particular, filled the room as though the person were in there with them, yet Sophie could see no one apart from the two of them.

"Do I do the same thing? How does it work?" Sophie asked, stepping before the scanner.

"Everyone has a magical signature. Your connection to magic and the specific energy reading it gives off is truly unique to you. Well, apart from identical twins, but that doesn't apply to you," Sariyah explained. "Try and channel your magic up to two fingertips, but don't release it in any form. Just let it buzz and gather there and swipe across, so it can take your reading."

Sophie nodded and attempted to do as she was told, tapping into the energy she felt in her stomach, letting it flow up into her right hand. She swiped across the screen just as Sariyah had done.

"Unrecognised signature" the voice rang out, "please identify."

Nerves prickled in her when she heard the voice, unsure how to proceed. She wondered where she had made an error in the process. But Sariyah simply smiled and entered a security key of some kind that approved Sophie's signature and the door unlocked for their entry.

"What did you do?"

"You're not on the system yet, so I authorised you as my official guest and responsibility until you can create your own Adytum profile."

Sophie nodded and entered the library proper behind Sariyah.

The sight that confronted her astounded her to the point of disbelief. She blinked multiple times to ensure her eyes were focusing properly. The interior of the warehouse resembled exactly that – a high roof with steel support beams, corrugated upper panelling, a sturdy yellow brick base and worn concrete floor. Placed and organised within the structure, however, were eleven extended aisles reaching down the entire length of the building, splitting halfway for a central walkway. Each aisle contained bookshelves on either side, which acted as all-encompassing walls. The bookcases reached almost twenty-five metres high, far into the recesses of the rafters.

Sophie approached one of the gargantuan cases, her neck permanently inclined upward in an attempt to make out the peak of these monstrosities. Smooth dark wood slid under her touch and she couldn't help but let her mouth gape in awe.

"How in the world do you get up there?" she gasped, staggered by the dizzying structure towering over her.

"Using one of those," Sariyah pointed.

Following her line of sight, Sophie could see identical wooden platforms at the base of the shelves, spaced every few metres. Each had a railing for safety and support, as well as a simple chair and small round table. Where there were oddly spaced gaps, Sophie realised that the platforms were in use, positioned at various elevations on the bookcases – each with a person far above sitting at the table, drinking morning coffee and reading a book retrieved from up high.

"Wow!" she gasped. The shock was beginning to wear off and excitement beginning to bubble.

Sariyah motioned for her to explore.

"Go on, have a blast. They're organised into categories and are alphabetical within those. Feel free to ask if you have questions."

Impulsively she hugged Sariyah tightly, who blushed at the gesture, then ran down the closest aisle to them, seeking out any marker for Necromancy. Five minutes of searching led her to a section on secondary Mage disciplines, where she discovered Necromancy was categorised. Each book in the section had a yellow tinge to the spine and she first took the section's index catalogue and read the contents before stopping at *The Beginnings of Necromancy* by Quincy Exanimate. Realising, however, that "B" would be situated almost at the very top of this particular shelving section, Sophie bit her bottom lip.

Guess I should try one of these lift things… jeez.

Forcing her unwilling legs to take action she moved to the nearby wooden platform and stepped onto it, glancing back to locate Sariyah, who was some distance back in an opposing section, though close enough to keep Sophie in view. Reassured, she looked around to see if there was an obvious way to operate the structure she now stood in. To the right-hand side of the railing, engraved on a flat board that jutted up at an angle just above her waist, were four symbols, constructed like Chinese characters, made up of various dots and slashes arranged around a focal point. They lay in a diamond shape on the board and Sophie instinctively channelled her magical signature into two fingers and pressed them hard into the top symbol – a horizontal crescent moon with the tips pointing down and a large dot above it in the centre.

Immediately, the symbol illuminated with the same pale blue light she'd seen at the entrance, and the entire platform, carrying Sophie with it, began to caravan upwards with terrifying speed. Alarmed and heart racing ten to the dozen, Sophie let out a shrill squeak and stumbled away from the engraved panel. This caused the platform to decrease in speed dramatically, then gradually drift to a stop after another two metres.

Taking a significant gulp of air, she righted herself and blew out.

Okay… maybe don't press as hard.

She repeated the process but pressed gently into the same symbol and the platform began to move steadily upwards, quickly but not uncontrollably so. She held the symbol until she arrived at the "B" section then let go, waiting for the platform to steady itself before continuing.

Trying her best not to look down she searched the shelves. She didn't consider herself afraid of heights, but sitting towards the upper end of a twenty-five metre structure with little more than a low railing to save you, would likely send any person woozy to a degree.

Soon she had found the book she had made the journey to find and took a seat in the provided chair to read. Despite being supported by nothing but thin air, the platform was surprisingly stable as she moved across it.

The book highlighted various topics that Apathy had referred to in their earlier meeting at the Adytum, alongside many techniques and concepts that were foreign to her. Under "Neophytes trials" lay information on concepts such as soul merging and harnessing raw death magic. It was clear that, despite the book being very informative, a base understanding of some of the applications of magic would also be needed.

However, some aspects of Necromancy she could understand, and they only served to feed her growing obsession. She learnt how the shadows of the necromancer were developed over time and adapted to the personality of their master, possessing a degree of autonomy but ultimately being bound in servitude.

Shadow pets, how delightfully deadly! I suppose some of Apathy's actions make sense now.

For around an hour she read, devouring the knowledge within the pages. She read of the application of shadows in combat and everyday life, as well as the importance of the soul to necromancy; how one must be in tune with, and entirely accepting of, themselves to truly harness its power. Throughout her perusal there were multiple references to ancient beings of significant power, named by what Sophie recognised as the creatures her father had attempted to summon – the Deorum.

Sophie considered her next actions carefully, debating whether discovering more of these creatures she had come into such close contact with was advisable or not. Her curiosity stood victorious, however, and she placed her current book on the small table, returning to the platform's controls. She used the other symbols to reposition herself further along in separate aisles. She failed to notice her disappearing from Sariyah's line of sight until she arrived, truly alone, along the back rows of books to the far side of the warehouse.

Here, each book's spine had the same violet colouring that had infused her father's church, and Sophie knew she was in the correct section. Delicately, she retrieved as many books on the Deorum as she could possibly find, scouring the contents for information.

Within their pages she learnt of the race of near transcendent beings who controlled the natural processes of the Earth, as much as the everyday lives and actions of the people that lived under them. Sophie read on, the world around her ceasing to exist as she lost herself in the words.

She learnt that around the start of the fourth century AD, the Deorum had become enraged at humanity's heretical proselytization and wide acceptance of new beliefs, and threatened to aggressively reassert control. These threats provoked a civil war of unforeseen magnitude, with the twins Solis and Luna, alongside a select few allies, defending the mortal race of which they had become guides and guardians.

The civil war, after decades of destruction, finally came to an end upon the twin's self-sacrifice, releasing their power into the earth and atmosphere, destroying themselves, and banishing the remaining Deorum – Tonitrua, Oceanum and Bellum – to the heavens.

Their residual power, shimmering and crackling around the atmosphere, was harnessed by the humans that remained and channelled into the magic that had been developed over the ensuing centuries.

Sophie stared in disbelief at the pages she read, attempting to fathom the reasons for which her father would want to bring back such destructive and spiteful creatures. With only a short few chapters remaining, she knew she couldn't stop now, despite the nauseating sensation washing over her.

Concluding the book, Sophie learnt of the so-called Aradian line, the worshippers of Solis and Luna; and of the revered three, who discovered and spread the use of magic, began the cult of worship alongside one Camilla Aradian and founded the first Adytum in Rome. The Aradian line continued from Camilla's descendants, each tasked with the responsibility of protecting the religion of the Adytum until…

Sophie gasped and swallowed to prevent herself from throwing up. The colour drained from her face and her eyes screwed shut in a futile attempt to shut out the reality of her history. In so doing, she failed to notice the evidence of torn and replaced pages toward the end of the book. Sophie wrestled in her mind, reluctant to believe that her father had drawn the worship of the church away and warped its values in line with his own interests of aiding the living Deorum to return.

Yet, not only had she received further confirmation of her father's malicious and malevolent intent, she also now held the knowledge that *she herself* was a descendant of the original line of religious leaders, the Aradian.

No! I won't be a part of this. Her mind raged in turmoil. *I won't let my father continue with his morbid distortion!*

It was then that the world began to return to her. Her senses awoke from their shock-induced numbness and she opened her eyes. There was fire and screaming. Chaos had engulfed the previously peaceful library. Sophie knew without the need for confirmation. They had come for her.

12 – ARADIA VASTATE

U tter pandemonium had consumed the building. Cries of terror and anguish pierced the once still air and sweat began to trickle down Sophie's cheek as the temperature steadily increased to a sweltering level.

The world moved with celerity around her, yet Sophie remained entirely still, fear binding her like the strongest of shackles. The fine hairs on her arms stood on end and there was a sickening tightness in her chest, returning for the first time since she'd left Atlanta. All the while her mind raced, fabricating childish, futile strategies to save herself.

Maybe if I stay still, they won't find me, won't see me. Sariyah will find me, I just have to wait for her.

A deafening crash caught her attention. Her head snapped around to locate the source of the nearby disturbance. She was greeted by the clattering of endless books, all falling in tandem, shelf by shelf, tumbling to the ground. Sophie stared in bewilderment until the realisation of what loomed ahead jolted her out of her paralysis.

Wood splintered and more books fell as the centre of the colossal bookcase opposite her began to bulge outward, splitting as if something were forcing it from the other side. The main structure's roots were anchored deep into the ground below, and steel struts supported the upper levels of the incredible structure, but the simple timbers of the centre and middle shelves had no such aid, and were crumbling under the unseen pressure exerted upon them. Sophie had but seconds to register the impending disaster before each timber simultaneously snapped, grinding with a sound that made her skin crawl.

She let out a primal scream from her perch on the adjacent platform, her brain unable to respond to the situation before her. Yet, instinctively, the magic that boiled in her stomach, fuelled by the overload of adrenaline coursing through her veins, forced its path down her body. It rapidly seized control of her muscles, pushing away from the chair where she sat and locking her knees bent, bringing her low to the floor – all this, in an intuitive act of self-preservation to protect its host.

Books and splinters hailed down upon her. Her handcrafted jacket proved effective in protecting her from physical injury, but the blunt force pain of the barrage prevailed despite it, causing Sophie to scream. After a significant weight bore down on her, the pressure suddenly relented and left her drawing laboured breaths. Gradually, Sophie regained control of her body, the reacting magic aiding in dispelling her terror-locked joints before returning to rest in her stomach, inactive but poised, ready to be commanded.

In one heaving movement she twisted her body, bringing her legs under her to push off and rise up through her prison. Breaking the surface, before her lay destruction and mayhem. Flames engulfed the lower levels, wrapping around any flammable timber, yet Sophie could make out figures on the ground floor. People she had seen previously enjoying a morning drink and visit to the library were now locked in vicious and deadly combat against men and women in deep purple robes. Sizzling beams of yellow energy were exchanged by both sides, alongside significant hand-to-hand brawling and occasional bursts of white-hot flame.

She quickly turned her attention to other avenues of escape and was almost tripped by a significant shift in the balance of the platform on which she stood, as it began to tilt due to the immense weight now inflicted upon it. Her eyes shot upward to see the fallen segment of the opposing bookcase, lodged less than a metre above her, bridging the space between the two constructions at a slight angle. Knowing each second she spent on the platform could be one too many, she surmised that it was securely wedged enough in the upper shelves to take her weight.

She reached up and wrapped her fingers around the now empty casing. Using the broken table edge as a boost, she hauled herself up and through the opening with a harsh groan. Upper body through, she renewed her grip and managed to crawl out onto the collapsed interlocking beams, her muscles straining to support her weight.

She let out a long exhale before steadying herself to stand. The beams, while weakened, were secure enough to hold firm under her and just wide enough to be walked across. Ahead of her, however, lay a fresh threat in waiting. As Sophie had correctly guessed, here was the cause of the recent explosion and the destruction of the bookcase's midsection.

"There you are, little girl."

The voice which barely reached Sophie through all the commotion, nonetheless chilled her to the bone, as if each word had fangs that eagerly ripped into her confidence.

"Come, your father is expecting me back with you tomorrow and we really can't delay."

"Go to hell!" Sophie screamed back. Her voice was breaking but she refused to go down without putting up some sort of fight.

"Let's not make this hard, shall we? I will take you – it's just a matter of whether you make me work for it or not."

The figure took a step forward, one foot directly in line with the other heading down a central beam. His indigo cloak swept behind him as he began to walk, revealing deep black armour underneath. Sturdy and heavily plated, each section overlapped the next to conceal any joints that might expose a weakness. The pattern repeated all over his body under the cloak, so that the armour resembled the scales of a mythical creature, joined by leather and steel.

A mask covered his head entirely, and it was this aspect of the being that struck the most fear within her. It was completely smooth grey metal, featureless apart from some engravings in a language that Sophie couldn't decipher, which ran down the very edges of the face, forehead to chin.

"Not one more step!" Sophie shrieked as the man edged closer.

"Or what?"

Sophie knew he was smirking beneath the mask. Then a thought dawned on her, a use of leverage against a superior foe.

"Or, I'll jump off… you… you need me *alive*. If you come closer, I swear I'll jump!"

Another step.

"You're bluffing."

"I'll do it. I'd rather die than let my father bring those monsters back," she cried, though she could see her attempt at a threat failing rapidly, realising what she might have to do to escape.

Another step.

"All you will do by running is wear me out a little and cause yourself a great deal of pain," he hissed. He was almost within arm's reach of Sophie's trembling form.

"Well then…" Sophie conceded, heart in her mouth. "If all I can do is make you tired, I might as well inconvenience you a bit." With that, she dove sideward as her assailant made a move for her.

Wind whipped at her hair, bile rose in her throat and the world spun. Mere seconds stretched to an age. Panic took her breath way as she tumbled through the air and stared at the concrete floor, eagerly rushing to meet her.

Impact.

Rather than the release of death or unconsciousness she had expected, Sophie was instead met with an incredible raging dagger of pain, rocketing through her side. Her mouth opened wide to scream but no sound came, pure shock freezing her reaction in time before the initial blow subsided and the intense stabbing pain took hold in her side.

Sophie sobbed as she felt a crash next to her and turned to see the boots of her attacker. He had simply hopped down from above with no effort. Reserves of energy came in uneven spikes that jerked her movements forward. Scrambling to her feet she careered around pockets of flame and debris in an attempt to escape. As she approached the corner of the aisle, Sophie risked a glance back. The man in the dragon scale armour had not even moved. He simply stood and watched as she ran. This was just sport to him.

Rounding the corner, Sophie begged for the sight of Sariyah, her thoughts and hopes centred on her saviour. But aisle by aisle her search yielded no result and the possibility that Sariyah may have been consumed by the madness around them provoked a twitching unrest unlike anything Sophie had ever felt.

She turned a final corner to find her path blocked by splintered timber, lit and burning. She shielded her eyes and sought an alternative route, but there was none. Sophie turned as her predator approached, striding forward casually and confidently.

"Nowhere left to run now, little Sophie," he chuckled spitefully.

She whimpered, desperately searching for a way of escape.

"I may need to bring you in alive," he continued, "but that doesn't mean I can't have some fun with you on the way home."

"You'll... you..." Sophie panted. Coherent speech failed her and she submitted to her fate, falling to her knees, weeping.

The man strode towards her, confidently goading her as he did so.

"Good, you made the right decision. You know you're helpless, powerless. The disgraced daughter of a forsaken lineage. Your ancestors may have been hallowed, but when you die, the future generations will curse your name for the trouble you caused in ushering in our rightful rulers. Even the Adyta will speak of you with disgust knowing your sacrifice sealed their fates."

Sophie continued to whimper and whine, her eyes red with terrified tears, her body exhausted from the pain and incessant trembling...

Until… something snapped within her. Another bone? Her sanity?

She couldn't think to tell, or tell herself to think. But she somehow became aware of a few simple, fundamental truths.

This isn't the end. My journey has only just begun, I'm on a vastation, a path of purification unlike any other. I'm Sophie Lockwood, my fate will be that of legend, but… I am no Lockwood, I am an Aradian. A descendant of the most revered religious leaders the magical world has ever known. My ancestors harnessed the power of Solis and Luna to honour their sacrifice… my father has destroyed this honour… I will not stop until I see it restored, cost it bone, limb or life.

I will not let my father succeed.

I will surrender to no opponent.

And I will not be powerless.

Ever again.

An incredible surge of energy sparked through her entire body, silencing fear, silencing pain, and jolting her upright. Rooted on legs of steel, Aradia held her ground. The magic in her core roared with untamed fury and streaked down her limbs into her fingertips as she brought her arms round in a wide arc. Further magic, enthralled by and attracted toward its new master, charged up from the Earth below her, synergising with the immense power already bubbling in her body, but she did not tremble.

With one herculean release, her magic sparked and infused the air particles around her hands, heating them, propelling them. An explosion of raw power launched that would crush anything in its path with savagery.

The scaled armour did nothing to protect the unsuspecting victim of this attack. Her aggressor was catapulted backwards as if he were nothing, along with piles of scattered books. Flames were extinguished in the wake of the air blast.

Aradia gazed at the carnage she had caused as the energy left her and she sagged. The entire warehouse seemed to have fallen silent from the eruption.

Sophie Lockwood had fallen in submission.

Aradia Vastate had risen to defend her legacy.

13 – The Honour in Duplicity

—⁓—

Sariyah awoke to the sound of muffled cries and a ringing in her ears. An attempt to sit up was met with stubborn resistance. Confused, her mind a blur, she jerked her head upwards and scraped across a jagged spike of wood, which opened a wound on her forehead. She cried out, but the sudden pain jolted her back to reality. Blinking, she could make out the barrage of dust, books and wooden planks tightly packed around her. The weight, bearing heavy on her body, set a panic rising in her throat, but she gulped it down.

Now isn't the time to panic – you've been in tight spaces before, you tunnel all the time!

With a grunting heave she attempted to raise her arms and push back the rubble that was slowly crushing her to no avail. Each limb was pinned under the immense density of her wooden grave.

Tunnel... tunnel!

Concentrating, she could feel that one foot and one hand were pressed against the concrete floor and thanked the universe for it. She employed the usual breathing techniques, attempted to quell any anxiety at her entrapment, and focused her attention on the cold sensation the concrete provided. At the peak of an inhalation Sariyah channelled her magic to the two relatively free limbs, attempting to manipulate the earth to part under the pressure she was creating. She exhaled as she did so.

She scowled, frustrated at the difficulty of attempting to tunnel in an uneven, uncentered position. Nevertheless, after thirty seconds of concentrated bursts and the breaking of sweat, the ground began to give way and a reassuringly familiar rumbling made its way to her ears.

Sinking at a sideward angle, Sariyah let out a grunt that was a mix of resentment and pain as she yanked her remaining arm and leg free of their bonds and sank fully into the earth, rotating and flipping onto her stomach as she did so.

The earth sealed behind her and light was banished in her underground domain. She let out a final long exhale before returning to normal breaths, soothed by the knowledge that nothing would ever find or hurt her within her earthly haven. Though acutely aware of her limited oxygen supply, Sariyah pushed off with a force that could level mountains. As she travelled, she repeated to herself:

Find Sophie, fight the bad guys, get to the car.

After travelling what she deemed a suitable distance to escape the rubble, she shifted her direction, crouching in her fabricated tunnel. She pressed her hands to the roof and closed her eyes, extending her magic in an attempt to determine what lay above the surface. An abnormal heat was reflected back to her. Correctly assuming the worst, Sariyah shifted once more, searching for a suitably safe location to surface.

Upon extending her magic upward for a fourth time she was greeted by a welcome coolness from the concrete flooring above. Taking a final breath of air, she released the energy needed to break the surface and light flooded her vision. But it was not a welcome light.

Righting herself and carefully rising to her feet, Sariyah was finally able to view what had transpired after her assault. The library was in ruins. Flame had consumed all that it touched and the bodies of fallen friends and foe littered the once opulent and respectable aisles of this fount of knowledge. Further into the building Sariyah could hear the immense blows and clamour of combat continuing and before heading to investigate, she gave a final glance at where she had previously stood down the aisle, reading a book peacefully before being taken round the back of the head and launched into the opposite shelving that had collapsed around her.

Coughing and parched, she moved through the smoke and sultry air. Sariyah pursued the signs of combative destruction until she found herself standing before the centre of a blast of epic proportions. Before her lay one of the most important bookcases of the library, previously containing information on the history of magic and culture. The upper and lower thirds remained fixed in place, held fast by their sizable and strengthened supports, but the mid-section had been entirely blown inward, separated at the edges, and now lay smashed against the opposite case, bridging the aisle at an angle. Sariyah stood astounded at the power one would have to exert in order to bring down such a colossal structure – until the blue flame that lapped at the newly formed edges of the charred wood informed her.

Gravely Sariyah blew out, goosebumps riddling her arms. She attempted to remain steadfast and stalwart in her actions, pushing down her emotions to hold back the burning anger and hysterical tears.

This time you aren't getting away. Not this time!

Her magic, violent and forceful, raged in her stomach. Its eagerness to be released was almost overpowering and Sariyah harnessed that energy while retaining her composure as best she could. Channelling the magic to her palms and fingertips, she released a significant burst of the thick air that surrounded her, allowing her to lift off the ground and launch herself some ten metres into the air, to land on the bridged section of bookcase. She retracted the magic and steadied it once she had touched down.

Steadily moving across one of the central beams, still mostly secure after the explosion, Sariyah skipped like an acrobat across a tightrope. She stopped in the centre to try and catch a glimpse of Sophie, dreading the thought that the Dragon of Erzurum may have gotten to her.

Her worries were startled into an abrupt end when her ears popped and her hair fluttered in a sudden strong breeze. Taken aback, Sariyah reinspected her surroundings. The gust of air seemed to have come from a couple of aisles across, with enough force to extinguish the great fires in its wake, as well as scattering debris. The only flames that remained, as far as Sariyah could determine, were the scorching blue infernos of the Dragon.

Without hesitation, she let forth a burst of air to propel her forward, then another to cushion her fall into a sprint. Within seconds Sariyah was upon the scene of the incident that had silenced the building. Vision now unimpaired, she could see Sophie, slumped on her hands and knees at the epicentre of the blast and attempted to dismiss the thoughts that pecked at her brain.

Did she...? Is that possible? Where is he?

Reaching Sophie, Sariyah knelt beside her and gently rubbed her shoulders.

"Sophie, what happened? Are you okay?"

A slight groan was the only response she received and Sariyah noticed the blood beginning to stain the vest beneath the girl's jacket.

"Don't worry, I'm here. Sariyah's here Sophie. I'm getting you out of here."

A laboured whisper managed to creep out of cracked lips.

"Not... Sophie."

Before Sariyah could question this statement, she detected a sudden shift in the air some paces behind them. She swung around, clutching the girl's body close to her chest, then set her to rest with a pained groan against the wall. As she rose to face her opponent, the voice that plagued her nightmares bit at her ears.

"When I heard that Sariyah Pierce was protecting Lockwood's daughter I didn't truly believe it. I told them, no not *my* Sariyah, surely? Why on earth would she accept such a dangerous mission? I suppose this has coloured me surprised."

Sariyah grated her teeth and dual orange flames lit up in her palms resting by her sides.

"I don't belong to anyone, certainly not you."

The figure chuckled.

"Oh, *you do*, and you'll realise that soon enough – just like the rest of your insufferable family."

Untamed rage continued to build within her, distracting her, leaving her open to attack.

"Don't… you…" A suppressed gurgle escaped her throat, the anger overwhelming.

"They all eventually agreed that I should have you. It took some painful convincing, but they all saw my side, as you know."

Beneath the helmet Sariyah knew that a sickening smirk dressed his handsome face. In her bestial rage, she quickly released a torrent of flame, closely followed by three rabid cries accompanying columns of air.

Burning blue flame rose to meet each attack with a poetic, steady swiftness and ease, deflecting them either side.

"Now, now, Sariyah, let's not get ahead of ourselves."

In her agonising rage, Sariyah had failed to notice multiple Mages closing in on her, barring the space between her and Sophie, who was still clinging to consciousness on the floor.

"I have an offer, a deal, just to show-"

Sariyah cut the man off and spat forward.

"I don't care about any sick deal, you pretentious murderous little pri–"

"Ah-ah… talking," he chided, holding up a finger to silence her, the action so jarring to Sariyah that it proved successful.

"Just to show how much I do care about you, I propose a Sorcerer's duel – by the book, as tradition would have it. If you win, you take the girl and we won't pursue you. If I win, you both come with me, the girl to her father and you, well… we can pick up where we left off."

"I'm not playing, your sick games, Saeva. No deal."

He laughed and shrugged in the way that never failed to make her blood boil.

"Alternatively, I could simply tell my fellows here to take the girl, knock you out and have you delivered to my chambers within the day."

The collection of Sorcerers and Mages surrounding her chittered amongst themselves and taunted Sariyah as she stood surrounded. Seeing no other option, Sariyah stamped a foot into the ground in anger, then slid it across the floor to assume a combat stance.

"I accept."

Saeva clapped and rubbed his palms together.

"Excellent, you Adytum Sorcerers have never been ones for an honourable duel, always looking for the cheap and easy way to best your foes."

Saeva's forces gathered around the two of them down the aisle, fencing them in the back and sides as he continued.

"Since I initiated the duel, I grace you with the courtesy of announcing the element."

Sariyah stared, anger now sharpening her senses.

"Fire."

Saeva removed his helmet and set it aside, revealing short black hair with not a single strand out of place.

"What a fascinating choice to select my speciality."

"Figured I would give you a fighting chance," Sariyah sneered.

"How kind." He nodded and smiled, bowing as he did so. Sariyah begrudgingly bowed in return before both resumed fighting stances. Silence descended and Sariyah awaited Saeva's first assault.

With a ferocious heat startling all present, Saeva took a commanding stride forward and threw two fast punches, each producing a blazing burst of flame. The step took him just shy of what had been determined to be the centre line.

Sariyah anticipated this manoeuvre, dropping to a poised crouch as the first ball of fire hurtled over her, closely followed by its twin. A successful defence made, she transitioned into her counterattack, propping herself up on her hands and one leg, while the other leg swept around releasing an enraged arc of flame to unbalance her opponent.

Her countering ambush proved to be a fruitless attack as Saeva simply swivelled on the spot, channelling Sariyah's fire around him as he spun. Flames wrapped and engulfed his entire body until all at once they were ignited into a bright sapphire which he launched headlong into Sariyah, catching her in the chest and forcing her back several metres.

She slid to a stop, crossing into the midzone, signifying a round break. Saeva strutted forward to where Sariyah had previously stood in response.

"I never remember you being so unbalanced dear. What's happened?" He smiled grimly, sneering down at Sariyah as she rose to her feet to take a defensive stance once more.

"I got distracted by your deformed face," she snapped back, but received no more than a sardonic smile in response.

"I would have thought insults below you."

No sooner had he finished speaking than the next attack was launched. Sariyah brought her arms up in front of her in a boxer's guard, dispersing the flames that barraged her. To counter, she broke her defence and swung her arms wide outward. The inferno produced engulfed the duelling ground, knocking Saeva off balance. She swiftly followed her attack with a quick burst of flame to knock him back. Saeva had recovered, however, and blocked the assault. She ignored his recovery and pressed on, piling the pressure onto her opponent, knocking him down and backward a zone.

The illegal manoeuvre caused disquietude in the gathered crowd who began to bellow and squawk their disapproval. Knowing she had been caught, Sariyah relinquished her place, retreating to the final zone, only a few steps from defeat as Saeva rose to his feet and brushed himself off.

"You cheeky scofflaw, that is certainly a violation!"

Sariyah made an undignified childish face at him before closing her eyes, focusing on her breathing and mission alone.

Win the duel, get to safety, protect Sophie.

Saeva began his next assault and the two became locked in turn by turn combat once more. Saeva held a clear mastery over his manipulation of fire and Sariyah's competence paled by comparison.

He's too strong, I'm going to lose. What then?

A blast caught her leg, taking it from under her and forcing her down to one knee, a mere stone's throw away from the final boundary and humiliating defeat. Saeva smirked down at her, taking his time in his concluding assault. As he did, Sariyah glanced over his shoulder, catching sight of a small number of Adytum aligned Sorcerers and Mages preparing for a surprise assault.

Protecting Sophie is more important than humouring this sick reprobate's code. I don't owe him a thing. Don't worry Sophie, I won't let anybody hurt you, ever.

Course of action decided, Sariyah twisted. She channelled her magic deep into the earth, forming cracks between the atoms of concrete, separating them until two uneven slabs burst free of the ground under Saeva's feet, blasting him into the air.

As if they had received a signal, the remaining allies descended upon the outraged crowd of Deorum forces and intense combat ensued for a second round.

Before turning to find Sophie, Sariyah stood tall and slammed one foot into the ground. Her magic amplified the vibrations and caused the concrete to split up ahead as Saeva impacted with it, causing him to become partially swallowed by the earth. It was a prison he could easily escape from, but she knew it would slow him down.

Evading bursts of flame, columns of air and multiple blasts of energy from all directions, Sariyah kept herself low to the ground. She spotted Sophie, doing her utmost to crawl away from the chaos and made fast for her.

Catching up, she scooped Sophie into her arms, aided by an opportune gust of wind, and made for the exit, swearing to herself that those who fell to ensure her escape would be suitably honoured once these events had come to an end.

Using air to propel them over multiple obstructions, the two finally reached the safety of the exit, thankful that with his destructive tendencies, Saeva had blown the reception doors off their hinges, inadvertently aiding their swift escape. A few more paces and she had Sophie safely back in the car. The engine roared and their escape was made good.

Before long, they coasted to a halt in the centre of mortal Dallas, parking in a lay-by.

"Sophie, are you okay?" Sariyah asked hurriedly, turning her full attention to her wounded passenger.

The girl's responses came in hushed murmurs through laboured breaths.

"Not… Sophie… anymore."

"What?" Sariyah stroked her arm reassuringly.

"Aradia…"

Sariyah arched an eyebrow, puzzled. Then the switch flicked in her mind.

"You've decided your name, haven't you?"

A gentle nod and a slight smile.

"They tracked us, I'm not sure how. Only we knew we would be at the library today, but I promise I'll look into it. We've just got to find somewhere to stay in the meantime. I'm so sorry Soph… Aradia."

Sariyah sat forward and found that Aradia's hand was in hers, gently squeezing.

"Necromancers," she wheezed.

"Huh? Wait, that's genius! You have an invitation from Apathy and she's an old friend of mine. The Deorum would never be so bold as to attack the Necromancers, especially not in their stronghold city."

The Mustang growled back into life. Sariyah put it in gear and pulled back onto the main road. The city churned like a habitual machine around them, people and vehicles moving along as if no intense destruction or tragic loss of life had occurred just minutes before.

Aradia settled her hands in her lap and took a shallow breath.

"Don't worry," Sariyah assured her, "first we'll get you patched up, then you can tell me all about your new name on the way. It's a long drive to Vegas."

14 – DISCORDANT LEADERSHIP

Donovan sat in quiet contemplation on the yellow cushion of a lavish bench that ran for a few metres along the outer wall of Imperator Orotund's office. His wait had already exceeded ten minutes and he was rapidly becoming more frustrated with the Imperator than he already was on a regular basis.

If you don't have time to see me immediately, then call me when you do! Otherwise, I end up here, sitting like an ass twiddling my thumbs. It would save us both a considerable amount of time, he thought, as he did precisely that.

There was nothing of interest to view while he passed the time. The pretentious golden corridors only served to anger him, and those who passed by would either stoop so low in reverence that their backs might break, or attempt to strike up a conversation that Donovan had no desire to entertain.

His mood lifted a little when a personalised caller ringtone liberated him from the depressing silence. Answering the phone, he addressed the caller warmly and with an audible smile.

"Hey sweetheart, I've got an important meeting soon. Is everything alright?"

The voice that responded had a naïve immaturity, but a sweetness that none could conquer.

"Yep, but you said you would be home earlier today. I was just wondering exactly what time that might be, so I can make lunch?"

Donovan gave a short chuckle.

"I can't say, it depends how long his majesty drones on for, and the implications of what we discuss."

"An important meeting, eh?" the girl teased.

"Supposedly," he sighed before adopting a more serious tone. "Is Vartija with you?"

The girl seemed mildly piqued.

"Yes, he never leaves my side, just like you told him. I really don't need to be protected twenty-four seven you know."

Noting her annoyance, Donovan adapted his intonation to be firm, but reassuring.

"Scarlett, you know why he's there. We can never be too careful when it comes to you, especially in light of–"

"Yeah, I know," Scarlett intervened solemnly as he approached the more sensitive subject.

"Sorry. I do like him, I just miss how things used to be."

"It's okay, now you get my ham and pickle ready, I'm starving!" Donovan jested, lightening the mood and causing Scarlett to scoff.

"Well now, you aren't getting anything," she mumbled in exaggerated dejection before returning to her cheery tone.

"I recorded a couple of episodes of Seinfeld for us to watch when you get home."

Despite the conversation being entirely verbal, Donovan smiled.

"Sounds great, but I have to go now. I can hear movement in old rotund's office."

Scarlett sniggered.

"Alright, bye Don, have a fun meeting."

"Hah… bye honey."

Call concluded, Donovan turned his attention to the door of Orotund's office. It stood proudly identical to the other doors in this wing of the

Adytum, with white and golden plates and skilfully made engravings of historical figures adorning its surface. The central knocker, similar to the one on Donovan's own office, was composed of two equilateral triangles with rounded edges, but contrastingly, the symbol of the head of the Adytum had a ring in the centre of the smaller triangle to distinguish it. It was connected via three thin supports to the shape around it, and in its centre lay a dazzling arrangement of elegant cloisonné – sapphires and emeralds arranged in a pattern and separated by thin gold strips.

While he had a strong dislike for ostentation and shows of wealthy arrogance, Donovan had always appreciated the emblem before him. He had never failed to notice how the blues and greens of its miniature had always complemented Emmaline's ginger locks when it hung around her neck.

After a further five, frustratingly long minutes, the doors opened autonomously onto the office of the Imperator. The extensive redecoration inside conjured up the same hubris that smothered the rest of the Adytum – with the exception of Donovan's and Montanaro's offices and the holding cells. The walls and flooring were identical to that of the main corridors, yet somehow impossibly brighter and more lavish than their counterparts. It was as if some unknown source were further illuminating the room beyond its natural extravagant flair, all in all creating a light far too intense for any regular eye.

Donovan entered with a strong but graceful stride and a mild swagger, with the specific intent of frustrating the Imperator, who sat behind his ivory desk in all his flatulent glory. The very same necklace that had previously accentuated Emmaline's revered beauty, now hung around his neck, a token of his power, but also the symbol of an immense reputation to live up to.

"Walk with purpose Consul Gesture, you're over one-hundred years old, not some brash teenager," Imperator Orotund spluttered, looking up from the sizeable collection of papers on his desk.

Donovan took a seat, dismissing the comment.

"You asked to see me, sir?"

"Yes, I did. Thank you for reminding me of the actions I took only twenty minutes ago," Orotund rebuked in annoyance. Inwardly, Donovan resigned any chance of an apology for the lengthy wait, though he would have been surprised if he *had* received one.

"What is the issue at hand?"

"The library, the one in Dallas," Orotund began. "A report from an officer in the field – that Officer Pierce of yours – has disclosed the details of a significant attack from the Deorum, almost entirely destroying the complex. Fronted by Saeva Dragoia himself!"

Taking the information in, Donovan cursed his negligence of the possibility that Sariyah and the girl could be followed, or at the very least spotted at a location so public.

"That… is an incredibly bold attack. Surely they are aware of the ramifications of such a blind insult? I will instruct my scouts to double their efforts in locating the church's many strongholds throughout the southern states. We will eradicate these extremist zealots before they can make any further moves."

Orotund shook his head in solemn contemplation.

"No, no, that won't be necessary. Leave the stratagems to me Consul Gesture. I say do nothing at all, perhaps proclaim our increased efforts as an empty threat."

Donovan raised an eyebrow, astounded by the Imperator's incredibly obtuse proposal.

"Do nothing? Do you want more people to die?" he practically growled.

A scowl flitted across Orotund's stocky features for but a second, before he returned to his regular mild frown.

"Lockwood clearly wants his daughter back, no? I say let him try to take her again and this time we will capture Dragoia. Then he will show us all the way home!"

He seemed doltishly proud of his witless plan and this frustrated Donovan greatly.

"And put the innocent girl in incredible danger? She has already gone through so much. Who are you to demand she suffer further?"

Orotund stood and replied in outrage.

"Don't you address me in that tone Consul Gesture!"

But Donovan gave him no chance to reply further.

"What of my officer? You risk her life with no regard!"

The Imperator's tone became one of stern accusation.

"Don't think I'm not aware of your, *affections,* for that Sariyah Pierce. Once we capture Dragoia he will tell us what we need to know!"

"Your skull is thicker than I first assumed if you think any man on Earth could extract so much as his mother's maiden name from Saeva Dragoia. The man is insane!"

Donovan rose to his feet also, towering domineeringly over the Imperator through sheer physical presence alone, quickly causing Orotund to reconsider and return to his seat.

"I will have a team of my most skilled Sorcerers and Mages be sent to track your officer in the field at a safe distance and neutralise Dragoia when the moment is right. For now, the northern Adyta are continuing to threaten intervention. Myself and Consul Montanaro are attempting to soothe their worries while the situation plays out."

Donovan scoffed and remained standing.

"A Sisyphean task you have set yourself. Once they invade, we shall see who will crumble first."

"Do not question my authority or my resolve, Consul Gesture, or you will soon find yourself without such a title."

The tension refused to alleviate as Donovan chuckled grimly.

"Relieve me of my position and behold the consequences. You're a smart man, I'm sure you can figure out what would happen then."

Gesture turned to leave, his former swagger gone, replaced by a tense but determined march.

Stupefied, all Orotund could manage was a belated bluster.

"W… Where do you think you're going?"

"I'm taking matters into my own hands," Donovan informed him. He exited the office leaving the doors wide open.

15 – FROM CAESARS TO CONSTANTINE

A radia remained unusually alert for the majority of the journey to the city of sin. While she had yet to become accustomed to being referred to by her new name, the change somehow provoked a peace in her she'd never previously felt at any time as *Sophie*. On the surface, the two personae presented themselves identically, but Aradia felt the more stable of the two – a character with purpose – and this was something they could both appreciate. This newfound synchronicity, for now at least, was able to quell her anxieties and distract from the sharp pain in her ribs.

The pair took a much needed and appreciated break from the incessant travelling, and stayed overnight in a motel outside Albuquerque, where they regained a small amount of energy. It allowed Sariyah to begin properly setting and healing the malefic wounds Aradia had sustained at the library.

Her rudimentary examination in Dallas had determined that Aradia's injuries consisted of a broken rib, a torn hamstring and some harsh bruising. Any expected psychological trauma seemed to be absent – a fact that Sariyah had explained was a by-product of Aradia's recent *magical maturation,* as she had so inappropriately described it.

Further respites were taken in Flagstaff, just north of Phoenix, and Kingman, before they took the final straight down Route 93 to reach their haven and Aradia's proving ground. The gambling capital of the world lay open before them, lights and fountains blinding in their affluence. The population seemed either keenly wealthy and vigilant, or drunkardly and recently penurious, but on the whole were living a dream only few could experience, even if only half of them remembered the thrill.

Aradia gazed in wonder at the sights around her, while Sariyah took them down the Vegas strip, and turned off to stop before one of the most renowned, or perhaps infamous, hotel casinos in the world, Caesars Palace. Practically giggling with excitement, Aradia recalled the times she had seen the legendary building in films and magazines. The reality of it seemed no different to her.

Sariyah pulled up and swiftly exited the vehicle, which was taken away by a valet without so much as a second's delay. Smiling faces with warm but hurried gestures offered to take what little belongings they possessed, before they were ushered inside, away from the incredible multi-layered overhang, its incredible orange glow further igniting the spark in Aradia's step.

Surely they can't be this nice to everyone who shows up? They would be here all day! Is it because we're recognised? Do they know Sariyah? Are these people magic?

Her mind buzzed with questions, theories, and a general feeling of ecstasy, each of which were amplified by the revelation of the lobby that now lay before her.

Not dissimilar to the Adytum in appearance, the room was made up of two main features. Indescribable decorations adorned the surface of the back wall; paintings and mosaics of blue, green and predominantly gold caught Aradia's eye immediately. Each one stood unique to its neighbour, creating an awe-strikingly asymmetrical, matchless work of art.

Though Aradia stared, she took note of Sariyah, who too appeared incredulous. Not by the brilliant artwork of the walls, but by the second notable feature. The central piece, that the entire lobby gravitated towards. A perfectly circular section of the lobby had been marked out with never ending bands of colour enclosing the area, built into a floor that shone with such vivacity that Aradia could see her and Sariyah's stupefied reflections staring back at them. Stalwart ionic columns bordered the area in which they now stood, internally supplicating to three marble figures that dominated the room from up high, all atop a fountain that drew them into the epicentre. Finally, the historical suspended lamps and central oculus directly above the towering statues brought a light that reflected off every surface and every person, fully completing the incredible glow of the room.

"Well, here we are!" Sariyah declared with an almost childish glee she couldn't seem to hide. "Caesars Palace – the hub of Necromancer activity in the United States. If I remember correctly…"

"I… it… they…." Aradia interrupted, attempting a response, but entirely lost for words.

"Come on, let's go check in!"

Following Sariyah, words finally came to her.

"But we don't have the money to do that, surely?"

"I'll just let them know what Apathy told you." Sariyah smiled reassuringly as they reached one of the many receptionists, a woman with light brown hair and kind blue eyes.

Sariyah spoke first.

"Hi, we're here to meet with Miss Apathy Crypt, if you could let her know we have arrived."

The receptionist seemed to take a moment to register the request, but soon enough nodded with a smile and dialled a number into the phone beside her. After a brief pleasantry was exchanged, she turned back to them.

"Your names please?"

"Sariyah Pierce, an old friend." Sariyah turned to Aradia and curled her lip in contemplation. "And, um… the young girl she met at the Adytum."

Aradia wondered how Apathy would react upon hearing her new name.

Something was different about me indeed! I'm an Aradian.

While she mused, the receptionist repeated Sariyah's answer and fell silent for a short while before hanging up the phone.

"Miss Crypt will meet you both here in the lobby at 9.00am tomorrow morning. She wants me to tell you that she is delighted to hear of your arrival and has provided you the Julius executive duplex suite to stay in while you are with us."

Sariyah raised her eyebrows, but completed the remaining formalities and took the room's key card.

"If there is anything at all you require, please don't hesitate to call. Our staff are here to make your stay as enjoyable as possible," the receptionist concluded.

Sariyah thanked her and made toward the elevators, Aradia in tow.

"You looked surprised. Why?" Aradia asked.

She received a casual shrug in return.

"Apathy isn't usually such a gracious host. I can't imagine she would be so welcoming if it weren't for you being with me."

Her first meeting with Apathy flooded Aradia's memory as she watched the floors tick by on the elevator panel. She found herself giddy with anticipation to meet her once more and, more importantly, to feel the shadows that had so astounded her.

Despite her anticipation of tomorrow's meeting, she couldn't ignore a dull ache at the back of her head. She had an urge to accomplish some kind of task, but what exactly, she had not the faintest idea. It was as if something was locked behind a door within her mind; a door she did not possess the key to. She mused that she had felt this ever since she had first awoken to Sariyah's face, but only now in the gentle humming of the elevator did the persistent presence of this relentless disquietude dawn on her.

The mirthful *bing* of the elevator as it arrived at the requested destination, and a gentle squeeze from Sariyah's hand, woke Aradia from her bleak reverie. The pair stepped into a well-lit corridor and, staying close to Sariyah's side, she realised she was blissfully humming a tune she recognised as *Magic* by Pilot.

How ironic.

She rolled her eyes in appalled amusement.

Before Sariyah could break into the verse, the double doors bearing the desired room number stood before them. They were well crafted and pleasantly stately, but paled in comparison to the grandeur of the Adytum. This fact caused her to reflect on the incompetence of the mortal world and its inventions in comparison with the magical.

Sariyah unlocked the room and glanced reassuringly at Aradia, as if to silently tell her that all was well, she was becoming used to this regular occurrence. Any remaining discomfort from her wonderings in the elevator was banished upon entering the apartment they would be staying in until further notice. Aradia couldn't help but let a wide grin break out from cheek to cheek as she entered the luxury that friends in high places could grant her.

More in line with the level of indulgent splendour she had been used to in her childhood home, the apartment was larger than any she had seen before in any media. A short corridor led directly into an open plan living space and dining room. There were two expensive, neatly arranged sofas sitting on a floral patterned rug, and another with its back against the all-encompassing window that let in the intensely warm light of the desert sun. There was a rotating armchair, a dense wooden coffee table, and an exquisite dining set, arranged for at least three times the amount of people present. There was even a chilled bottle of champagne and two glasses, already prepared and on display atop their own glass stand, eagerly awaiting the guest that would arrive to the room. Sariyah being that guest, she made no delay in pouring herself a glass with gleeful cheer.

As visually stunning as the living space was, Aradia's attention was captured by the staircase that clung to the wall at its side and curled up onto a railed balcony that overlooked everything, allowing the entire space to have a double height ceiling. She raced up the stairs, taking them two at a time, before rapidly slowing to a walk. The sharp stab in her ribs flared up once more, catching her off guard.

"Don't get too excited or you'll hurt yourself!" Sariyah called after her. "I haven't finished patching you up yet!"

Aradia screwed up her face and replied with mock teenage vapidity, "Okay *mom*." Then she continued her exploration, travelling at a sprightly hobble, one arm to her side for support.

"Still not feeling any pain?" Sariyah inquired softly for the fourth time in the last hour.

Aradia gave the identical reply she had to each posing of the question.

"Still none, I don't feel a thing."

She let out a long sigh as she straddled one of the dining chairs, wrapping her arms around it and resting her chin on its back, apathetically regarding the wall-mounted flatscreen while Sariyah worked. The substance Sariyah had been administering to her lower back and sides, textureless as far as Aradia could sense, had numbed every cell it touched to beyond any feeling. Her entire midsection felt as though it was a separate entity; nearby perhaps, but certainly not part of herself. According to Sariyah it was also covered in a vivid green moss, which was the source of her cells' comatose state.

The brief flashes of Sariyah's reflection she would occasionally catch in the flatscreen presented her hard at work, almost picking away at something on Aradia's back with the medical supplies she kept in her satchel. Aradia's mind could only conjure ghastly images of what Sariyah could be up to, fixing a broken rib in so little time, and from behind somehow. But she assured herself that the reality was most likely far more gruesome, so she dared not look too closely to save feeling faint.

"How much more do we have to do this?" Aradia asked impatiently. As fascinating as the out of body sensation was, she was beginning to become quite sick of it.

"I'm pretty much done," Sariyah promised, "There isn't much more I can do, since I'm no doctor, but that should be good as new with a of couple days rest. Let's just not get into any more fights for the time being?"

Aradia gave a slight shrug.

"I'll try, but people really like trying to kidnap me, so we'll see how that goes."

She managed to produce a chortle from Sariyah which pleased her, but even as she joked, she realised that what she had jested was indeed true – she may well have to fight for her life again in the near future. That unsettled her greatly.

After a few more minutes Sariyah stood and took a pace backward. All regular feeling began to return to Aradia's body.

"You're free, I'm all done!"

"Thank you," Aradia nodded as she stood properly, pulling her top back down and turning to give Sariyah a smile of gratitude.

Sariyah returned the gesture and moved to an open space, where she began to do the routine stretches she had done at each rest stop they had taken on the journey so far. Aradia on the other hand, unable to sink the feeling of anxiety that was building within her, moved to the main bathroom that branched off the living space.

Once inside she stared at her reflection intently, almost expecting it to be different somehow. As she did, the harassing ache returned in the back of her head.

Why won't this headache go away!

She seethed, dismissing it as a common vexation.

All bloody day it's been bothering me.

She brought her hands to her head, resting both palms on her temples, and almost growled in frustration.

Then she noticed her arm. Until now, the bandage had been tightly wrapped around her, concealing the horrors of her father's mark since the day she was saved. She had been too fearful to investigate what lay beneath, and had allowed Sariyah to change the bandage while keeping her eyes firmly closed. But now she could see. Due to the day's commotion, the bandage had slipped – the fault of a hurried wrapping in the morning – and Aradia could plainly see a slight marking.

Part of a larger pattern, two carved lines created grooves in her arm, almost parallel and just beginning to come to a point. The space between the sable lines was about as wide as her index finger, and a morbid temptation urged her to test that theory. All common sense and reason abandoned, the ache that dwelt at the back of her mind grew, its purpose becoming gradually clearer and she reached for the bandage. Fingers seeking the end, she grabbed hold and began to unwrap her wound and her fate. It was the signifier of her entrance to this new world, and the mark to present her true ancestry to any who viewed it.

The material gently fluttered to the floor and Aradia couldn't breathe as she stared. The symbol that had been so excruciatingly carved into her skin was made up of three elements – two completed, one unfinished. The symbol in its entirely covered the majority of her upper arm: a jagged oval of the deepest black was etched into her, alongside what appeared to be ancient script of some kind down each side – a language that she recognised on second glance as Latin from her private tutoring.

Vocant Deos, and on the opposite side, *Ad lucem.*

Finally, completing the nauseating and harrowing disfigurement, there was what appeared to be a lightning bolt chiselled into her, running down through the oval shape and exiting at the bottom. Where the lines should have met to complete the spark, however, there was only her pale skin, the symbol incomplete, imperfect.

Entranced by its grotesque piety, Aradia moved her outstretched hand further and watched with unblinking eyes as her fingers came to gently rest against the surface of the wound.

Blinding pain coursed through her veins like a black poison spreading to her very nervous system, causing every nerve and synapse to fire in rage. A scream she could not hear for its pitch erupted from her lips and her neck snapped back with such startling ferocity it might give her whiplash.

Her father stood before her in her mind's eye, his towering presence dominating her, the blade piercing her skin, making her scream, and the abhorrent creature presiding above. The previously dull ache in her mind had now become a roaring fire that encompassed her entire being. It brought fresh visions of her mother and those needle-like cerulean eyes.

Aradia could only stare, jaw unhinged in the voiceless scream, as her mother came closer, silk gown trailing her, across a blank plain, devoid of light and substance. Her father, the creature, the hotel... all life had vanished and her soul lay vacant. All that remained was wilted grass, grey in colour, spread out for miles around her, and even that was trodden under her mother's bare feet. Any brain function became useless to her, and the pain only grew as her mother neared, reaching a pinnacle as she stopped a hair's breadth away, looking down upon her daughter.

"I see you."

Cecilia teased her as one would a small child, her voice filling the void, the only presence that existed, the only one that mattered, for she was all there was.

Cecilia extended an elegant finger and pressed it into her daughter's face for a second.

"We'll be with you soon dear."

She gave a murderous smile, malice painting her face, and a white light coupled with an equally burning white pain grew from the depths of the horizon, rapidly encompassing all until it blended with her very body. Reality and fantasy morphed and contorted until...

Aradia let out a shrill, terrified scream and jerked upright in bed. The scream was sustained until Sariyah leapt into action from where she sat in an armchair alongside the king-sized bed.

"M... Mommy..." Aradia managed, the first words to escape her lips in a desperate plea.

There was a hesitation that felt like an eternity before the response resonated in Aradia's heart.

"I'm here, Aradia... Sophie. I'll always be here, I promise."

She felt the warm embrace of Sariyah, her haven, her security. The scream died into a gentle sob as they lay on the bed, both shedding a tear for Aradia's pain.

16 – Assertions of the Dead

It took three hours, two showers, a hot meal and a significant amount of comforting for Aradia to feel confident enough to be left alone for more than a few minutes. The vision of her mother, while in the past, echoed in her mind and each viewing brought a fresh bout of tears and intense fear. Sariyah had already assured her that her nightmares and irregular moments of nervousness were most likely due to psychological trauma, a remnant of the attempted sacrifice. But Aradia remained doubtful and ever vigilant of another assailment on her mind.

The remainder of that day and evening passed without incident, and a feeling of quietude began to descend on Aradia as she calmly ate the breakfast Sariyah ordered to the room the following morning.

"You're looking much better by the way," Sariyah smiled, her hand on Aradia's.

"I feel a little better. It all feels… more distant now."

Sariyah let go and moved to the coffee table where her satchel rested.

"Probably a bit of PTSD, and to be expected perhaps. But we can get you help soon."

"Yeah," Aradia nodded, lying unconvincingly, "just some bad mental health."

"Hey, it'll be okay," Sariyah encouraged. "You get to meet Apathy to learn a bit about Necromancy today. That's exciting, right?"

Despite the intense feeling of weakness she was experiencing internally, Aradia's anticipation to begin learning the aspect of magical discipline that intrigued her the most did bring a slight smile to her face.

"Definitely."

Sariyah slung her iconic grey jacket over her shoulder and gave Aradia a quick hug from behind.

"There's that lovely smile I like to see. Finish your breakfast and we'll head down to the reception."

Aradia wolfed down the remainder of her cereal and stood up slightly too fast.

"Ready, though I'm not sure I'll be much good feeling like this. And how I failed at being a Sorcerer like you."

"Pah!" Sariyah exclaimed, "you'll be amazing, I can tell. From birth your magic is tuned to be better at a certain style of use. Being a Sorcerer just isn't for you it seems, apart from your amazing display at the library, of course."

"You think I'm more of a natural Necromancer?" Aradia asked.

"Well, if you aren't naturally a Sorcerer, there are only two other options as far as we know – a Mage or a Pure Born, but the second is incredibly rare, so... yes!"

Sariyah patted her on the back.

These simple words provoked a deep feeling of pride and encouragement in Aradia and she put on her custom jacket, eager to begin learning. She did her utmost to dispel the misgivings the previous day's visions had brought.

"Ready then? Let's go!"

Sariyah took her hand and led her toward a new beginning.

Returning to the magnificent reception, Aradia bubbled with excitement when she caught the first glimpse of Apathy since they had met at the Adytum. Leaning casually against one of the pillars around the central fountain, she wore near identical attire to that Aradia had previously seen; boots capped at the knee and her flowing overcoat, considerably too warm for the weather, with its void of wonder and trepidation within. The only difference in her presentation were her lips, now a soullessly deep purple, and black nails that rapped rhythmically against the marble pillar.

Apathy noticed the two approaching and beckoned them with a subtle flick of her head and a sly smile.

"Looking frightfully guileful today, Apathy," Sariyah began, stopping an appropriate distance away, Aradia by her side.

"Thank you, I'm glad you noticed," she replied in a tone that suggested an indifference to the art of small talk and pleasantries. She retained a stately British politeness, however. "I trust your accommodation was acceptable?"

"A damn good service you lot provide," Sariyah confirmed before moving on. "You won't be taking her to the Pantheon, will you?"

Apathy seemed to casually disregard the question before turning to address Aradia.

"I think that would be up to my new prodigy to decide, would it not? Tell me, have you decided upon a name for yourself in this big bad world yet?"

Aradia gave a confident nod and stood a little taller.

"I have. Aradia Vastate, a pleasure to meet you."

"*Aradia Vastate*, what a peculiar but fascinating name. I think I like it," Apathy grinned. "So, Aradia. Would you like to see the grand chambers where us Necromancers gather and learn?"

Resisting the urge to jump on the spot, Aradia nodded quickly.

"Definitely, yes!"

"I'm not sure I like the idea of you two running off too far," Sariyah interjected. "I'm supposed to be protecting her." She rested a hand on Aradia's shoulder.

"It isn't dangerous, right?" Aradia protested. "Apathy can protect me and you said my father wouldn't dare to attack the Necromancers. Please?"

Through pouted lips and a conceding sigh, Sariyah caved to Aradia's pleas and gave her a short hug.

"Alright, but I want you right back here no later than 2.00pm. And Apathy, ease her in, she is still recovering from some pretty serious injuries."

"I wouldn't dream of hurting my new star, don't you worry old friend."

Sariyah refocused her glare.

"I'm serious, I don't want you playing any of your games. Do so and I'll make sure to play a couple of my own."

"What a titillating offer!" Apathy smirked as Aradia skipped to her side. "But I'm afraid I have no time to explore such an avenue. I have the teaching of a bright young girl to be seeing to. Follow along!"

Apathy swivelled on the spot, raising one hand above her shoulder and snapping her fingers as if to call Aradia to heel. Before doing so, Aradia gave a gentle wave and smile to Sariyah who returned the gesture, and the two went in opposite directions.

Approaching the door, it was only now that Aradia realised this was the first occasion she had been separated from Sariyah for any length of time since occupying this new world. The state of perpetual disquietude that had seized her since the previous day's vision retained its understated strength in the back of her mind, but strangely Aradia felt secure.

As long as I'm with someone then I'm safe. Apathy can protect me, and I'll see Sariyah again soon.

Presently they emerged into the stifling air of the city. Apathy continued to lead the way, walking past the valet, who had few arriving guests to attended to at this early morning hour. Walking alongside her, Aradia made note of the contrasting mannerisms and tendencies of the two authority figures that currently presided in her life. Sariyah carried a careful but meaningful stride, always walking squarely and entirely in tune with her surroundings. Furthermore, she would regularly glance back to Aradia with a reassuring smile, never straying further than an arm's reach, and always ready to jump to her defence at a moment's notice.

In stark comparison, Apathy travelled almost blasé to the world around her, focused on the single goal of her destination. She was always a few paces ahead, moving at a speed that Aradia had to almost skip to keep up with. Despite the boots she wore having a significant heel, Apathy walked predominantly on her toes, perhaps due to her determination to advance with such unnatural speed.

Aradia found respect for both methods of directing her. One allowed her to feel as safe and as cared for as possible; the other allowed her to adopt the kind of walk that caused people to move out of one's way, rather than forcing you to detour around them.

"I think I know what it was you saw in me that was different," Aradia informed Apathy, just keeping up with her as they approached the fountain just ahead of them.

"Oh, and what would that be?" Apathy glanced to the side of her, catching Aradia's eye with her artful smile.

"I'm an Aradian, descended from the first religious leader, Camilla Aradian," she proudly proclaimed.

Apathy gave a slow nod and turned her head to the sky in contemplation for a few moments before rapidly returning to her original disposition.

"No… that's not it."

Aradia opened her mouth to protest but decided against it as she watched Apathy climb onto the edge of the fountain and stare down into the water. Instead she raised a more appropriate question for the situation.

"Um, what are you doing?"

"Come… come and join me."

Apathy beckoned and Aradia did so without complaint, carefully balancing herself on the low wall, peering at her own reflection in the shimmering ripples.

As if via a miraculous, inaudible cue, the attendants that patrolled the entrance to the hotel and complex moved with startling efficiency to shut off the route for cars to enter the premises and ushered any remaining guests inside.

"What's happening?" Aradia asked, a tinge of anxiety mixing with general intrigue and excitement.

"We're entering the Pantheon of Necromancy, a significant improvement to the original in Italy, I might add."

As she spoke, she rested a slender hand against a slab of stone to the side of them. A handprint flashed yellow and remained on its surface for a short time before dissipating.

Aradia raised a perplexed eyebrow.

"How? By jumping in the fountain?"

"Pre*cisely*!" Apathy replied, heavily emphasising the word. "Take my hand if you would like an untroubled journey."

Her heart rate steadily increasing, Aradia reached out and took Apathy's hand. Her skin was cool to the touch, despite the roasting temperature of the morning. It almost made her shiver.

"Are you sure about this?" Aradia gripped Apathy's hand tightly.

"Certainly," she confirmed. "Now, I don't wish to drag you, that would be incredibly uncomfortable for both of us. You'll have to work with me here. When I say the word, give me an impassioned leap for joy right into the water. No faffing, understand?"

Aradia composed herself and nodded.

"Good, and off we go!"

Aradia jumped and suddenly felt an extreme chill shudder down her arm, originating from Apathy's hand. The shadows within her coat began to react to their falling, bursting forth and parting the water below them, forming an impossibly dark, narrow tunnel in a split second.

The entire world was a roaring void of darkness as they fell. Aradia felt an intense rush of adrenaline and exhilaration. She turned her head to glance at Apathy by her side, who simply gave her a wink as they fell through space for a seemingly impossible distance from where they'd begun. Aradia felt the dark walls of their tunnel begin to narrow and press against her shoulders, but the discomfort proved short lived as a striking yellow light rushed to meet them and the two emerged into a sizeable chamber, bursting upward with force.

Aradia felt her polarity shift in a sickeningly volitant moment, but once she had regained her sense of direction and her stomach settled, she found herself standing in an eerily similar position. Her hand remained in Apathy's and she stood on the edge of a fountain identical to the one outside Caesars.

"Wow!" She exhaled for the first time, the adrenaline of the experience still coursing through her. "That was…"

"Positively fantastic?" Apathy finished for her. "It is rather fun, even after your hundredth time."

While she caught her breath, Aradia examined the chamber in which they stood. Carved out of limestone, the entire space held solely the replica fountain from which they had emerged. The walls retained a dampness to them, due to the moist chill in the air, and rose up high, gradually coming to a point in the centre of the ceiling to create the appearance of a beehive tomb. The room emitted a cold light and adjoining corridors, branching off in four directions, were lit by hanging lamps of yellow flame.

Aradia let go of Apathy's hand and the two stepped off the fountain onto the damp limestone floor. The chamber gave Aradia the impression of a series of ancient, dangerous catacombs, wrapped in mystery and perhaps containing the decrepit remains of bygone times.

Perhaps not as resplendent as the Adytum, but it's definitely eerie!

Apathy led her down a series of corridors with irregularly spaced doors down either side. Each path was near identical to the last, save for engravings of Latin words at each turning. They indicated the name of that particular section of the Pantheon, Apathy informed her.

As they traversed the complex, Aradia thought it prudent to ask the questions she had now, to avoid interrupting her lesson to come.

"So, what kind of things am I going to learn first? I read a book in the library before I was interrupted that talked about the shadows and the soul."

"Ah yes, it seems we are cutting to the chase. I may as well inform you of some aspects of your training now to save time."

Apathy slowed her pace just enough for Aradia to remain consistently by her side.

"While we Necromancers use magic with a strikingly similar method to the common Mage, we also hold one fundamental difference."

"What's that?" Aradia asked, her attention sharpening.

"A Sorcerer channels their magic with a connection to the magic of the Earth. A Mage draws their magic from the air and atmosphere around them, to store within themselves. We Necromancers, and our sister order the

Vitamancers, use the magic that resides within our very souls to influence and manipulate the presiding powers of life and death," Apathy concluded.

Utterly captivated, Aradia let out a gasp that she quickly stifled. "There are Vitamancers too? They're like, *life* Mages?"

"Indeed," Apathy confirmed. "There are less of them, due to the art of Vitamancy being incredibly niche, difficult, and almost strictly defensive, but we work in tandem for the most part with the eventual goal of conquering both phenomena."

Apathy continued to explain the union of the two orders, and the hierarchical council made up of two representatives from each order, which collectively decided the actions and delegated the resources of the union. She also explained her own role as Adytum liaison and recruiter.

"Just one more question," Aradia timidly asked as Apathy finished her explanations.

Apathy chuckled and sighed in unison.

"A curious soul, aren't you? Go on then."

"Can Necromancers raise the dead, like in movies?"

"It has been attempted in the past to raise creatures lately expired to act on our nefarious needs," she explained. "However, the last attempt resulted in the creation of Vampires and was universally recognised as quite an abysmally dreadful result to our experimentation. Ergo, it has not been attempted since the fifteenth century."

"Oh… I see." Aradia quietened down, having heard first-hand from Sariyah of her encounter with the vampiric groundsman.

As they approached what appeared to be a grand archway in the style of corbel vaulting, Apathy rounded off her initial informative lesson.

"The Vitamancers have created new life successfully, however!"

"Really? That's amazing!"

"Indeed, the Axolotl they called it. Mind you, whoever came up with the idea of a fish that can walk but never makes the transition to land is beyond me."

The exchange came to a close as they passed through the arch into the grand main chamber of the Pantheon, and Aradia stared in wonder.

The Pantheon had clearly been constructed as a successor to its more well-known counterpart, with multiple details of its architecture being fashioned in a similar or identical way, only grander. In the first of three prominent sections, high reaching Corinthian columns separated the space between archways that branched off at each compass point in the perfectly circular space. The second segment of the colossal structure held alternating inset and offset rectangles, each with styled patterns comprising differing shades of yellow. Bringing the true encompassing effect, and adding to the incredible acoustics of the chamber, was the third and final section. An incredible dome loomed above them, constructed of a tessellation of stone squares, identical to the original pantheon, and an oculus in the exact centre of the dome.

This oculus, however, rather than allowing sunlight to enter the chamber, instead channelled a single stream of bright yellow energy, illuminating the entire space. It also brought the main source of contrasting light to the materials that made up the Pantheon, which had so far been mostly shades of grey.

"Wow, I definitely see why it's called the Pantheon, but this place is even bigger! Less colourful though," Aradia judged, examining every precise detail.

"The original Roman Pantheon was constructed for the benefit of Necro and Vitamancers when we formed as an order," Apathy explained as they passed numerous figures dressed in attire in styles from across the world. The contrast in culture was incredible to see. Despite this they were all unified, brought together by the single truth that all Necromancers must apparently wear black.

"But wasn't the original Pantheon built way before the fourth century, when mankind abandoned the old gods?" Aradia queried, recalling the knowledge from her private tutoring in the classics.

"My, my, someone is full of surprises. Yes, you are correct. Our orders were formed before the common man was able to manipulate the magic left behind after the civil war," Apathy informed her, as they exited the main chamber to walk down further corridors toward a final door that stood against the far wall.

"Before they passed on during the civil war, the gods who presided over life and death were the three fates."

Aradia nodded. "I think I've heard of them."

"Good, they commonly influenced the dawn of new life, the passage of time within that life, and finally the eventual ending of that life. The original Vitamancers worked closely with, and worshipped, the first fate and studied life, while we studied death."

"I see." Aradia continued to take the information in, fascinated by the immense history magic was steeped in.

"Well, I am positively parched. You can always learn more of our history at a later date."

Without further conversation, Apathy guided Aradia to the door and deactivated the magical lock. It glowed the same quality of yellow that lit the chamber. The two entered what appeared to be an office of some kind. Apathy's office evidently, by the comfort and familiarity with which she traversed the space.

The office was made up of two main chambers with high ceilings and the same hanging flames that brought light the rest of the Pantheon. The initial space had the feel of a quintessentially English drawing room. Cabinets of fine wood and antiquated seating from the 1920s brought a warmth and life so far unseen to the Pantheon, most of which had been clearly modelled to simulate the coldness found in death.

Apathy took a seat behind a courtly wooden desk and relaxed with a long exhale. The shadows that Aradia so greatly desired began to emerge from the recesses of Apathy's flowing coat, and quickly made themselves busy gathering a mug, some liquid and other devices. It took Aradia a moment of staring to realise they were in fact making tea, while Apathy herself simply took her repose.

"That's handy," Aradia chuckled, gesturing to the shadows at work.

"Indeed, it is!" Apathy replied as the kettle was brought to the boil. After a brief mixing, she gently sipped the tea that was brought to her lips by a collection of shadows.

"Now, in order to truly harness the magic of death you are required to be at peace within yourself, and you must also merge your soul with another who already has the power of death within them."

Exasperated, Aradia stared.

"What? What does that mean?"

"Calm, calm now. The merging will not change you as a person, it will simply bring the feeling of death to your senses so that you may harness it."

"Oh… okay," Aradia conceded, none the wiser.

"Listen closely," Apathy began. "The merging of another's soul with yours is a rapidly intense process, but the result will be an enlightenment like none you have felt before. To gain the best results, you must merge with the soul of one who has witnessed a heightened amount of death, the more so the better. In fact, when I was younger I myself merged with the soul of a fallen comrade, a fellow Necromancer, and the results were a staggering surge of power."

The thought that such a process was not only feasible but regularly practised sparked Aradia's excitement once more, though in the back of her mind she felt misgivings on the topic of being at peace with herself – especially after all she had experienced in the last week.

"In the next chamber you will find a room that contains all the souls of people I have killed myself, or witnessed the death of, and promptly took the opportunity to collect a sample," Apathy continued. "They are all serial killers, war veterans, and the occasional awful surgeon. Each receptacle holds the required concentration of death within. I want you to go and retrieve one to your liking and we can get started."

Aradia pondered this thought for a moment. While she yearned so desperately to reach a level of power in which she could stand up for herself, the thought of taking the soul of another being and denying them the release of death troubled her. While she considered her options, a realisation dawned upon her, and she raised her query to Apathy.

"What about yours?"

Apathy raised an eyebrow.

"What about mine?"

"You said that bonding with a Necromancer made you more powerful. What if I bonded with you? I'd get two times the power, surely? If it wouldn't kill you, of course," Aradia proposed.

Apathy seemed taken aback by Aradia's words for the first time since they had met. She leant back in her chair in silent rumination, head cocked slightly at an angle and lips puckered. After what seemed like an age, she stood and approached Aradia.

"Now *that*... is an interesting theory. I'm not exactly sure what would happen. It may kill me and make you incredibly powerful... or nothing could happen at all," Apathy surmised.

Disheartened, Aradia hung her head.

"Sorry, it was just a thought. I know I'm new to this."

Apathy let out a long and almost maliciously curious laugh.

"Let's do it!"

17 – A Girl's Best Friend

———～～———

Having happened upon the five-hundred dollars that Apathy had so insincerely gifted her, Sariyah first made her way into the casino. She tried her luck on the variety of games and spent hours dwelling on the disingenuity of Apathy's actions and offers since they'd arrived at Caesars. The inconsistency of Miss Crypt's nature irritated her immensely and only served to stoke the fires of her paranoia.

I know her, she's playing an angle. She has to be! She needs Aradia but I'm not sure why… a new apprentice, for what purpose? It definitely isn't for the gratification of imparting knowledge to the next generation, that's for sure.

Her musings continued for the remainder of the morning, before she left the casino with four-hundred dollars less than she had entered with.

With her pockets lighter but insecurities weighing heavy on her chest, Sariyah made her way back to their suite to pass the time until she had to pick up Aradia from the lobby. She cast away thoughts of Aradia for now – they would only hasten the decline of her mental health – and decided to take a short break to set her mind in order. As a concluding note, she vowed that Apathy would sincerely regret her choice, should she be tardy in returning Aradia to her at the agreed time.

Sariyah let out a long exhale and her worries with it. Closing her eyes for a moment outside the door to their room, she recited a relevant selection of her usual mantras.

Breathe, stay calm, worry later. Someone will help and I am not alone anymore.

She opened her eyes, but the usual tranquillity these utterings brought were instantly dispelled. The door to their opulent room stood ajar and murmurs emanated from within.

Focus snapping to attention, Sariyah slipped inside and shut the door silently, locking it. She moved along the wall, travelling as light footed as she could manage, simultaneously harnessing her magic to increase the air pressure around her hands, ready to put to use in blasting any clandestine assailant.

Turning the corner into the main living space, Sariyah's nervous adrenaline quickly converted to intense irritation and seething anger. Before her, making incredibly discourteous use of the room's facilities, were three figures Sariyah recognised in their black armour with signature yellow band around the arms. Mage soldiers and the commanding officer of the Adytum militia, Plagoya Stonewall.

"What do you think you're doing?" Sariyah growled at the intruders.

Stonewall turned in an irritatingly casual manner and spoke with a dismissive laugh.

"Making sure everything is in order. I see you finally came to join us, Pierce."

"Why are you here?" Sariyah scowled. "I have this entirely under control. I don't need you and your goons getting their dirty hands all over my mission, nor my hotel room!"

"We are here under orders from the Imperator himself, to oversee and assist you in protecting the girl, of course. Where is she? I must say you are an awfully terrible guardian if you aren't by her side in times such as these, Pierce." Stonewall spoke with a strident cadence, uttering Sariyah's last name with clear spite.

"It's *Officer* Pierce. You're all for formalities, so I'd at least expect you to address me by my rank, even if nobody else does. And with prudence to your state of mind, Aradia is with Miss Crypt, the Necromancer liaison… perfectly safe."

The various medals that adorned Stonewall's lapel glinted in the afternoon sun. Sariyah knew for a fact that Stonewall had positioned this encounter so that the sun would be behind her, just catching the good side of her features and glaring head on into Sariyah.

"Fine, *Officer* Pierce. Now that we are conducting ourselves formally you must refer to me as Commander. By your own request be it."

Sariyah nodded and moved across the room, interrupting one of the two soldiers who was making himself at home on the sofa, forcing him to stand despite his complaints.

"When can we expect this girl to be returning to us? It is vital she remain in sight at all times, should Saeva Dragoia make another attempt to capture her."

Stonewall began to pace the room, hands behind her back.

Frustration continuing to bubble, and her magic writhing, Sariyah stood her ground.

"There is no *us*, only me and her. She hasn't left my side until now and is perfectly safe with Apathy. If you must know, I am picking her up later and all will return to normal then."

Stonewall gave a curt nod.

"Acceptable this once, though I will not allow it to occur again. We will make ourselves comfortable until then."

She motioned to the Mage soldiers who mumbled to each other and began to leave the room.

"No!" Sariyah raised her voice, taking a commanding tone in the confrontation. "Aradia gets very nervous and scared around strangers after what's happened – especially strangers from our world. This is still new to her and I am one of the only people she can trust. If that trust is damaged by bringing new hostile figures into the fray, you'll lose her."

Stonewall seemed mildly taken aback by the sudden dominance and stumbled slightly over her words before resuming her casual disregarding demeanour.

"Right… well, we will simply take adjacent rooms to keep a watch over you both."

"With respect, *Commander*, you'll stay in a hotel down the street or so help me I will get the Necromancers to remove you for disturbing a guest." Sariyah dealt the finishing blow.

Infuriated and a little intimidated, Stonewall backed down.

"Fine, but you will make contact with me the moment any suspicion is aroused of a possible attack, and you will inform me of your every move while in the city." She regained a slight footing of confidence as she ushered the soldiers from the room. "Once this trouble is behind us you, will find yourself spending a week in the cells for taking that tone with me Officer Pierce. I'm sure you're familiar with the degrading reprimands you will face there."

Sariyah resisted the urge to spit as Stonewall moved toward the door.

"Oh, and Pierce… I know you are facing a lot of pressure right now with this assignment. Try not to desert and take flight when things get tough. I know you're rather good at that." Stonewall gave an unpleasant laugh and left the door open. Sariyah promptly slammed it shut and locked it.

So much for a moment of peace.

⁂

Aradia sat up dazed and took a moment to find her balance again.

"I wasn't expecting that to be so… explosive," she muttered, one hand on her aching head.

Standing, but supporting herself with the aid of a table, Apathy brushed ash and soot from her snow-white hair.

"Neither was I! And it seems I have lived to tell the tale someday. You must tell me, how do you feel?"

"My head hurts, but other than that I'm… I'm not sure."

"Right, right… well that is a usual by-product of a soul merging. I mean, do you feel power, a little cold perhaps?

Considering Apathy's query, Aradia rose to her feet and composed herself. On the surface she felt no different, perhaps slightly singed. However, on the inside things did seem to be lying in disarray to the norm.

The magic that spent its time at the base of her stomach and core now felt… *dispersed*. It was as if she were more at one with the magic, rather than utilising a substance that just so happened to be inside of her. Furthermore, when she investigated this magic, attempting to channel it through her body as she had done before, a mild coldness set in under her skin wherever the magic passed.

"I feel, chilly, I think… when I try to use the magic. But something is blocking it from coming out – it's trapped inside," she explained to Apathy, who had now steadied herself and was making her way back into the main office chamber toward her desk.

"Hmm, it will most likely need some time to acclimatise. Some of my essence and magic is in you now – quite the foreign environment – an adjustment would be an expected side effect, I suppose."

Aradia nodded as if she fully understood and sat back down on the floor in the centre of the scorch marks that newly decorated the floor. In this moment of rare quiet, Aradia decided to fully analyse how she felt, to detect any hidden or subtle differences in her reality. First, she noticed how her magic, now flowing through her as if it were her own blood, was drawn toward the row of jars that sat upon the table Apathy had leant on. It seemed excited or eager to act when she approached the table, and calm again when she moved away. This new phenomenon confused her a great deal until the penny dropped.

The magic of death, and those are the souls of people who've died… this is going to be interesting.

Before she could continue her investigation, a sudden discomfort arose around her xiphisternum behind which, Apathy had informed her, was the location of the soul. This feeling of discomfort, while an annoyance and unsettling, was not painful and felt as though it was not her issue, but a form of heartache for another. In her mind she knew that the feeling was a mild annoyance and a twinge of pain, yet she couldn't place where the feeling originated from or why.

Brow furrowed in bewilderment, she moved back into the main chamber to be greeted by Apathy tenderly rubbing her knee. Noticing Aradia enter, she voiced her displeasure.

"I really should get a round desk, these edges are far too sharp for my liking."

Aradia stood with her mouth gaping at the realisation of the new bond she shared.

"What are you gawking at?" Apathy frowned.

Aradia quickly closed her mouth and perused the room for a demonstration that would not prove too painful, before resigning and pinching herself on the forearm.

"Why are you…? Oh my!" Apathy glanced down at herself and then back at Aradia. "How interesting indeed. Come here and hit me!"

For the remainder of their allotted time, Apathy caused herself varying degrees of pain in a multitude of places in a morbidly curious experiment to test their connection. Aradia herself had discovered that, even without a form of distress, they could focus their attention in on the soul and determine a rough gauge for the other's current mood or general feeling. Much to Aradia's relief, and Apathy's disappointment, these insights applied solely on an emotional level, rather than to the very thoughts of the other.

A childish glee continued to bubble within Aradia, and despite her magic being unable to leave the confines of her body at this moment, she remained positive for the future of her path into Necromancy.

Bidding a fond farewell to Apathy at the reception, Aradia spent the next few hours regaling Sariyah with the details of the day's events. Once finished, they went out for a brief stint of shopping and enjoyed an expensive prepaid dinner. A note from Apathy that read, "You deserve it, soul sister" was left for them on the table.

Finally, concluding the day, Aradia changed into newly bought pyjamas and climbed into bed. She was left in the dimming light, alone with her thoughts.

In her solitude, Aradia could already sense the nervous ache at the back of her head once more. It crept upon her in every moment of quiet, like night chases day. She began to breath faster, her anxiety of another vision building, until the sudden and welcome intrusion of the room's phone ringing on the bedside table broke the silence. Aradia dived to answer it, if only as an alternative to the encroaching nightmares.

"H…hello?" she spluttered.

"Ah, I sensed it was you."

Aradia frowned, rubbing her head.

"Apathy?"

"You're no fun," Apathy moaned, "but I did feel like you were in some distress. Is everything alright?"

A welcome smile.

"Oh, thanks. Yeah, I'm okay, I–"

"Very good, very good."

Apathy cut her off immediately after receiving confirmation.

"Now, I forgot to mention earlier in all the fascination of our new discovery… I have acquired two tickets to the most prolific magical performer in the world. His show is touring and making a stop in sin city. Would you like to attend with me, 9.00pm start?"

"Oh, um, sure, sounds fun," Aradia replied, the thought of leaving Sariyah for a second time pressing on her anxieties. "Is it possible to get a third ticket? For Sariyah? She feels a bit left out I think."

Apathy seemed slightly irked by the request but gave confirmation.

"I suppose I can request a third ticket. They will be slipped under your door in the morning. I trust you will not delay in arriving, it truly is a magnificent show. I would hate for you to miss any of it."

"Okay, I'll tell Sariyah in the morning. Goodnight… soul sister."

They shared a giggle at their new situation and ended the call.

The world's most prolific magical performer? Is that magic tricks or actual magic?

Aradia debated the possibilities that could await her. The only shows she had seen thus far had been at the theatre when her parents had taken her years ago, usually to old musicals or high class plays. After the significant fighting and fleeing she had experienced lately, a fully-fledged Vegas magic show would be a much-welcomed change of pace.

She was just nearing sleep when the second interruption of the night caused her to almost leap out of bed. A slithering feeling crept its way across her arm and Aradia let out a startled squeak, swatting at the source. Her hand connected with a substance that had no apparent texture and resembled all three states of matter at once. Realising what she had just splattered, she cried out and quickly searched for the shadow.

Timidly wiggling its way back into her T-shirt sleeve was a small sliver of a shadow, about as long as her middle finger. Aradia pulled the fabric up, so it bunched around her shoulder and meant that the shadow couldn't escape. Then she picked it up, holding it in the palm of her upturned hand. It was impossibly dark in her hand, darker than the blackness of the night that occupied the room, but Aradia flicked on the bedside lamp to get a better look at the specimen.

Light now flooding the bedroom, she observed the shadow, curled into a childishly defensive ball, almost afraid to come out. Concerned, and feeling sorry for the poor thing, Aradia gently stroked the shadow with one finger.

"Hey, it's okay little guy. I'm sorry I scared you. I thought you were a spider or something. You startled me for sure!"

The shadow remained curled and motionless, and despite a part of her mind thinking it idiotic to continue to talk to what may as well be a black worm, she adopted as soft a tone as possible and continued to reassure it.

"It's okay, I won't hurt you. You're my little shadow, my first one! Apathy told me the magic would have to get used to my body and you made it out first."

Aradia smiled, taking note of her magic. She now found herself able to extend its reach further, to just past her fingertips.

Hearing Aradia's voice and words seemed to soothe the shadow, causing it to gradually uncurl and turn one end upward, as if to observe her.

"Hiya."

Aradia continued to smile down at the shadow in her hand, and immediately felt a connection between herself and it, an almost motherly bond.

The shadow moved about in her palm, taking in its surroundings. It seemed significantly more methodical and slower than she remembered Apathy's to be, but she figured it was simply due to it having only just been created.

"I made you!" Aradia beamed and chuckled. "You're my baby and we're going to destroy all our enemies together, aren't we?"

Hearing its master's command the shadow immediately stood upright to attention and the tip bent slightly, like it was nodding in approval.

Aradia giggled watching it.

"You're cute, I think I'll call you… Virbius. You are a boy, right?"

Virbius gave no indication either way.

"I guess shadows don't really have genders like that." Aradia was giddy with the thrill of her own magic. "But you do respond to what I say and do, right?" She extended her index finger and gently rubbed the top of Virbius' head. He wrapped around her finger, clinging to it happily.

"Aww, I love you," Aradia sighed with a smile. She cuddled Virbius close to her chest, lying back down and switching off the light, plunging the room into darkness once more.

Virbius stayed in close contact, never leaving the surface of her skin. Aradia was unsure if he even could break contact. Either way, she had always wanted a pet.

If all magic is this beautiful, my life is going to be amazing someday, she thought as she drifted off to sleep, her new pet cuddled close to her face.

18 – A Plan Into Motion

Half past eight and precisely on time… This was the sort of punctuality that pleased Donovan greatly. He had pulled up in the Amerson River car park outside of Macon on Interstate 75, only an hour after he had received the call to do so. The time spent on the road had given him the freedom to finally get his thoughts in order, and the soft hum of his electric car's tyres on the freeway had helped him avoid the unnecessary white noise one would usually encounter at such speeds. Despite despising pompous shows of wealth, especially expressed through cars, he felt this had been money well spent. And, of course, he was improving the environment – not simply making up for sorely lacking qualities of attraction.

Flicking the engine off, he gazed out the windscreen, hoping to catch sight of Montanaro in the distance, as was expected. Before he could make any progress in his searching, his phone rang, shattering the calm of the morning he had thus far enjoyed.

Donovan answered immediately, a crucial habit he had briskly developed in the wake of being appointed Consul of the Adytum.

"Gesture?"

"Mr Gesture, sir," a timid voice called out, so faint it almost failed to reach his ears on the speaker phone.

Donovan raised an eyebrow in speculation at who his bashful caller could be and what reason they had have to call him.

"Speaking. Who is this?"

A short sniff preceded the reply.

"Aradia... Lockwood's daughter, sir."

At this, Donovan instantly switched to a more comforting approach, taking the phone off speaker and raising it to his ear.

"Ah yes, Sariyah informed me of your new identity. What can I do for you?"

"I had another nightmare... my parents coming to get me across a dark field." Aradia let out a slight sob as she explained.

Donovan sighed.

"Don't worry, Aradia, me and my partner are doing our best to track down your parents. This will all be over soon and you'll no longer have anything to fear. Where is Sariyah? She should be with you."

"She's downstairs, getting breakfast. She should be back soon," Aradia answered.

"She'll know what to do to make it better, I'm sure. I'll stay on with you until then. How does that sound?"

There was a slight pause, then, "Okay."

"Nobody can hurt you with me here, I can have a whole team of Mages at your location with a single phone call. An entire army at your beck and call."

Aradia gave the slightest of laughs through her tears.

"That sounds nice."

For the next ten minutes Donovan stayed on the line with Aradia, doing his best to distract her from the recent terror, and learning about her less perilous activities since their last meeting. Aradia had just finished explaining her adventures in the Pantheon with Apathy when sounds of commotion could be heard in the background of the call. Sariyah's return.

Before signing off, Aradia expressed her gratitude for Donovan's aid, though remained rather timorous in her speech.

"I'll call again another time, if that's okay, sir?"

"Of course it is, anything you need. You remind me a lot of my niece you know, confident and strong but... gentle at heart."

Donovan didn't have to be present to sense the smile on Aradia's face before hanging up.

He exited the car and made his way down the path in search of his partner. It wasn't long before he located Montanaro. He was stood to attention, his focus fixed on an imperceptible far off spot, his dark, handsome complexion keenly highlighted under the fresh morning sun. As Donovan neared, he turned on the spot, long coat swaying in the breeze.

"Phone call?" Montanaro asked. "Could see you chatting away in that fancy Tesla of yours."

"Don't start," Gesture chuckled. "Lockwood's daughter, she's been having nightmares of a dark field and her parents striding toward her. Sound familiar?"

Montanaro nodded gravely.

"Sounds like a psychic attack to me. Dark field? Could easily be the astral plane."

"Exactly," Donovan agreed, folding his arms in displeasure at the idea. "I've dispatched a psychic who will investigate to see if the girl's mind is being infiltrated. It's a distinct possibility."

"Still doesn't explain how the bond was made to perform such a feat. Even a mortal will notice if their mind has been entered, it's nigh impossible to hide."

"Indeed, it doesn't explain it," Donovan nodded.

The two stood in relative quiet for a few minutes. The morning had become rather brisk, to the point where a passer-by might wonder why these two men were standing so still, out in the cold air without so much as the cover of a tree. Donovan resumed the conversation, broaching the subject that had warranted their meeting.

"So, what are your leads?" he asked.

"My various scouts and I have found multiple small villages, no more than a couple of streets, entirely absent of mortals, yet they all go to church on Sundays. Keeping up appearances? Why, when there are no mortals around for miles?"

Donovan gave a satisfied smile.

"It's possible they could all be worshippers. How many have you found?"

"Eight so far, and a ninth that was far larger than its siblings. Rumour has it that Lockwood has a stronghold somewhere here in the south, so we're looking for something similar to the larger town we found as a possible location where he could reside."

Montanaro finished his report with a sigh.

"Dangerous times we live in."

"Has it not always been that way?" Donovan nudged him. "Very good work so far, but it's vital that even if you locate Lockwood, you must *not* engage. If a single cell of worshippers survives, then their actions can continue subversively. We need to be sure we have them all before striking simultaneously."

Montanaro agreed before turning to leave.

"Oh, and Don, thank you for meeting in person rather than over the phone. If Orotund…"

"I know," Donovan reassured him. "If he heard we had located Lockwood, he would strike immediately and blindly – cut the head off the beast."

"We aren't dealing with a beast, just a worm that'll live on without the body," Montanaro asserted. He headed off down the path towards the treeline. Donovan turned the opposite way, back to the car park to plan his next course of action.

19 – Omen Couture's Spectacularly Odd Circus Show

O h my god, oh my god, oh my god!" Sariyah practically screamed. "We're actually here, I can't believe it." She had been boiling over with intense excitement ever since Aradia had shown her the tickets that arrived under the door.

"Why are you so excited again?" Aradia asked with a chuckle. While the raw energy Sariyah was outputting disconcerted her somewhat, it certainly lifted her spirits to see her friend and carer so elated.

Sariyah stared as if the question posed was one of unbelievable stupidity.

"*Why?* We're only going to see the number one magic show in the entire world, performed by actual Sorcerers and Mages. Omen Couture is a genius!"

Aradia listened intently to Sariyah's words as they approached a looming tent, almost twice the size of a regular circus, but just as extravagantly flamboyant, if not more so. Spotlights lit the blackened sky in a multitude of colours, like mighty corridors to the heavens, and the occasional flurry of fireworks popped Aradia's ears as they moved down the line. Crowds of mortals and Mages alike battled over places in the queue, and the hustle and bustle would have drowned Sariyah out, had she not been shouting.

"He brings the wonders of magic to the whole world – shows them every new discovery and they are none the wiser!" she yelled, then put on a stereotypically posh accent as if to mimic a pontifical mortal. "Oh, ho-ho, good show, good show... but it's all real to us and equally as amazing to watch."

Observing the crowds ahead, Aradia could feel the anticipation in each person as they poured into the gargantuan tent. Three separate entrances, each with a ticket office and hundreds of clamouring audience members, stood before her. Everything had a distinctly blue hue to it in varying shades. The walls and lining of the tent had large stripes of alternating white and deep blue, each stripe about a metre in width. As they entered the tent itself, the signage directing guests to various facilities and sections of the seating were a light blue.

"This Omen likes blue, does he?" Aradia smirked.

Sariyah shrugged. She was occupied with taking in her surroundings, analysing every single detail for perfect recall at a later date.

"How come you've never been before?" Aradia asked.

"It's very expensive! And the show tours the world every two years. With my job sending me all sorts of places too, it never seems to be in the same place I am," Sariyah complained. "But now I'm cruising!"

Before long they had checked their tickets and taken seats in a prime location at the centre of the middle stand; precisely positioned to view all the action of the show simultaneously and with perfect clarity.

"How on earth did Apathy get such good seats!" Sariyah exclaimed in wonderment. "These must have cost a small fortune."

"You'd be surprised the sort of discounts I can get," a voice chimed in.

They turned to see Apathy arriving in their row. She gave a winsome smile as she took her seat next to Aradia, who now sat in the middle of the three.

Now seated within the main ring of the circus, the atmosphere and appearance of the tent had changed dramatically. In stark contrast to the incredible clangour that rang in every direction on the outside, within the stalls all seemed relatively quiet, the tension beginning to heighten. There was a faint smell of what might be gunpowder lingering in the air and Aradia gazed at the lights which faced away from the main ring, illuminating the oak stalls so that people could locate their seats without difficulty. As a result, the centre remained in relative darkness, the structures within it obscured from Aradia's vision. However, one feature of the act that Aradia could discern was a platform constructed high in the rafters that bridged the entire space, just under where the overhead lights were situated. In the centre of this platform, suspended by delicate support beams, was what resembled the face of an antiquated but luxurious Victorian house. Its equally opulent red door, equipped with a knocker, had its name and postal code written to one side:

Couture Manor, SW1A 1AA.

Aradia observed the door with keen interest, wondering what manner of creation might emerge from it during the show. It wasn't long before her pondering was disturbed by a chuckle from Apathy, seemingly directed at her.

"It's almost as if they know they're siblings," Apathy whispered, continuing to titter away. It took Aradia a moment to realise what she was referring to.

Craning her head around, she saw Virbius sitting on her shoulder, apparently playing with a shadow tendril from Apathy's collection. The two were twirling around each other and occasionally butting heads in a playful manner. Aradia was both delighted and alarmed. What if someone spotted them? But she also marvelled at the fact that, despite the two shadows appearing identical, she knew via a deep-seated instinct which was her own and which was Apathy's.

Over the next fifteen minutes, the remainder of the crowd took their seats. Adult parties and full families alike were amongst those who came, all of them divided by age, race, sex, culture and religion. Yet all of them were united by the same desire to take a couple of hours to be thrilled and enthralled by the wonders of magic – whether they believed it to be real or not.

Many of the children and even adults were wearing matching top hats, and had various other souvenirs and oddities. Aradia began to feel slightly left out without them. She was about to interrupt Sariyah's babbling to ask if she could buy something from one of the many stalls set at each entrance to the ring, but her request died on her lips as she felt the tension grow and the lights begin to dim. It was starting.

The lights cut out entirely and blackness consumed the arena. The tension palpable, Aradia could only hear her own breathing and feel Sariyah's hand in hers, squeezing tightly in excitement. All vision useless, one arena full of hundreds of people, all silent... Aradia felt as if every sense and cell in her body were heightened to the experience and goosebumps riddled her arms. Her entire reality was a tension so intense and delicate it could be shattered by the slightest sound.

Aradia flinched when the overhead lights suddenly burst into life, blinding her temporarily until her eyes refocused. Every light was now angled to illuminate only the upper walkway that held the house front, leaving the rest of the arena in darkness. Every sound emitted in this moment seemed to echo with an unbelievable clarity, from the light switch to footsteps. Footsteps? Aradia could hear them echoing around the circus, coming from every direction at once. She turned her head to determine the source, but was entirely unable to detect their origin.

Aradia silently counted ten steps, then there was quiet once more. The calm was soon disturbed by the exaggerated sound effect of a battered door opening, its creak piercing her ears. Simultaneously, the stately red Victorian door atop the platform opened, revealing an indistinct figure behind it.

Out of the door stepped a man, possibly in his mid-to-late thirties, and rather handsome looking. He wore a classically stylised 1820's Victorian suit, closely resembling that of a circus ringmaster. Among his less extravagant features were dark pinstriped trousers, silky white gloves that caught the light at every possible angle, and black shoes polished to a gleam. Judging by the incredible volume of the footsteps, the latter were most likely also designed for tap.

While unconventional, these aspects of his outfit did nothing to distract from the spectacular suit jacket he wore. Its colour was a combination of a vivacious, passionate red, mixed with a brilliantly intense blood orange. Furthermore, the dazzling jacket had a deep black lapel and lining, travelling down the centre of his chest to be joined via many black and yellow buttons. Even the cuffs were adorned with exquisite embroidery.

Identical to a significant number of the crowd, upon his head rested a top hat, absent of any colouring but an intense sable. The rim covered his eyes and the greater part of his face as he held his head tilted forward slightly – perhaps in an effort to retain the mystery of his true identity.

Finally, and most intriguingly, in his right hand he held a long, narrow black cane. Aradia could only speculate what feats of wonder this simple item had the capacity to carry out.

The man travelled to the very edge of the bridged platform and stood perfectly still. Both hands were resting on the top of his cane, concealing the golden figurehead that topped it, as the booming tones of a stereotypical voice-over filled the arena.

"Over the last twenty years, Omen Couture, like his father and ancestors before him, has dedicated his life in servitude to entertainment. He has used his elite expertise in the arts of magic to bring the gr–"

As if via an instant command, the voice-over ceased as the man on the platform, presumably Omen, lifted one gloved hand into the air and tilted his head upwards.

His blue eyes sparkled into the crowd and he spoke.

"Enough, enough. Let's get the fun started already!"

Omen's accent was similar to Apathy's, but with an ever so mild Greek twang to it. Voice echoing around the arena, he swiftly took a step backward and tossed his cane off the platform. Smoke enveloped Omen and his cane began to twirl through the air, rocketing toward a set of stairs used to navigate the stalls. Impossibly stepping out of a second puff of smoke onto said stairs, Omen caught his own cane perfectly and slung a wink to the crowd as a chorus of brass instruments erupted into a classic 1930s swing number. Amid gasps from the audience, Omen gave a delighted laugh and once again tossed his cane, only to catch it just in time, appearing out of smoke at the foot of the stairs.

Dancers dressed in a variety of colours and fabrics swiftly made their way to accompany him as he moved out onto the ring floor, now lit fantastically. A large circular podium stood proudly in the centre of the ring with ramps up either side, and various barricades and obstacles were scattered about the floor. Suspended above this were multiple balance beams and small platforms, now revealed to have had people standing on them the entire time in equally fanciful costumes. The music reached the verse and Omen began to sing. The song appeared to be his own eccentrically unique creation, containing references from various other songs of a similar style, and even some staple Disney classics.

As the song progressed, the performers on the platforms began firing flames and beams of yellow energy down on the dancers, who twisted and twirled with an unnatural agility between them all. All the while, Omen continued to sing in time and appear in various spots around the arena, seeming incredibly pleased with himself. The action provoked roaring cheers from the crowd and Aradia giggled with excitement. Looking at her companions either side, Apathy simply sat and observed with a smile, eyes tracking Omen precisely and looking to locations before he would appear there, as if she knew the routine. Sariyah, meanwhile, was almost losing her mind in glee and exhilarated laughter.

During an instrumental segment of the song, the dancers formed a moving ring around one incredibly tall armoured man, and Sorcerers who had now joined the floor sent columns of air to disrupt and levitate the occasional performer for added flair. Omen swiftly leapt into the arms of the large man, who proceeded to cradle him almost as softly as one would a baby. As Omen added the occasional extra line, he tapped the man on the shoulder with his cane. At this, the man swiftly launched him into the air with immense strength, causing him to fly high into the rafters and out of sight. All eyes that had been fixed on the place of Omen's disappearance were suddenly wrenched away to the top of the exclusive stalls where he now stood, looking just as dapper as before, making his way down the rows of seats seemingly looking for someone.

Aradia watched with uncontainable giddiness as he scanned the rows searching for a suitable candidate – for what purpose she had not the slightest idea. Her heart leapt, however, when he began making his way down their very row of seats, delicately tiptoeing between the legs and belongings of those seated there. Aradia couldn't seem to close her mouth, gaping up at Omen who now stood before the three of them, Apathy smirking and Sariyah so pale she might faint.

"Hold this for me dear," Omen asked with a wide grin. He bent down and carefully handed his cane to Aradia, who cradled it as if it were made of porcelain. "I'll be back in just a tick!" He laughed before blowing a kiss to Apathy and vanishing, only to emerge from the main tunnel down in the ring followed by the final procession of performers.

While he sang the last chorus, Omen led an army of Sorcerers, Mages, and even a few Pure Born around the entire ring in a dazzling display of raw power and wonder. As this took place, Aradia's trembling hands held his cane. It was constructed of a wood Aradia didn't recognise and had a golden ring about a third of the way down. The tip looked as though it could be unscrewed, and the head of the cane was a most intricate and peculiar design. It was made up of two intersecting half-moons at a diagonal angle to each other, with a thin golden mesh spanning the space between them, connecting and forming a globe. What fascinated her the most, however, was the way she could feel the magic within it, and the way it vibrated gently in her hands. It was practically humming with energy, though she was still unsure what it actually did. As the procession completed its lap of the ring, Omen vanished, appearing before Aradia once more as the song began to build to a mighty conclusion.

"Thank you kindly. Still intact I see," Omen smiled, taking back his cane and ruffling Aradia's hair before appearing at the foot of the ramp to the central podium. Every instrument in the orchestra built the tension of the piece, yearning to release and resolve to the tonic note. Omen climbed the ramp, almost sliding as he arrived at the top, and bent backward to release a mighty finishing note, holding it with perfect pitch until the finale of the song almost popped Aradia's ears with its ferocity and the lights cut out with it. Only a single spotlight remained, illuminating Omen from behind. He now stood in an eccentric but striking stance, one hand on the rim of his hat angled downward and the other out behind him balancing his cane. He was clearly short of breath and his mousy brown hair was slick with sweat.

The crowd let out a deafening roar and tumultuous applause, Aradia joining in wholeheartedly. The mortals among the audience were stupefied in utterly perplexed delight at what they had just witnessed. Those who knew better were equally impressed, despite their understanding.

Omen took a gratified bow. A grin from cheek to cheek spread across his face like butter as the lights came back on, revealing the other members of the act taking their bows and applause. Twenty seconds passed and the commotion restarted, performers travelling in all directions clearing the floor for the sequenced acts to begin. From this point on, Omen practically teleported about the arena, taking on the role of commentator and announcer to the diverse and mythical acts that shared their moment in the spotlight.

Throughout the first half of the show, Omen presented astonishingly skilled Mages, and a lightshow like no other infatuated the people gathered to watch – the entire spectrum of colours clashing and combining through the crystal-clear air. This act was closely followed by Sorcerer's in their prime, manipulating the earth and the elements to create spectacles unseen. This included men engulfed by flame and dazzling displays of levitation via the air – not to mention the manipulation and use of water to deliver the spectators in the *splash zone* the dues they expected.

Finally, Omen himself and a selection of Pure Born presented their own unique abilities, each with their own typically inelegant circus title. Aradia stared in wonder alongside Sariyah as they watched men and women with strength and speed beyond belief. Omen himself demonstrated his ability to miraculously materialize in any location he wished, dodging bullets by appearing behind the gunman, or vanishing only to reappear with genuine items from famous locations across the globe.

Aradia found herself particularly fascinated by one young girl, a short blonde in her late teens, who seemed to be able to communicate with and instruct even the most untamed of animals. She spent her act prancing with wild horses, play fighting with lions and tigers, and swimming alongside sharks.

"This is incredible!" Aradia marvelled during the intermission, her ears still ringing from the almost violent applause that had preceded this break.

"I am the happiest I have ever been my entire life!" Sariyah shouted, feet stamping on the floor in delirious ecstasy.

Apathy regarded them both in the manner that reflected her name, while she quietly ate an ice cream pot purchased from one of the concessions.

The show's second half proved to be a unique experience, even more than the first. It was starkly dissimilar to the first half's act-after-act structure, and followed the more logical flow of a story. Told through multiple scenes with a recurring cast of characters, the tale was one of a forbidden love *à la Romeo and Juliet* and how the discovery of magic in the world would influence such a story. Stunts and feats of wonder were central to conveying the tale in each scene and various musical pieces were performed throughout, one of which, Aradia felt, had a profound effect on her.

In the song, *A Lover's Insecurity*, the line, "*How could I love when my heart's brimmed with strife? Take you in my arms and say, it'll be alright*" resonated powerfully with her, and she pondered this very question during the short break between scenes. The performance ended on a resolved and rather jovial note, which worked to dispel Aradia's feelings of insecurity that the lead role had so convincingly evoked.

She took Sariyah's hand once more for the final act of the show, a second original song. An oddly bohemian performance, it contained solos by Omen and other actors and underwent multiple shifts in genre and mood but concluded on a significant high.

Aradia grinned and rose to her feet alongside hundreds of others, and applauded the intrepid thespians for their incredible work. She took her seat as the arena's lighting adopted a neutral palette and members of the audience began to retire. Ears ringing and heart hammering in her chest, she marvelled at the fresh memories of what she had witnessed. Omen and his troupe had provided her with the most enlightening and joyous night of her life thus far… and Sariyah's too by the sound of her energetic screams.

"Come along then," Apathy motioned, rising to her feet and making her way down the stairs towards the entrance of the ring below.

Aradia rose and followed blindly, Sariyah following suit before questioning, "Hold on, the exit is up there."

"The exit for *normal* people is up there, yes," Apathy confirmed. "But we are VIP's and I have business with Mr Couture."

Sariyah almost collapsed, steadying herself on one of the nearby handrails. Hearing Apathy speak these words, Aradia awoke from her delirious stupor.

"Wait, what?!"

20 – Meeting the Maker

They passed by the security watchman, who delivered them a consenting nod, and Aradia was caught profoundly off guard as she stepped into the circus ring. The second she set foot inside, she felt the residual magical energy in the air, practically sizzling with unreleased tension. It felt as though she could grasp a handful of air and it would hold its shape, such was the raw power trapped within. Then there was the temperature. This caged magical tension created a powerful heat, which radiated from every surface around them, bringing a stiflingly hot but thrilling temperature to the ring.

"Ouch, hot!" Sariyah exclaimed and laughed while hopping from foot to foot, her glee most likely absorbing the pain.

Aradia considered offering to carry her friend and carer, but decided against it. She wasn't sure she currently had the strength to support another human being.

Besides, she did choose to take the unshod life, be it for her magic or not! she figured.

Apathy guided them up the very ramp on which Omen had stood and performed several times in the past couple of hours and placed herself in the exact centre of a marked out square.

"Come, stand here," she instructed, indicating for them to follow.

Aradia and Sariyah obeyed. The allotted space had clearly not been designed for three, so they linked arms to ensure none of them would slip.

"Hold on tight, you wouldn't want to fall to an untimely demise now," Apathy asserted, followed by an unnecessarily callous chuckle. Immediately, the section on which they stood broke away from the ramp and began to levitate upward, much like the platform Aradia had used at the library.

Aradia clung on for dear life. Fear and adrenaline created a mixed feeling of enjoyment for the ride, but it was over no sooner than it had begun. They had been transported up to the bridged platform, and Apathy stepped off first and headed toward the facia of Couture Manor. Sariyah took a moment to stop and feel each and every material, her connection to the earth aiding her sense of touch.

Aradia stared over the edge of the platform at the ring and stalls below. She mimicked the stance Omen had made before the start of the show and gazed out at a now vacant crowd, imagining what it would have looked like to him. Despite the absence of an audience to view her, Aradia still felt a great degree of empowerment, stood atop the entire circus as if she were queen of the world.

"Hurry up, we don't have all night!" Apathy complained, holding the door ajar like a mother waiting for two inquisitive children.

"Sorry, sorry," Sariyah mumbled, hastening her pace to catch up. Aradia followed after.

Where are we actually going? Aradia wondered in puzzlement. *This is a fake house in a circus tent, after all. What can possibly be behind the façade?*

Quite a lot, it transpired. Defying the laws of physics, they were confronted with a flight of stairs. After descending them, Apathy continued to lead them down a corridor with walnut floorboards and green wallpapered walls, divided by a dado rail. Many doors symmetrically led away from this central corridor, each with a specific act's name above the frame, and Aradia could hear the distant sound of drinks and merriment coming from one of the adjoining corridors. Before long, Apathy stopped outside one particular door, identical in design to the others apart from the name plaque that read, much to Aradia's excitement, *The Magnificent Omen Couture*. Without a moment's hesitation or a courteous knock, Apathy turned the handle and entered the room.

The dressing room resembled an expensive hotel room. While it contained the expected makeup bench and mirror, plus a rack of varying costumes to match any style or mood of performance, it also had a seating area in front of the door and a king-sized bed, recently disturbed, against the left-hand wall. The colour scheme was predominantly blue, in contrast to that of the corridor, and this only caused the man himself to stand out even more starkly against it.

Omen Couture sat calmly at the makeup bench observing himself in the mirror, attempting to carefully thread a large splinter of wood out the lapel of his jacket. He turned when they entered, half in surprise, half in gratitude to have guests.

"Stacey!" he exclaimed. "So glad you came, and you brought friends."

Apathy's eyes grew narrow. She glowered at Omen as if he had grossly embarrassed her.

"We agreed we wouldn't use that name in the presence of others, did we not?" she muttered as he rose and approached them.

"Why? They're your friends and you have such a bewitching name. I couldn't let you forget it."

He gave a slight chuckle and wrapped his arms around Apathy's waist, who leant in and pressed her head into his chest. Without leaving his embrace, she angled her head slightly to address her companions.

"Sariyah, Aradia, may I introduce Omen Couture. I've tried countless times to rid myself of this positive plague of a man, believe me."

"You know you couldn't get rid of me, you're the rhythm to my rhyme! Rebel all you want; you'll still always be mine."

Omen took a step back and gently caressed Apathy's cheek. She smiled and blushed pink. Looking on, Aradia realised she had never seen Apathy smile before – at least not with the genuine warmth she expressed now – much less blush.

Aradia could better study Omen's features now that he was within arm's reach and without his top hat or the glare of show lights. He was clean shaven, had deep blue eyes and a rather fair complexion, despite his heritage. His mousy brown hair had very little styling to it upon first glance, but on closer inspection, it became clear it had been *made* to appear as if it were naturally unkempt.

Omen turned to face them.

"Apologies, I'm getting distracted again. A pleasure to make your acquaintance."

He proffered a hand that Aradia swiftly accepted and gave a firm shake in formal greeting. While she was astounded and overjoyed to have the opportunity to be acquainted with the pioneer of the night's performance, she was adamant she would retain her dignity and not become starstruck.

Turning to Sariyah, he offered the same handshake, to which she timidly attempted to raise her shaking hand, eyes locked with Omen's and lip bitten in swoon. Omen noticed this and found it mildly amusing and endearing. He took her hand for her, raised it up and gave it a tender and traditionally polite kiss.

Sariyah's eyes widened further, if that were possible, and she fell backwards losing all strength in her legs, landing on one of the nearby sofas with a heavy thud.

"She's a really big fan, sir," Aradia explained. "Probably a little overwhelmed."

"I can tell!" Omen beamed in response, as Apathy moved to a collection of cabinets by the bed and rifled through them in search of something.

"Thank you ever so much for holding my cane earlier," Omen said, gesturing behind him to where the cane rested, propped up against his desk, still buzzing with energy.

"It was my pleasure!" Aradia smiled, glancing over to it, then added, "I didn't realise Apathy had a partner."

Apathy called out from under the bed as she searched.

"Just a boyfriend. Flirting really, I assure you."

Omen shook his head with a light-hearted scoff.

"Can I interest anyone in a drink perhaps? It's been a successful night, how about something to celebrate?"

Having gathered her strength and composure, Sariyah stood once more and came to Aradia's side.

"I'll have one… if that's okay."

Omen nodded and began diligently searching the minifridge tucked into one corner of the room. He withdrew a bottle of Dom Perignon and gathered four elegant glasses.

"Okay with you, Aradia? Or something a little less intoxicating?"

"Anything else is fine," she smiled back to him, grateful for the consideration of her age. She hated feeling as though she was left out.

The night progressed to be one of great ebullience. Stories of past misadventures were shared and drank over, so much so that Sariyah eventually fell unconscious due to her inebriated state. Aradia's beverages contained no ingredients other than fruit, so she was able to observe her companions without the hinderance of alcohol. She deemed Omen to be a character of significant buoyancy and decided she particularly enjoyed his company. He had commented upon even the most concealed positive aspects of her personality, and his compliments had brought smile after smile to her face.

Glancing toward the clock in his office and reading the time as 3:00am, Omen rose to announce, "Alas, time has travelled on as it always must, and it has come the time that we shall part in trust." He moved to the door, a slightly drunken sway in his step. "How I am able to do so, you may wonder why; for I will have us home before we see dawn's fresh sky."

Aradia laughed at his flamboyance before skipping to his side.

"Are you going to use your smoke bomb teleporting?"

"Minus the smoke, that's simply for theatrical flair."

With an expression that lay Apathy's irritation plain across her face, shadows began to flow out of the recesses of her coat and split into multiple tendrils. Each coil found its target, gently wrapping around the sleeping body of Sariyah and lifting her from the sofa. She then rested a single slender hand on Omen's shoulder to form a connection.

"Do I have to cling on?" Aradia asked inquisitively.

Omen gave a cheeky grin.

"Not at all, only the slightest second of connection is required."

As he spoke, he reached a hand forward and gently tapped Aradia's nose with a single gloved finger.

An incredible surge coursed through Aradia's body from head to toe, electrifying every inch of her person, causing her hair to pulse outward as if attracted by static. The feeling was exhilarating, yet an uncontrollable reflex forced her to kick out and leap backward in shock.

The clangour of a bucket tipping and multiple brooms clattering to the floor caused Aradia to cry out when she narrowly avoided tripping over them. She pressed her back against a wall, steadied herself and realised she now stood within a cleaning cupboard of some description, shelves of products stacked high, and a single overhead light illuminating the room. Any possible indication of their previous location was now vacant, vanished. Only she and the three entirely unphased passengers she accompanied could provide any form of evidence.

"Ehwha?" was the only sound she could produce in response to the experience.

"It's quite startling the first time, I forgot to caution. Here, this'll level you out a smidge." Omen itched the back of his neck as he spoke and handed Aradia his cane once more.

No sooner had she taken the item than the residual energy in her body seemed to evaporate, transferring itself into the mystifying cane, causing it to vibrate ever so slightly just as it had done during the earlier performance.

Aradia let out a relieved sigh.

"I knew what was going to happen… but I wasn't prepared for *that* to happen."

"Very few are," Omen informed. "You do grow accustomed to the feeling after a while."

After ensuring no mortals were still on the premises at this hour, Aradia was elected to lead Omen and Apathy, who still cradled the sleeping Sariyah with the help of her shadows, to the location of their room, which they arrived at promptly and undetected.

Brief farewells were exchanged, and Apathy linked her arm with Omen's in preparation for their travel.

"I will be arriving promptly after lunch to begin your first lesson, Aradia. I expect you to be prepared and awake," Apathy instructed from his side.

"I'll drop by too; it'll be interesting to watch," Omen laughed as Apathy snatched his cane from his grasp and he hoisted her into a bridal carry. "Besides, I can bring some genuine Caribbean cocktails, make a day of it! Forecast says it'll be sweltering later today."

Aradia nodded with a shy smile and watched as Apathy gave an elegant wave of her fingers. Then they both vanished, leaving nothing beside a momentary heatwave that rippled toward the ceiling in their wake.

21 – TRIALS OF STRENGTH

A radia awoke around 1.00pm and immediately sat up in bed, sweating profusely. Her recurring nightmarish affliction seemed to have no end, but she found some morbid comfort in the fact that she was becoming accustomed to the experience of terror coursing through her on a nightly basis.

As her senses began to reactivate, she became aware of the faint smell of exotic fruit and the strains of what sounded like the song *Break My Stride* drifting through the partially open bedroom door. Perplexed as to the source, Aradia slipped out of bed and reached for the curtains to provide some light.

Stifling a scream, she jerked backward and collapsed onto the bed, staring at her outstretched hands in shock and horror. They were engulfed in an impossibly dark black, skin-tight substance. Remnants of it were dispersed unevenly covering parts of her forearm.

What in the world?!

She turned her hands over multiple times to view both sides. Flexing her fingers, she noted how the substance bubbled and shifted ever so slightly in reaction. It reacted somewhat like a Necromancer's shadow.

Could this have something to do with my recent soul merging?

She decided to make her way directly into the studio's main living space – the source of the scent and music – and speak to Sariyah about it.

"Ah, finally awake," Sariyah called as Aradia reached the bottom of the stairs, still staring at her hands in disbelief.

"Well, would you look at that." Aradia heard Apathy's eldritch tones from across the room. "You're growing up already."

Apathy approached her excitedly, while Omen and Sariyah sat at the dining table. Multicoloured drinks in tall glasses and bowls of various foods were spread across it. Apathy took Aradia's hands in hers.

"Fascinating… mine didn't do anything like this. How does it feel?"

Once more examining her encased hands, Aradia noted the almost slimy but somehow comforting texture her shadows provided while in this form.

"It's creepy, but alright now that I'm over the shock of it," she confirmed.

"Most Necromancer's shadows coalesce in a place that is unique to them," Apathy informed her. "Mine reside in my coat as I'm sure you've seen. Yours seem to prefer a more direct contact."

"That's cool but… how do I get rid of it?" Aradia asked, the thrill of her magic tempered by the thought that she might have to go through life with shadow covered hands from now on.

Apathy pondered this for a moment.

"Well, you are their master, they respond to your whim and emotion. I felt a slight disturbance within you overnight; perhaps you were reacting to a feeling of impending doom?"

She expressed her theory with a unempathetic frankness that would be considered insensitive by most.

"Right," Aradia nodded. She took a step back and focused, shaking off any residual tension and fear left over from her nightmare. Holding her hands out in front of her, she concentrated, willing the shadows to retract. Without a second's delay, each and every tendril trickled up her arms and disappeared up her sleeves, where she could feel them no more. Pale hands revealed once more, she gave them a close inspection to ensure all was as it should be.

"That would have been cool if it wasn't really unsettling," she sighed.

The four then proceeded to have lunch together. Omen joyfully presented his purchases from a short visit to the Caribbean earlier that morning, and they relished a multicultural meal. A short instructional lesson on Necromancy from Apathy came thereafter.

Under Apathy's tutelage, Aradia managed to master the control of her now numerous shadows, summoning and dismissing them. She even managed to perfect the summoning of specifically Virbius, who acted in an endearing but irritatingly converse way to his siblings – an unexplained phenomenon that Apathy informed her was peculiar to all Necromancer's first-created shadows. They seemed to possess an enhanced degree of free will.

As the evening sun began to set, and mere seconds before the lesson on simple combative usage of shadows was about to start, there was a sharp knock at the door.

Sariyah moved to answer the call as Omen raised a query.

"Is there a film you'd like to see Aradia? I have a rather large screen in my home on Kos. I'm sure it would be much preferable to this little thing." He gestured towards the substantial TV that hung on the wall.

"I don't think we're allowed to," Aradia explained with a tinge of annoyance. "Sariyah doesn't want to leave Vegas. I'm not sure why though, other than safety."

Omen shrugged as Sariyah returned, an incredibly formal looking man behind her.

"Aradia, this is Enkefalos. He's the psychic I promised would check you over."

"Oh, hi," Aradia greeted him, a mixture of apprehension and relief seizing her all at once.

Sariyah didn't attempt to hide her seething indignation in the slightest when Stonewall summoned her presence. She marched through the grounds of the Flamingo hotel opposite Caesars, mind entirely preoccupied with thoughts of Aradia.

Having your mind entered is an incredibly intrusive process. I should be there to comfort her... And I would be if it weren't for this prick and her inconvenient meeting schedule!

She moved through the many trees, passing multiple mortal men and women, out for an evening stroll, or perhaps heading to the pool for a swim. Each and every one seemed to have an innocence, coupled with joyous holiday glee, written plainly across their faces. Many times in her life, Sariyah had yearned for nothing more than to join them in their ignorance, perhaps even abandoning magic altogether.

Before long, she had worked her way to a more secluded section of the gardens, toward the north-east end – the rendezvous point Stonewall had dictated. Turning the corner, she was met with no indication of her presence. This unfrequented area of the gardens was entirely vacant of human life.

Is this some kind of joke? Ask me all the way out here then just don't show up?

Sariyah immediately retrieved her phone and dialled Stonewall. She prepared to be deafening, foul and not in the slightest respectful. The call failed and Stonewall's irritating voice requested she leave a message, only serving to anger her further. She called a second time. Before the call failed again, a muffled buzzing caught her attention. It was barely perceptible, but she could hear a faint buzzing... the vibrating of a phone somewhere nearby. Tucking her phone in her pocket, she hurried further down the path, conflicted anxiety beginning to rise.

A few metres away, a mobile phone lay tucked into the grass to the side of the path. She picked it up and two missed call notifications from her cell lit up the screen. It was Stonewall's phone. Thoughts hopeful and macabre immediately filled her head. Had she dropped it or had something more sinister caused her apparent tardiness?

Then she saw it and her heart sank...

A solitary hand protruding from the bushes. Sariyah leapt to investigate. Moments later she was using all her strength to drag Plagoya Stonewall's lifeless corpse free of the underbrush. After this she retrieved the two Mage soldiers who had flanked her. Sariyah inspected the cadavers, religiously keeping watch for any unsuspecting mortals who might happen upon her as she worked.

Stonewall and her underlings each had distinctive burn marks around the neck, so severe that the skin had partially melted. It was one of Saeva Dragoia's preferred methods of unsuspecting execution.

The weight of her heart in her chest was almost too much to bear. She began to conceal the evidence of the crime, utilising her magic to provide the three bodies a fast and temporary burial. Her priorities were now simple: *warn the others, protect Aradia.* The fallen soldiers would be honoured once the situation had been handled. Saeva's transgressions concealed, Sariyah took flight, sprinting back to Caesars.

Experiencing a psychic probing for the first time, Aradia realised, was a harshly intrusive process. But it was not as blindingly painful as she had imagined it might be. Enkefalos had so far been examining her closely for around fifteen minutes. He had remained silent for the most part, only occasionally muttering an incantation or two. Aradia felt as though she could sense where his presence was affecting her, searching her mind, in even the deepest of crevasses, bringing memories both joyful and harrowing to the surface.

Omen had recently left to procure dinner supplies and possible entertainment options for the evening, which left Apathy to oversee the process alone. Standing to one side, her soulless grey eyes remained fixed on Aradia, not wavering even for a second.

Thus far, Aradia had not detected anything of interest that had been uncovered, and seemingly neither had Enkefalos. That was until a dull ache began at the back of her head, identical to before, and instantly she felt Enkefalos focus his attention on the pain.

"Is this a regular occurrence?" he asked plainly, a transparent attempt to mask his concern.

Aradia nodded.

"Every night after a nightmare."

Putting it into words and stating the facts aloud, Aradia began to register what should have been obvious before, piecing together the puzzle herself.

"Oh no."

"I should have come sooner," Enkefalos admitted gravely, stepping away from Aradia. His psychic bond to her depleted as his distance from her grew, gradually dissipating into nothingness.

"Someone has created a psychic link with you," he explained, a slight quiver in his voice. "They can visit you in shared dreams if they are powerful enough… even discern your location after a couple of attempts perhaps."

Aradia's heart grew cold and anxiety began to bubble within her. With a glare as sharp as a dagger, Apathy stepped between the two of them.

"Well, go on then, break the connection!" she demanded impatiently.

"I can't, not here, it would take a long time. We would have to find the source of the connection."

Enkefalos put up his hands in defence and backed away from the seething Apathy.

"Forgive me, but I do not find it prudent for you to speak in such a way that we cannot understand," Apathy retorted. "How about we use layman's terms so that both of us can contribute to aiding *my* apprentice?"

Enkefalos drew breath to speak when Aradia cried out, clutching her arm in reaction to a sharp pain that had seized her. Almost falling from her chair, she grimaced in agony and instinctively clawed at the scar on her arm, presently concealed by her jacket. It felt as though a naked flame had been applied to her skin.

Apathy dropped to her knees. She slid towards Aradia, clutching her xiphisternum in clear sympathetic pain, made possible by their connection.

"Aradia, what is it?" she questioned, alarm raising her voice as she attempted to get the attention of the squirming girl.

"Someone's coming…" Enkefalos warned, terror paling his complexion.

Apathy turned, her mind racing to determine the most appropriate course of action. She pressed her phone into Aradia's chest.

"Bedroom, now. Call Omen."

Apathy lifted Aradia from the chair and pushed her towards the stairs. She began to climb, falling twice in her scrambling. Upstairs, she dived under Sariyah's bed – the nearest place of safety – and fumbled with Apathy's phone, attempting to find Omen in her contacts. There was no answer. Eyes brimming with tears, and with no answer from the circus master, Aradia called him a further two times before leaving a sobbing voicemail.

"Omen help, they're here... they're here. Please!"

Aradia abandoned hope of a reply and curled into a defensive foetal position. Shadows coursed out of her sleeves in an aggressively constant stream, covering her hands and forearms as they had done before, eager to protect her should it be required.

She waited motionless in the darkness of the room. Presently, sounds of commotion and screams of death emanated from the main living space and rang shrilly in her ears. All the while she felt every single blow Apathy took in battle. An incredible rush of adrenaline mixed with pain and seething anger filled Aradia's soul, and she knew Apathy was not on the winning side. Utter dread consumed her and a lump formed in her throat. This time the fear was hers, not Apathy's. She heard a window shatter and experienced a dim sense of falling within her soul.

Oh god, please don't let them find me!

Aradia sobbed, tears streaming down her cheeks.

All fell silent. The battle was won and lost. Aradia lay curled in the darkness, her heart beating so intensely in her chest she thought it might burst free of her ribcage in terror of what might come next.

Light burst into the room as a switch was flicked. Heavy footsteps echoed, each step driving daggers into her mind with its thundering. A substantially armoured boot came into view, a mere hair's breadth away. Aradia silently begged for its owner not to inspect her hiding place, though she knew the chances of such luck were incredibly thin.

They're going to find me. They will, I know it...

She began to abandon hope, before taking a deep breath in and remembering who she was.

No, I'm not Sophie anymore. I'm not weak, I won't be. But I can't beat them… can I?

Clinging to improbable and fanciful scenarios that could see her to safety, a mental battle raged that would decide her course of action.

No, you can't, don't be stupid… they will find me or catch me if I run. But I'll be damned if I'm going down without a fight. Aradia Vastate doesn't surrender. That was Sophie's weakness, not mine.

Aradia released a primal, adrenaline-infused roar and thrust her arms forward, launching a torrent of shadows which burst outward from her palms, knocking the intruder to the floor. She knew the commotion would immediately raise the alarm and that she didn't have a second to waste. She rolled out from under the bed and rose to her knees.

The prostrate man wore armour similar to Dragoia's, though clearly less regal. He was already stirring from the shock of the assault. Aradia reacted solely on instinct, clenching her fist and striking him across the face. Her shadows responded to her every whim, conscious and subliminal, forming an unyielding rigid surface around her hand to help knock her enemy unconscious with one clean blow.

"Okay, come on," she encouraged herself, acting as her own Sariyah in her absence. She quickly examined the room for an escape route. There were only two possibilities, both unfavourable. Her first exit was the door leading back to the main chamber where an unknown number of Dragoia's men awaited her appearance. Second was the window on the far wall – certain death if she plummeted to the ground, or simply a delay to her capture if she managed to scale the building somehow.

Before she could process the information further, a figure loomed in the doorway – another of Dragoia's soldiers, a woman this time. She immediately raised her hand to fire a sizzling beam of yellow energy that narrowly missed Aradia, scorching the wall behind. Aradia's response relied entirely on gut instinct. She dived forward and splayed her shadow covered hands outwards. She turned her head in discomfort, the discharge of energy creating some painful pressure under her skin, but she impacted fiercely with her assailant, knocking her over the balcony into the living space below.

Through one open eye she saw the empty space where her attacker had stood. She let out a small cheer and reverted her attention to her escape, deciding on the window as the lesser of two evils. Hurriedly she opened it as far as the safety lock would allow, then once more utilised the solid state of her shadows to shatter it completely.

"Don't fall, don't fall," she repeated quietly, easing herself out of the window and perching on the ledge.

She looked up in hope of anything she could grasp onto to help her climb, but there was no point of leverage, and the roaring thunder of multiple armoured footsteps charging up the stairs filled her ears.

She raised her hands upward, barely keeping balance on the window ledge, and allowed her shadows to seek security of their own accord. Without a second's delay, the shadows rocketed upwards until they almost vanished from view into the night sky. She felt them latch onto the hotel roof and become as taught as climbing rope.

A hint of a smile at her shadow's ingenuity flashed across Aradia's face, but it faded just as quickly as soldiers began to spill into the bedroom. Seconds from disaster and with no care for safety, Aradia took a leap of faith and pushed off the windowsill into the chill night air.

Weightlessness seized her for a moment before her feet collided with the solid wall. The shadows held strong. Aradia let out a long exhale of nervous energy and terror. She dared not cast a glance behind her or she might falter. Instead, she began to climb, relying entirely on her upper body, for rarely did she find any footholds on the journey up.

"God…" Aradia strained. She quickly realised that she did not have the strength to lift her own weight for very long with her arms alone, assisted by magic or not. The shadow's grip on the roof began to loosen, and the tendrils tightened and thinned like elastic under the pressure of her weight.

"Don't break!" she commanded them uselessly, for she knew they had no choice in the matter. Muscles burning, she attempted to at least pull herself up to the next window. Perhaps she could get another guest to summon help.

Her efforts were fruitless, however. She focused on her soul as she began to slip, little by little.

Apathy's alive, I'm sure of it. Does that mean a fall from this height is survivable?

She desperately hoped and turned to view the immense number of stories she would inevitably fall at a moment's notice. With shadows straining, their tensile strength rapidly depleting, Aradia let out a cry. She had come so far only to fall now, hanging by a thread.

A sharp jerk jolted Aradia from her despair. Flicking her head upward, she could feel her shadows being aided, hoisted up to the roof. Relief washed over her as she was gradually pulled up the side of the building, passing many windows, trying to avoid detection from unsuspecting guests. She had no idea who her rescuer was.

"Thank you!" Aradia gasped as she crested the roof and crawled out onto it, her shadows retracting into her sleeves, exhausted. "I couldn't hold on any longer."

Only then did she look up.

"You're very welcome," Saeva Dragoia's agonising tones rang out, shattering Aradia's hope and relief in one fatal blow.

Saeva towered above her, dragon-scale armour polished pristinely, and mask removed. Aradia could make out his features accurately for the first time. His hair was almost as black as her own and styled to perfection. Deep brown eyes slashed into her very soul.

"You shouldn't be so surprised to see me," he sneered. "My dear Sariyah committed an act of the most heinous misconduct and disrespect to our Sorcerer's traditions. You should have known I'd be coming back for you soon."

Every syllable he spoke pierced the night with a coldness that gave Aradia goosebumps. Resisting a second bout of tears, she remained silent and unmoving, attempting to focus on a second escape plan. Saeva cast his eyes over her shoulder momentarily.

"Oh, I wouldn't recommend jumping off any more high platforms. You caused me an awful lot of bother chasing you down at the library. Do yourself a favour and don't cause any more trouble, lest I have to punish you for insolence."

The last dregs of adrenaline firing through her, Aradia summoned her magic a final time, channelling it up through her arms, alongside weakened shadows. She struck Saeva across the face, as she had done his soldier.

Eyes fixed, staring into hers, Saeva barely moved and immediately caught her wrist in an iron grip making her squirm.

"Now *that* was an exceedingly stupid error little girl," he snapped.

Intense heat began to burn into her wrist and Aradia screamed in agony, submitting to his will. Saeva released her and she slumped to the floor, clutching her wrist.

"Consider that a cursory demonstration of what punishment will entail for you."

Kneeling in defeat, Aradia attempted to formulate a heroic line to utter in defiance, but all she managed was a sob.

Saeva stepped back as a collection of his soldiers joined them on the roof and pulled Aradia roughly to her feet.

"Where's our teleporter?" Saeva asked impatiently.

"We rendezvous in five minutes, sir," one of the soldiers replied.

A sharp whistle pierced the air and Aradia stared across the rooftop to determine its source.

"Here's a teleporter for you," Omen announced, stepping up onto the roof, cane supporting his walk. "Maybe not the one you were hoping to see, but here I am nonetheless."

Saeva turned to face Omen who remained a safe distance away, and for the first time seemed to be genuinely perplexed.

"What are *you* doing here Couture? Since when did you involve yourself with matters of the Adytum?"

Omen took another step forward, casting a subtle nod to Aradia as if to direct her to prepare.

"Since you've begun kidnapping teenage girls. That's enough to make anyone turn against you, surely?"

"I have done far worse things you've found no sense of morality to challenge before," Saeva growled.

Aradia noticed that his countenance with Omen was significantly more bitter and formal than the condescending manner in which he treated those he believed he held advantage over. This fact gave her a spark of hope. Saeva clearly deemed Omen an equal.

"Go back to your circus and retain your independence."

"I've never been inclined towards fighting," Omen began, ignoring Saeva's ultimatum. "The drama and plight, all awfully exciting, but it has never truly captured my interest."

Saeva's hands ignited into fists of blue flame and his glare never left his opponent.

"I don't have time for your rhymes, circus act. This is your final warning. Leave and I will consider not hunting you down for wasting my time."

"I think not, my irritating friend. Despite my distaste for it, I can hold my own and you will be my witness."

No sooner had the words left his lips than Omen teleported, reappearing behind Saeva, a wooden dining chair in his grip. He splintered it over the back of Saeva's head sending him reeling then teleported again, this time to between the two soldiers holding Aradia. He quickly separated and launched them either side as their beams of energy missed him hopelessly.

Aradia stumbled forward in reaction, crawling to the side of the rooftop as Saeva rose to his feet, an expression of seething anger across his face. Fists igniting once more, he fired two punches into the air sending blue flames to engulf the rooftop. Aradia took cover behind a ventilation unit, peering around it to view the fight. Omen simply teleported sporadically around the rooftop, each action bringing him closer to Saeva who was becoming increasingly frustrated at his inability to make contact with his enemy.

Reaching touching distance, Omen paused to begin an assault using his cane as if it were a brutish yet elegant mace. He battered Saeva's armour before abandoning that approach and aiming solely for his exposed head. Saeva blocked each swing and fired back with a burst of flame and a column of air to fan it, forcing Omen to retreat from the encounter and teleport to the further end of the rooftop.

"Argh, hold still and fight me, coward!" Saeva roared.

Omen chuckled, immensely enjoying the irritation in his opponent.

"But then you'd win! This is my main advantage."

"Don't worry, I'll take you on just fine," a new voice called out.

It was Sariyah, entering the fight through the rooftop access door. Aradia's spirits lifted, but she could see blood partially staining her jacket. She had clearly fought her path up to aid Omen.

The absence of a snide retort from Saeva confirmed to Aradia that he no longer felt he had the advantage. As Sariyah and Omen simultaneously rushed to engage, he released a wide arc of flame, knocking both of his opponents to the ground and creating a heat that flushed Aradia's face. Omen's cane slipped from his grasp, spinning and coming to rest near Aradia. Saeva immediately strode across the rooftop aiming directly for her.

Fumbling for a grip, Aradia dived onto the cane, clutching it in two hands. Its natural hum was now far more aggressive than she had ever felt it before. It was like a caged animal of energy, clawing to be released. She held the cane toward Saeva as he arrived upon her, hoping and praying that it held offensive capabilities. She willed the magic to burst forth, adding her own to propel it.

A bright blue spark careered out of the head of the cane, impacting Saeva full in the chest. He hurtled backwards, armour smoking. Aradia dropped the cane immediately. The heat that had been created almost burnt her hands. Touching it seconds later, she saw that the vibration had stopped entirely, its energy reserves drained.

Saeva attempted to rise, but was met with a hailstorm of blows, rained down by Sariyah who straddled him, fists flying. Under the pressure he lifted his arms defensively and soon twisted his hip, flipping her over onto the ground. He stood once more as Omen retrieved his cane and Sariyah retreated, each fighter ready to resume. Even Aradia sought to summon her shadows.

Sariyah made to charge first but was interrupted by a sudden darkness that blocked out the star-filled sky and lights of the city. The blackness consumed all on the rooftop, blinding Aradia's vision entirely until it subsided. Left in its wake were at least fifteen Necromancers, each clad in the deepest black attire. At the head of them, Apathy stood firmly, blood smearing her coat and a large cut running down her left cheek. Her expression was full of malice and intense hatred.

"Next time your men throw me off a building, remind them to ensure I have expired. If you are going to kill me then at least do a thorough job of it." A tone of intense, bitter anger replaced her usual plain address.

Observing the small army of Necromancers Apathy had brought in her wake, Saeva let out a sigh and knelt, resting his hands behind his head in submission.

"A fine choice," Omen chuckled, laying a kiss on Apathy's unwounded cheek. "In time, as always, dear."

"Indeed," Apathy replied, eyes fixed unwavering on Saeva.

The Necromancers surrounded Saeva, each with their shadows ready to strike. Sariyah stalked up to Saeva, barely resisting attacking him once more.

"You'll pay for taking so many lives… you're finally going to pay." Her voice wavered slightly as the others joined her.

"I suppose, if anything, it will be interesting to discover how you Adytum rats treat your prisoners," Saeva goaded, unimpressed.

"Not very well in your case," Sariyah snarled before turning away and attempting to compose herself.

Aradia rushed to her friend and protector's side, instinctively enveloping her in a tight embrace.

Apathy was the next to address the prisoner.

"Not that it would usually concern me, but I have quite the vendetta against you people after this."

She pointed at the large slice in her cheek, infuriated.

"So now I must know, where is Lockwood based?"

Saeva chuckled.

"I wouldn't think I should tell you that. I would tell Sariyah happily, of course, in the right setting."

Aradia gripped Sariyah and held her in place as she lurched to turn and strike Saeva once more.

"Oh, that is a shame… then I suppose *we* will take you into custody," Apathy smiled connivingly, gesturing to her fellow Necromancers.

This threat caused Saeva some genuine concern. His eyes darted to the side and back.

"Well, consider this one free then. Our Bastion operates mainly in the Kisatchie National Forest in northern Louisiana."

As he provided his answer, chaos returned as Saeva suddenly kicked out, sweeping his legs around to create an incredible arc of blue flame before diving off the side of Caesars to the streets below and vanishing from sight.

22 – An Unfortunate Hypothesis

———— ∽∽ ————

The news of Dragoia's attempted kidnapping of Aradia, and the murder of a high-ranking militia commander and her subordinates had only contributed to the growing list of pressing issues Donovan was currently faced with.

He walked the halls of Caesars the morning after the attack in search of the party's new quarters, having been summoned to take care of the fallout in person. Since Omen Couture had provided him with instant transport to the scene, he had personally seen to the interrogation of any surviving soldiers under Dragoia's command, and took part in a brief meeting with the head of the Necromancy order. During this meeting they discussed the implications of the attack and the involvement of Necromancers in the search for Lockwood and his followers. It was a rather pleasing result to balance his mostly negative outlook on the current situation.

Good thing these Necromancers are so proud. An attack on their own turf has only encouraged their involvement. Did Dragoia truly not consider this?

He pondered these matters further as he arrived at the replacement room that had been provided to Sariyah and Aradia, while their original suite was "refurbished".

He knocked on the door and Sariyah answered, quickly transitioning into a respectful stoop as she registered who stood before her.

"Sariyah, can I come in? We have a great deal to decide," he began, face absent of a smile but tone friendly.

"Of course, Aradia's resting in the bedroom." She stepped back to allow him entry, still nursing a wound in her side with an icepack.

Donovan took a seat in the lounge space and let out a relaxed sigh, sitting for the first time since he had arrived in town.

"What do we know of how they are tracking Aradia? To tail you perfectly from New Orleans to Dallas to Vegas is too much of a coincidence."

Sariyah sat opposite as she explained.

"Well, before he… unfortunately passed away during the fight, Enkefalos, and Aradia too, came to the conclusion that a psychic link has been created between herself and Lockwood by means of the marking etched into her arm."

"A scar like that is rather permanent. A fiendish yet intelligent idea by whoever created this link," Donovan admitted solemnly. "Until we determine a way to disrupt the link, or deal with Lockwood, she should be moved to a secure location."

"But sir, we thought that Las Vegas would be secure, due to the protection from the Necromancers. Where else could we possibly stay?"

Donovan remained silent for a moment, contemplating the security risk he would take in sharing the location of his home with anyone other than those who resided there. After a brief pause, he continued, deeming the secret to be secure with Sariyah.

"My personal residence… it has a significant defence structure in place. Some of these features are specifically designed to hamper psychic effects and disrupt them."

With a concurring nod, Sariyah inquired, "Are you sure they're strong enough to block any connection? It's a big risk opening up your own home to possible discovery and attack."

"They're strong enough. I had them designed and implemented by the best in the business. The bond would have to be more robust than that of a pair of psychic identical twins to surpass my defences."

"Right," Sariyah smiled. "Once we're there we can work on ridding her of the connection for good."

As they reached an agreement on Aradia's new living arrangements, Apathy Crypt entered. She wore her usual attire, long black coat swaying with her step, bubbling activity emanating from within, and her boots clicking as she approached. She also had a large patch of vivid green moss pressed against her cheek – presumably to numb the pain of her recent injury.

"Consul Gesture, what a surprise to see you here so soon."

Donovan rose to meet her and shook her free hand.

"Miss Crypt, I hear from Sariyah that you are rather involved with our young Aradia's development. A pity we haven't had the pleasure of spending too much time with one another."

She flicked her head upward with indifference and continued her address.

"Yes, indeed. Now, I am developing rather the vendetta with these fanatical zealots, and I would much appreciate it if I were included in all discussions regarding tracking them down… and subsequently eradicating them, of course."

She gave a smile that was entirely homicidal as she finished speaking.

Returning to his seat, Donovan nodded for Apathy to take one of her choice, and permitted her request.

"The leader of your order has committed fully to aid in the hunting down of Lockwood and his followers. As the official liaison between our peoples it is only appropriate that you are present."

"Excellent," Apathy acknowledged and sat next to Sariyah.

Whether it was the callous way in which she spoke, or simply the body language she exhibited, Donovan didn't know, but he certainly knew that something unsettled him about Miss Crypt. He couldn't help but wonder if her apparent lack of empathy was a consistent trait, or reserved only for those who displeased her.

"So, what's our next move?" Sariyah asked, breaking the silence.

"You told me that when you stormed the church that day, one of the Deorum was in the process of physically entering this world to possess

Aradia. If that is the case, then Lockwood is perfecting his strategy and we desperately need to know how he is accomplishing this."

Apathy agreed and contributed.

"In order for him to actually summon one he would need a connection to the heavens, no? An impossible feat for all but the most experienced inter-dimensional travellers."

"Indeed," Donovan continued. "I have my suspicions about how he has managed to break the walls of reality down to summon the creature. There are places in this world where the fabric of reality is especially thin. A highly skilled dimensional traveller could possibly break through to allow passage, as long as a strong enough call was made to the Deorum so that they would hear. However, we would require empirical evidence to confirm such a theory."

"And how are we going to get that evidence?" Sariyah asked doubtfully. "There aren't many dimensional travellers left in the world and none of them work for us."

"As much as it would be difficult for her..." Donovan began, Sariyah already shaking her head in dismay, "Aradia has witnessed these creatures and felt their attraction. If anyone would be able to determine this, it's her. We must take her back to the church in Atlanta."

Sariyah held her head in her hands for a moment before inhaling sharply and sitting up once more.

"Sorry... you're right, I know it. I just wish you weren't."

"As do I, dear Sariyah."

"I can break the news to her. She's strong, she can manage," Sariyah decided. "We'll investigate the church then head directly to your residence so she's secure and can finally relax."

Donovan rose to leave and Apathy confirmed she would accompany the trip to the church with Omen as transport, should any apparent danger arise. With a reluctant sigh, Sariyah headed to the bedroom to wake and inform Aradia of their next destination.

23 – Turbulent Connections with New Faces

———

Driving… oh how I despise it," Omen complained as the scenery flashed by on the I-20 out of Atlanta.

"Honestly, this is the fifth time you have moaned since we left the city," Apathy hit his shoulder in the back of the Ford they had rented after teleporting into Atlanta proper. "You may not enjoy conventional travel, yet it is the only option available to *us*."

Omen grumbled under his breath about alleged travel sickness and turned his attention to any source of entertainment he could find out the window.

I guess for someone who can teleport anywhere they can remember instantly, regular travelling must be a strenuous exercise, Aradia pondered, gazing out the passenger window much like Omen behind her. She had remained silent for the entire journey thus far, contemplating the tribulation of returning to the scene of her terror and betrayal. While her mind was cast entirely with doubt about discovering anything of note within the church, she felt slightly more secure because she had her friends with her. They could provide capable protection or evacuation if the need should arise.

After several more minutes of travel, she spoke for the first time.

"You're sure it's safe?"

Appearing mildly surprised, Sariyah turned to her quickly and smiled.

"Of course. Consul Gesture informed me himself that the church has been abandoned ever since I first rescued you."

She cast her eyes back to the road. They had just turned off the main road and were transitioning to country lanes.

"Okay," Aradia nodded curtly, attempting to convince herself that she would indeed be *okay*.

"Don't worry, Aradia," Omen comforted, reaching forward and stroking her shoulder. "Nobody will hurt you while we're around. I'm not letting you out of my sight!"

But their surroundings, which were becoming increasingly familiar to Aradia, only served to disconcert her further. Then they turned onto the road where her mother's car had previously been ambushed by Sariyah and her late partner.

Sariyah shifted down the gears and slowed to a crawl along the dirt track that was supposed to lead to the mortal Sophie's demise. Upon reaching the end, the church loomed into view, decrepit and démodé. A surge of foreboding ravaged Aradia's confidence.

They exited the car, Omen thanking his maker that he was free from the incessant travelling, and made their way toward the door of the structure. A small path had been cleared through the rubble of the entrance way. Moving inside the church, Aradia couldn't believe it was the same structure she had seen little over a week ago.

The altar was cracked in the centre, the pulpit collapsed in, and the pews splintered and awry. The only aspect of the previously magnificent, menacing church remaining intact was its central columns, which still proudly supported the roof among the ashes of its former opulence.

Aradia gazed around the structure. The deep purples of the walls were now obscured by ash and the windows shattered. The splintered, broken nature of this place subdued the majority of her anxieties. She almost found a satisfying irony in the comparison between her memory and what lay before her now.

Despite her relief, as she approached the crumbling altar, she could not help but picture herself, innocent and exposed for the malice of ancient gods to claim. She had kept her eyes firmly fixed, either level or downwards, since they had entered, for she dared not take the chance that the image of the Deorum might still be unbroken above her.

"What am I looking for?" she asked, stopping by the altar and detecting nothing out of the ordinary during the cursory investigation.

Omen was ignorant to the sensitive information of the Adytum, and Apathy had exited the main chamber into a side room, which left only Sariyah to answer her query.

"Anything at all that feels wrong within you. Where you're standing now is presumably where reality is the thinnest, so focus on how you feel with different objects or surfaces."

Following her instruction, Aradia moved around the altar, running her hand across its smooth yet unforgiving surface. She attempted to search for any indication of celestial interference around it. Omen dusted off the contents of a table to one side, but deliberately stayed within touching distance at all times for her assurance and safety.

Footsteps echoed, emanating from one of the side chambers, heavy and striding. At first, Aradia dismissed the sound as Apathy's return – that was until she heard Sariyah's exclamation and quickly turned her attention to the source, breath caught in her lungs.

Out of a door that had been blown off its hinges stepped a man of around six foot five, human features masked by a myriad of textured armour and leather. He was dressed head to toe in soulless black and light grey, textured plating creating the effect of incredibly streamlined protective clothing. He had what appeared to be a sword strapped to his back, alongside two pistols, and a small baton at his belt. His head was entirely encased by a helmet similar to a motorcyclist, but attached to the suit and sewn at the neck.

Aradia's heart pounded, while Sariyah called out.

"Who are you? You aren't getting anywhere near Aradia!"

Sariyah's hands ignited into flame as she adopted a combative stance. Omen stepped in front of the altar, teleporting multiple times, side to side a metre apart, presumably to charge the offensive capabilities of his cane.

The masked man didn't reply, he simply observed the three people before him, assessing them as if to determine an avenue of attack.

"Answer me!" Sariyah demanded, raising her voice. Her cry summoned Apathy back to the nave. After another moment of silence, the man answered in a thick accent resembling that of northern Finland or Russia.

"Death."

He burst into motion, charging forward and drawing his sword. He made three slices at Sariyah in rapid succession, the skills of an expert blade master evident. Sariyah narrowly avoided the steel and leapt backward, hurtling a column of air after her in hope of knocking her assailant off balance. The masked man, however, seemed to move into the blast, twisting around the intense wind and continuing his charge.

"Aradia, find some cover! We'll handle this nimble ninja," Omen ordered. He teleported forward and caught the man with a sharp burst of lightning from his cane that sent him tumbling.

Aradia followed his command, ducking behind the altar but keeping an eye on the action so she wouldn't be caught unawares.

The masked man came to a stop, armour smoking, but executed a swift acrobatic flip and stood ready to engage once more. Apathy, Omen and Sariyah stood at the opposite end of the church, barring the path to Aradia, awaiting his next move. If he was such a capable attacker, they dared not test his resolve in defence.

He took a moment to catch his breath then launched his next assault. He attempted to bridge the gap between them using the rubble of the church for cover as Apathy sent a barrage of shadows forth from her coat. Apathy's defence held and he was forced to retreat behind the cover of a column. While effective, her efficiency marked her as the priority target and the masked man spun from his cover, drawing his pistols as he did so. He took two fast shots at Apathy, both of which found their mark through the shadows. She fell backward with a cry of pain and surprise as the bullets perforated her coat.

With a roar, Omen advanced into an ambush but his attack was easily deflected. Aradia watched in horror as the assailant made swift work of dismantling their party one by one.

She kept as low to the ground as possible in the hope that he would lose sight of her. As she did, she felt a sickening attraction to the floor, causing her to jerk away from it, seeking relief. She swiftly recognised that the attraction was the same one she'd felt under the influence of the Deorum.

Something is under the floor...

She took a deep breath, overwhelmed by the rush of emotion; disturbed by the return of the vile feeling in her soul and fearful for the wellbeing of her friends and her own safety.

The masked man disabled Sariyah with several jabs to the side, dominating her in the discipline of martial arts and sending her careering to the floor. With only Omen remaining, he squared off against his final opponent.

Omen teleported in various equipment to aid him in the fight, but not a single attack found purchase as the man deflected each and every swing. Backing off, Omen gave a determined grunt and dived forward. He made a feint and teleported behind the man to deliver a blow to the back of his head. Unbelievably, this manoeuvre was predicted, and the masked man spun rapidly catching Omen in a chokehold before he could register the situation. Omen attempted to teleport, but he was held fast and the lack of oxygen to his brain hampered his abilities. Instead, he flickered between locations like a buffering video.

"Stop, STOP!"

An alarmed voice unexpectedly cut through the air and the masked man immediately disengaged. He took several paces back and stood immobile, as if not a single action had transpired.

"Oh my god, I'm so sorry." The voice belonged to a young girl who had entered by the same means as the deadly attacker.

Omen staggered back, clutching his throat. Sariyah had recovered and scrambled to her feet. Then Apathy appeared, seething with anger.

The girl who now stood at the masked man's side was relatively tall, with strikingly vibrant, thick red hair that hung just below her shoulder blades. Aradia noticed it contained multiple streaks of white which complemented the stunning auburn. She wore a cherry red puffer coat, despite the heat of the afternoon.

"That bastard shot me twice!" Apathy growled. "What is the meaning of this?"

The girl had deep blue eyes that seemed to Aradia to hold a rare innocence and beauty. She spoke again, her voice full of concern.

"Please forgive me, he was just trying to protect me; he didn't know you were good guys." She cast her eyes across the group and recognised one of them.

"Oh, Sariyah!"

Sariyah took a closer look at the girl then exclaimed.

"Scarlett?! What are you doing here?"

"Trying to help investigate. Uncle Don said that the church they found may hold secrets we need to find out." She hung her head sheepishly.

Apathy strode over to her and spat her retort.

"You're lucky my underclothes are bullet proof, you gormless twit!"

"I know… I'm really sorry, I swear."

Aradia noticed that she spoke with a neutral accent – the sign of a significant amount of travel in her life – and that despite her youth, she stood her ground in the face of an irate Apathy, and didn't cower away.

Apathy strutted away to compose herself, while Sariyah gave Scarlett a tender hug. She explained the situation before expressing her concerns in her usual maternal way.

"If your uncle knew you were here and not safe at home, he would flip his lid you know."

"I know," she nodded. "I just got so sick of being cooped up there and I wanted to be useful. I know I can be. Magical history is one of my specialties."

As they spoke, Aradia tentatively made her way over, still fearful of the assassin in black. She could identify with Scarlett's frustrations, feeling trapped at home with few options for some variety in life. She spoke up.

"Umm, I think I found something by the altar, under the floor."

Sariyah nodded and made her way over to inspect, joined by Apathy and the still startled Omen. Aradia was left alone with their new acquaintance.

"I hope you weren't too scared? Vartija is just very good at his job. He really didn't mean to hurt anyone, only to protect me. I'm Scarlett by the way. Scarlett Fable."

"Aradia Vastate," she smiled slightly in return. "It's okay... I'm getting used to being attacked now. It's just Apathy who will have a hard time forgiving."

Scarlett raised her eyebrows at the mention of Aradia's name.

"I've heard so much about you from uncle. I didn't think I'd ever actually meet you in person. You're so brave for what you've gone through."

The comment brought a smile to Aradia's face, genuine and broad.

"Thank you, it's nice to actually meet someone my own age... unless you're secretly old too. Everyone around here has deceptive looks. I don't even know how old Omen is."

With a nod Scarlett clarified.

"Aha, no I'm seventeen. But Omen Couture has been a famous name for over a hundred years."

This revelation staggered Aradia, despite expecting to receive such an answer.

Speaking with someone her own age for the first time in many a month granted her a significant amount of comfort and relatability. She also felt a strange synergy with Scarlett, despite having only just met her. She felt as though they could connect somehow, on a spiritual level perhaps.

They all gathered around the altar, searching for anything of peculiar note. Omen remained uncharacteristically quiet and Sariyah spent the majority of the time hushing Apathy's regular insults and complaints, directed toward Scarlett and Vartija in particular. A couple of minutes passed before Scarlett declared a discovery.

"Here!"

She pointed to a line of inscription that ran along the very base of the altar, faded but still legible despite the damage and wear.

"It's Latin. It says, *those who seek it shall find peace in the gods.*"

Aradia knelt next to her, peering at the writing.

"What's the significance of that?"

"Well, it's one of the ancient passcodes used by the cult, dating back to Roman times, when it was first gaining traction in the magical community," Scarlett explained. "It means there should be some way to get under here."

Like an overexcited child, she frantically searched the floor around the altar until she pressed on a small slab of stone which gave way. It was the key to an unseen locking mechanism. Stone ground against stone and the altar opened up, revealing a narrow entrance down into a passageway – just big enough to squeeze a person through.

"I knew it!" Scarlett's eyes grew wide with excitement and she attempted to climb into the hole that revealed the murky depths of an underground passage below them.

Before she could progress, Apathy pulled her out by the collar and set her down beside them.

"Not so fast, I'm going first. Can't have you attacking anything else down there with your one-man army."

With an expression of mild discomfort, Apathy squeezed herself into the tunnel below through the tight gap.

Scarlett gave a slight shrug and entered next, followed by Aradia and then Vartija. Sariyah and Omen remained on the surface.

Within the tunnel, darkness consumed all. The only source of light was the entrance they had descended from, and even that provided little aid to determine what lay ahead. Even the senses of smell and hearing became useless, as the air only smelt of undisturbed musk and, apart from their breathing, all was silent.

"Does anyone have a light?" Apathy sighed, the sound of her voice emanating from somewhere up ahead.

"I'm on it!" Scarlett replied eagerly. She scuttled up to Aradia's side then, as if the Lord had spoken the first immortal words of creation, white light flooded the passage, illuminating even the most veiled crevasse and crack in the stone walls. Aradia rubbed her eyes in response to the sudden contrast before searching for the source of the light. Utterly astounded, she saw that it was the white streaks in Scarlett's hair, shining impossibly bright, that illuminated the passage – so bright that it hurt to look at them for too long.

Before Aradia could express her amazement or raise a query, the streaks of white sank down, seeping out of each strand of Scarlett's hair, and coalesced into an orb that floated in her palm, leaving her hair its natural red colour.

"Thank you," Apathy spoke without sincerity and began making her way down the tunnel.

Aradia recovered her wits and realised the meaning of the connection she'd sensed between her and Scarlett.

"You're a Vitamancer aren't you?"

Scarlett gave a nod and a wide smile.

"Yep, and you're a Necromancer. I felt it too."

Aradia grasped onto the feeling, for it was a pleasant one, and focused on the warmth and reassurance of their combined power. Before she could inquire further as to what a Vitamancer's abilities entailed, they had reached the end of the passage, which opened out into a small chamber.

Irradiated by Scarlett's light, the chamber seemed not much different to the rest of the church's sublevel – cracked stone walls, a low ceiling and musty air that made it difficult to breath properly. But, one key aspect greatly unsettled Aradia.

In the centre of the chamber stood another altar – identical to the one Aradia had found herself bound to. Atop it lay the body of a man. He was presumably deceased, given the way her shadows keenly rushed and writhed beneath her clothes.

He appeared to be in his late twenties, dressed in deep indigo ceremonial robes. He was entirely bald, without a single hair on his head, or even his arms from what they could determine.

"What is it?" Aradia asked, voice hushed, backing away slightly in discomfort.

Scarlett moved closer, inspecting the body with morbid fascination.

"I think… it's the body of a person who was touched by the Deorum once… many years ago. I read about cases like this in some of the old books my mom had."

Apathy raised an eyebrow and approached the body, resting a hand on its chest.

"Fascinating… I sense the death, yet life prevails, even if inactive. I suppose that is how they formed a connection to the heavens. They wished for you to become this man's twin, Aradia." She let out a slight chuckle and scoffed at the absurdity, as well as the conniving ingenuity. "Why leave it here for us to find?"

Still uneasy, Aradia remained silent, bemused as to what humour could be found in the situation. Scarlett theorised…

"Usually these bodies carry a lot of energy, but I can't feel as much life as I should do in this one – barely any in fact. I think it's out of battery, so to speak."

"They only had one shot. It seems our task is complete, since they failed with your sacrifice Aradia," Apathy resigned.

Aradia remained unconvinced. She wanted nothing more than to put a great deal of distance between herself and the body before her.

"We can't just leave it here. Maybe I could test it a bit in my workshop back home, then destroy it afterwards," Scarlett suggested eagerly.

Seeming equally excited by this prospect, Apathy gave a callous grin.

"Oh, of course. That would be truly fascinating." She immediately reverted to a more irritable tone. "Though this does *not* mean I have forgiven you."

Scarlett made another shrug as Vartija carefully lifted the body and hoisted it over his shoulder. The group moved back through the tunnel to make their exit. In Aradia's case, it was a much welcomed one.

24 – Riches and Wonders

aving regained his usual jovial disposition, Omen teleported them all to a rooftop in Yonkers, before hiring another mode of transport. The group had grown considerably in size, so two cars were required to facilitate their travel and they split up for the journey. Scarlett, Sariyah and Aradia were in one car and the others trailed close behind in the second.

From the city, the road north was taken into the Catskill mountains, per Scarlett's direction. As if passing over some sort of boundary, the dull ache that had occupied the back of Aradia's mind for the past few days vanished. There was not a single trace of its presence left except in memory, and this brought significant comfort to her. Sariyah drove on, and in a little over two hours they arrived at a most sumptuous estate.

The mansion itself implicitly reminded Aradia of her childhood home. It was simply more mature and understated in its prosperity, though it certainly did not fail to emphasise the abundance of its rooms, due to the innumerable windows that reflected light from the evening sun. Symmetrical in structure and layout, Aradia marvelled at its beauty. The walls of assorted, smooth cut stone; the contrast of warm orange light emanating from within, set against the grey structure... all this added to the immense impression it made.

She turned her attention to the entrance to discover yet more masked extravagance. While her previous home had an ostentatious glass doorway,

Scarlett's family abode remained steadfast and secure. Paved steps led underneath symmetrical white columns that propped up a front facing overhead balcony, which itself was overlooked by a portico that attracted the majority of her attention. In all of its robust opulence, this acted as the mirror line in which the house was reflected, and dominated the entire entrance.

"Here we are, home!" Scarlett beamed as she climbed out of the car onto the light gravel driveway, sizeable enough to accommodate the vehicles of an entire stately party. It made the two modest rentals that perched upon it look incredibly meek.

"Wow!" Sariyah chuckled, following behind, her neck craned in an attempt to view the roof. "I knew that Gesture's family was wealthy, but nothing like this."

Scarlett shrugged as she hopped onto the paved porch.

"Uncle Don doesn't really like it. I think he would happily live in a farmhouse somewhere. But it's definitely the nicest place I've ever known."

Aradia joined Scarlett's side as the others exited the second vehicle and Vartija unlocked the front door, allowing them entry into the glowing mansion. The lights had been turned on remotely in preparation for their arrival.

"I like to think of it as my princess' castle," Scarlett giggled as they entered.

Walking into the main reception, Aradia was immediately met with a space that extended all the way to the rear terrace, passing by a curling staircase and through a gallery that was overlooked by balcony walkways and modest chandeliers on the way. Scarlett immediately skipped off into the kitchen that branched off the main chamber of first floor.

Vartija made his way around to the back of the premises. The body of the young man – the harrowing image of which weighed heavy on Aradia's mind – had been retrieved from the trunk of the car and slung over his shoulder once more.

Murmurs of admiration from the group echoed around the gallery. Rather than explore on her own, and inevitably become lost in the maze of rooms and archways, Aradia followed in Scarlett's steps to the kitchen. As she did, she ran her fingers across the dark wooden Georgian style walls and took in deep breaths, devouring every sensory experience the building could muster. As a result, she almost tripped over the shoes and coat Scarlett had hastily discarded.

Aradia found Scarlett excitedly pottering in the kitchen, preparing drinks for everyone.

"You're an eager host," she smiled, watching her.

Scarlett turned, almost lost for breath to speak.

"Yeah... I don't have many guests. It's mostly just the three of us."

"Glad you're happy to have us then. I think I'm going to be staying for a while."

"Perfect, then we can get to know each other. I hope you're okay with cranberry because it's all we have in."

She poured out six glasses as Omen and Apathy took seats in the lounge which stood opposite the kitchen. Sariyah used her magic to light the fireplace and bring some warmth as the sun began to descend behind them.

An hour later, after significant drinks and revelry had been indulged in, Aradia heard footfall from outside on the terrace, and presently the French doors opened. The room turned its attention to the new arrival as Donovan Gesture entered the lounge, as passively smooth and imposing as the first day Aradia had met him.

Scarlett broke the silence first, leaving her seat next to Aradia to hug him.

"Glad you're home, but you're late for dinner. We've been waiting!"

"Sorry," he apologised. "I was a little caught up in the Adytum masking my recent actions. Then I had the journey home, of course."

The dialogue continued and Aradia listened keenly. She pondered how Gesture had managed to arrive home in such a timely manner, travelling all the way from Louisiana to New York, and as she did so, she noticed slight wisps of smoke coming off his suit jacket.

"I'm glad to see you have all arrived safely," he began, remaining standing and addressing Aradia and Sariyah specifically. "Scarlett will see you both to your respective rooms in due course. And the rest of you, of course, should you wish for a place to stay in order to be nearby – though I know distance is a fickle concept to you Mr Couture!"

Omen chuckled and Gesture continued, an increasing gravity to his tone.

"Preceding this, there are some things we must discuss regarding Aradia. I'm sorry to unfortunately make your protection the topic of debate once more," he said, glancing in her direction.

The group turned their attention to absorbing the information Gesture presented.

"Aradia should be perfectly safe here, guarded from the psychic link that was created between her and a currently unknown source. However, that does not mean we should lay off our responsibilities. Miss Crypt, if you are truly dedicated to your student, and resolute in your efforts to remove Lockwood and the cult from their position of power, I ask that you remain here with us to train Aradia to as high a level as possible in the time we have. In the event that she is discovered, it is vital she is able to defend herself – or at least until aid can be summoned.

Apathy gave a confirming nod.

"I'm more than willing." She turned to give Aradia a reassuring wink. "We're going to have so much fun together, aren't we?"

Though she knew that everyone was doing their utmost to ensure her safety, the ambiguity of what life would entail from this point forward unsettled Aradia and disrupted her feeling of security. She worked up the courage to disrupt the flow of Gesture's speech and raise a query.

"Umm, for the time we have… how long is that exactly?" She spoke tentatively, dismissing a childish thought that she should raise her hand to draw attention and await permission before speaking.

Gesture turned to her with the same respect he afforded every person in the room.

"I cannot say for certain, but I would assume at least a few weeks, while we uncover every holding that the cult has in their wicked community."

This settled her misgivings to a small degree.

I suppose a few weeks learning with Apathy and living in this incredible mansion will be good... I'm safe now... relax.

For a further five minutes or so, Gesture continued to delegate responsibilities and informed the group of his activities for the weeks to come. Sariyah was designated the task of keeping a stalwart watch on the activities of the neighbourhood and ensuring Aradia's safety, along with Vartija. Scarlett was to make certain that their new guests were satisfied with their stay and that every aspect of the house and grounds was accessible to them, should they need it.

"As for you, Mr Couture," Gesture concluded, "you are not officially affiliated with the Adytum and therefore have no responsibility to aid us. However, I am staking my hopes on your good nature and charity to aid me in a task I have down south that would be greatly progressed by someone with your specialty."

Omen nodded his assent with obvious contentment to be useful.

"As long as I'm free on weekends for my professional commitments, I'd be more than happy to help," he said. "It reminds me of some old times."

"That won't be an issue," Gesture assured. "Now, if we are all well informed, I will be in my study should anyone need me."

With that, he exited through the gallery and climbed the stairs to the upper levels.

Two hours passed by in a crawl and Aradia savoured every moment of that evening which, she decided, was her favourite so far. Scarlett and Sariyah had seen to the preparation of dinner, and the party had eaten together on the extensive rear terrace, basking in the orange glow of the setting sun. During the meal Aradia had felt the true warmth of companionship and love. She enjoyed the way each member of the group brought their unique flair and opinion to any discussion, and it created a lasting impression on her. They were a family, united by diversity. It was an experience she knew she'd never forget – especially since she had *never* felt this way when she'd spent similar evenings with her parents. Perhaps *this* was the perfect image she had been seeking for so long after all.

The discussion continued until the sharpness of the night air took over and darkness rushed in, taking them unawares. It was decided that the journey thus far had been long and that a restful night's sleep was much needed and would be appreciated by all.

"If you need me at all, I'll be out in my house," Scarlett said kindly, leaning up against the doorframe of Aradia's designated bedroom.

"You have your own house too?" Aradia chuckled, astonished at the extreme wealth this family had accumulated.

Scarlett nodded, craning her neck to peer over Aradia's shoulder out of the window.

"Yeah, it's a converted barn. My mom and Uncle Don built it for me with some help, so that I could have my own little escape."

"I wish I had one of those, so I could pretend everything didn't happen," Aradia sighed, a little hopelessly.

Even as she spoke the words, she found herself doubting their veracity. Truly, despite the significant hardship and suffering she had undergone in the past week, she found herself almost thankful that she had been thrust into this world, to meet the incredible people she had, and to escape the circle of abuse she had lived through.

"Well, goodnight then," Scarlett concluded before slipping out into the corridor. Aradia watched from her window as she strode up the lawn toward a brilliantly lit structure at the bottom of the garden.

Now alone in her elegantly designed bedroom, Aradia changed into some pyjamas and sat herself on the double bed. The walls were a brilliant white that reminded her strongly of her childhood bedroom – a room that, despite the now tainted memories of it, she had always appreciated. The impression it had created on a bright summer's day remained unrivalled in her opinion. As time passed, Aradia spent the majority of the time with her own thoughts.

I used to love being alone, free to act as I wished, nothing to control me. But now all I want is to be with people. The vice of loneliness is tightening and I've only been here for an hour.

Rapidly becoming sick of her newfound tribulations, Aradia gave herself a metaphorical slap and made her way out the room and down towards the garden.

As she crossed the luscious garden lawn, illuminated with night lights, she observed the landscape about her. Flowerbeds and bushes of a wide variety were organised into neat rows, creating pathways to follow, each confined to its space. The great treeline that surrounded the estate acted as a natural barrier to the property.

She approached the door of Scarlett's private abode, the slightly moist blades of grass tickling her ankles, and knocked hesitantly, then firmly a second time.

Scarlett's rosy face answered the call, staring at the ground for a second, entranced, before looking up with a smile.

"Oh hey, what's up?"

After a hesitation, Aradia asked, "Can I stay here for a bit? I don't know why but I don't want to be alone right now."

"Oh, of course! Come in, it's chilly out there."

She ushered Aradia in, closing the door behind her and welcoming her into the tender warmth of the room.

Scarlett's converted barn, while sizeable, constituted a single room that acted as all aspects of the small dwelling. Aradia was impressed by the natural wooden support beams that crossed overhead, retaining the building's structural integrity while acting as the basis for a balcony that spanned a third of the space, providing a ceiling of sorts to the kitchen and living area. Scarlett led her past the staircase and small bathroom, tucked into the left-hand corner by the door, and into the main space of the home – a lounge and dining room, separated by nothing but a simple pathway that led straight from the entrance.

"Make yourself comfortable, I was just about to watch a film with Vartija," Scarlett smiled, moving to the kitchen's small breakfast bar. This was constructed from the same natural wood with a granite surface, on which were gathered an assortment of stereotypical movie snacks. Vartija was seated silently at the dining table.

"Thanks," Aradia nodded in return, taking a seat in the corner of a brown leather sofa opposite the wall-mounted TV.

As Scarlett set the food on the coffee table in front, Aradia appreciated the considerable glow the room exhibited – a well-aged saffron that blended well with the natural browns of the wood.

"It's really nice here," Aradia complimented. "They did a good job of making it, your mom and uncle."

Scarlett took her seat next to Aradia, curling her legs underneath her.

"Yeah, I spend a lot of time in here… helps me to remember her."

Aradia's eyes widened a little at the realisation of tragedy.

"Oh, I'm sorry…"

"It's alright, it was a while ago now," Scarlett sighed. She seemed solemn but unaffected by the topic of her mother.

"How did she…?" Aradia began, silently swearing at her inappropriate curiosity.

Surprisingly, Scarlett answered without complaint or issue.

"She used to run the Adytum, if you can believe it. Imperatrix Emmaline Gesture – a really strong leader, but she had a lot of ideas that were too progressive and extreme I think… so a lot of people took a disliking to her."

As she spoke her tone became increasingly downcast.

"So, she went the way of Lincoln and Kennedy, I guess."

"Oh," was all that Aradia found herself able to muster in response.

"Yeah, but that was how we got this house. The job pays very well. Before, we were living all over in rentals and small houses. But she always cared for me."

Realising she had opened a set of floodgates that Scarlett wouldn't be able to close on her own, Aradia acted accordingly.

"I'm sorry, she… sounds amazing," she said, feeling it prudent to not inquire about Scarlett's father at this moment. "But you've got your uncle now, right?"

Scarlett replied with a melancholic smile.

"Uncle Don is the best too. He's always there for me and we get on more like best friends."

"That's good," Aradia smiled, attempting to bring some light back to the conversation. "You know… you're the first person I've met that is my own age in months. I didn't really have any friends before this, home schooled in the country and all."

"Really? I hope I made a good impression of a somewhat semi-normal teen," Scarlett chuckled. She showed her compassion for Aradia's plight by giving her a tender stroke on the back.

Aradia leant back a little, absorbing herself into the sofa.

"Definitely. I guess it's the fact you're a Vitamancer but I feel at peace near you."

Watching her companion's face, Aradia gave a small laugh when Scarlett blushed.

"It's been said that Necro and Vitamancers feel best rested and in tune when there is a pair of them together. I think it's something to do with the completing of the soul," Scarlett explained, masking gratified embarrassment.

"It's nice how life can work like that."

"We truly thrive off the riches and wonders this world provides. Guardians of its beauty, yet seeking shelter under its tender wing."

"Poetic," Aradia chuckled.

Scarlett shrugged with a snicker. "I try."

Leaving their discussion on a more sanguine note, Scarlett decided upon *Forrest Gump* for the film and the two watched together, each curled into their own corner of the sofa, legs overlapping slightly in the middle. It wasn't long after Forrest had arrived in Vietnam that Aradia's eyes began to droop, the exhaustion of the day finally taking precedence over her. Slowly she turned her head, the softness of the cushions aiding her descent into sleep. Resting peacefully, she would have to let Scarlett inform her of the film's ending in the morning. For now, she was content to lie, finally, in restful and undisturbed slumber.

25 – INTANGIBLE ATTACHMENT

⚬⚬⚬

As she stirred, Aradia became dimly aware of a smell – an aroma as sweet and fresh as the morning she had just awoken to. After a moment she opened her eyes and slowly sat up, realising in the process that she was neatly tucked into an incredibly warm, cosy bed atop the balcony of Scarlett's barn – the fragrance from the sheets that surrounded her.

An untroubled smile marked her face as she gazed around the upper level, spotting Scarlett curled up on a nearby sofa, a bright yellow blanket ensuring her warmth, and a pair of pink slippers protruding from underneath.

Taken aback by her new friend's kindness, Aradia slipped out from her haven and tiptoed past the sleeping girl. She smiled as she approached the stairs. She had never known anyone act in such a way for her, apart from Sariyah, and now there was Scarlett too. The lengths that some would take to make certain others were comfortable never failed to astound her. It was a trait she desperately wished to reproduce herself for the future.

"Ahhh!"

Aradia exclaimed as she reached the bottom of the stairs and was met with her own startled image reflected in the visor of Vartija's helmet. She took an instinctive step backward, but Vartija moved on, heading into the kitchen, where he set about preparing some simple ingredients, entirely unphased.

It's creepy that he never takes that suit off... but it's nice that he does the chores!

Aradia slipped out the front door and headed back to the main house. Upon arrival, she was greeted by a sight that provoked nothing but bewilderment. Omen Couture stood before her, dressed in his usual ringmaster's attire, and was busy pressing pineapples, one after another, extracting as much juice as possible into separate containers.

"Isn't that enough juice for one man?" Aradia smiled, lifting herself onto the kitchen counter and perching on the edge.

Omen turned to her with mild surprise.

"Early riser I see! And this is for a specific purpose, I assure you... I'm not *totally* insane."

"Sure," Aradia shrugged. "A magical power that I'm not accustomed to yet?"

"In a manner of speaking."

He finished his work before tidying away any spillages and joined her, leaning against the opposite counter and resting his cane atop the central kitchen island.

"Settling in fine?" he asked, nothing but sincerity in his voice.

"Scarlett took good care of me," she replied, before taking a slightly more dispirited tone. "Everyone is so nice to me and I've done nothing to deserve it."

"Oh, don't say that! After the platter of sour grapes life has served you thus far, you deserve some charity," he encouraged. "I'm glad people are treating you well. You should join me on one of my escapades sometime. I can tell just by looking that you have that *bon vivant* streak in you too."

Aradia raised her eyebrow doubtfully.

"Go on adventures? How would that work?"

"*C'est simple comme bonjour!*" he laughed. "All you need do is say the word, no need to be deterred... after the current situation is taken care of, that is."

She nodded, resting her hands in her lap. Observing him, she couldn't help but notice the unpretentious manner in which Omen held himself, despite his fame in both mortal and magic worlds. He carried himself with an almost childish glee, yet had a firm grounding in reality when it was required. Aradia wished she had such control over her demeanour.

"Can I ask a… *personal* question?" Aradia said, the pitch of her voice raising mildly in discomfiture at the request.

"Of course. Though if it's about my choice of attire, I'm afraid I refuse to dress otherwise. This suit was the height of fashion when I was younger."

A slight titter brought a degree of levity to her question.

"You and Apathy are together, but… she doesn't seem like the sort of person who would want a relationship to me. She just seems different when she's not around you."

By the expression on Omen's face she could tell this question had been asked frequently and she immediately regretted her decision to inquire.

"Apathy is a remarkable woman, and she has had a significant number of pressures in her life that have shaped her," he explained earnestly. "She wasn't always as you see her now. The Stacey Church that I met many years ago was quite the unsullied flower."

Aradia smiled, imagining times past when Apathy was young and probably somewhat naïve, like herself. It gave her hope for her future in magic.

"That's sweet, I bet she was beautiful."

Omen searched his inside pockets for a moment, drew out an antique pocket watch and handed it to Aradia.

"A cliché I know, but it wasn't when I first got it."

With a satisfying click, the latch opened to reveal a pristine watch, keeping perfect time as far as Aradia could tell. But most notable was the picture set into the reverse of the lid. It was a young girl, perhaps in her late teens or early twenties, smiling as if none could do wrong, her hair styled in a classic 1920s look.

Despite the picture having an absence of colour, Aradia could tell the girl's cheeks were blushed slightly and that she had eyes that could light a path in the night. As she handed back the watch, she couldn't seem to acknowledge that Stacey Church and Apathy Crypt were one and the same. Perhaps now they truly *were* different entities, changed with the passage of time.

"An angel, isn't she?" Omen smiled. "She still is, just in a different way." He returned the watch to the safety of his jacket.

The two remained in silence for a moment before Omen continued.

"Right well, I'm going to pop to Greece quickly and get this juice in the fridge. Back in ten!"

Aradia chuckled at the madness of it. As soon as Omen had gathered his things, he vanished, leaving nothing but air and empty space in his wake.

Aradia returned to her room and dressed in some clothes that had been provided by her host, more personable in nature than her usual handcrafted leather attire. She shared a breakfast with Sariyah and, hunger satiated, organised a 2.00pm lesson in combative Necromancy with Apathy. Then she made her way back to Scarlett's barn to see if she was awake, to thank her for taking care of her the previous night.

Making her way across the garden once more, she noticed a second structure, almost enshrouded by foliage off to the side of Scarlett's barn. The dark of night had concealed it until now. It resembled some kind of garage or workshop as far as she could tell, and she stopped near the door to the barn and turned to take a closer look. She felt an unnatural attraction and urge to investigate its contents.

I'm sure Scarlett wouldn't mind me taking a look… she didn't say I couldn't go in here; didn't even mention to me that it existed!

Her inquisitiveness consumed any better sense and she hopped off the main path and made straight for the building that had so unusually enraptured her attention.

Aradia was met with a workshop taken straight from the 19th Century and brought to the 21st. All manner of tools, unrecognisable to any mortal, hung from hooks on the walls and ceiling. Books with spines of yellow, blue and red were stacked on a shelving unit in the corner, and various workbenches lined the back wall behind a central table. The exposed wooden beams across the ceiling and naturally dusty floor all contributed to the aesthetic of a carpenter's workshop, and the room had an air of chaotic order and stability to it. Though perhaps messy in appearance, she had no doubt that every tool and splinter of wood had a place that was solely its own, and Aradia appreciated that sentiment.

Scarlett's handier than I thought. There are all manner of things in here for magical experimentation.

Aradia entered further into the space, toward a table that stood at the very centre of the room. A thick beige sheet covered what appeared to be a body. Realising where the body had come from and its purpose, she wanted to back out of the room and make her way to Scarlett, acting as if she had never entered the workshop. But she couldn't. A foreign attraction was gripping her, pulling her toward the table and she was helpless to prevent it, a slave to its wishes. She stood beside the table drawing short, rapid breaths as she felt an ethereal force increase in its intensity.

"No... no, no," she mumbled, even as she reached forward to grasp the sheet tightly, the force entirely in control of her body. As if a switch were flicked by her contact, Aradia immediately felt a sickening, draining sensation – as if all the energy in her body was being channelled through her arm and out of her. The magic in her stomach was writhing in an attempt not to be taken away, along with the rest of her lifeforce.

The body began to rise. Atrophied muscles rejuvenated, and it began to sit up, slowly turning its head towards Aradia. She screamed in desperation for any soul to hear her, but her voice sounded distant – a far off reality that was rapidly dimming, ebbing away with each second. The only reality she knew was the endless draining, then she felt the hard floor of the workshop slam into her back.

There was blackness, but for a few specs of light in her eyes, as she lay on the floor. She became murkily aware of another presence in the room – a black figure with a gleaming blade striding across the periphery of her fading vision, striking down the body that sat on the edge of the workshop table.

Energy began to return to her gradually. Her vision began to clear a little, and she concentrated hard to focus on the sight of the now acephalous body. The figure standing over it was Vartija, who sheathed his blade and observed her impassively.

"Aradia!"

Scarlett's voice rang out and her vibrant auburn hair filled Aradia's vision. She felt the immediate relief of safety.

"Don't worry, we've got you," Scarlett told her.

Still delirious, Aradia gave a weak nod and blinked, attempting to banish the spots of darkness in her eyes that sent her dizzy.

"This will help."

The brilliant strands of white in Scarlett's hair began to glow as they had done at the church. Slowly, they trickled downward, parting with every strand and coalescing in the palm of her hand. Scarlett observed the perfect sphere of light and enclosed it, forming a fist with her hand which began to glow. She pressed her open palm into Aradia's chest.

Not dissimilar to a defibrillator, Aradia received a sudden jolt of energy that brought her rapidly back into the conscious world. Her physical ailments were banished, before the light retracted into Scarlett's palm and, from there, returned to provide her hair with highlights once more.

Struggling to find words Aradia stammered.

"I… didn't…"

"Shh, it's okay, Vartija saved you. We heard the scream through the wall," Scarlett reassured her as the rest of the group came charging into the workshop, alarm written across their faces.

"What happened?" Apathy cried out. "I could sense you were in peril."

Vartija took a step back and gathered the severed head of the body, efficiently concealing all evidence of the events.

"I don't know, we heard screaming and the body was getting up when we got here!" Scarlett exclaimed. She sat beside Aradia, providing her ample space to breathe and gather her wits.

Gesture stepped forward and knelt before Aradia.

"Are you okay? What happened?"

After a brief pause, Aradia shook off the final dregs of the awful draining sensation she had experienced.

"I… couldn't stop myself. I *had* to touch the body. But when I did, I felt drained, like I was dying… and it sat up like it was being filled with life or something."

He gave a grave nod in response and helped her to her feet, assisted by Scarlett.

"How does it feel now?"

Steadying herself, she took a moment to focus on how her body was responding to stimuli at that moment. Her magic remained, and had begun to settle in her stomach and limbs once more. Apart from the psychological strain of the experience, she felt perfectly fine in every physical way that she could examine.

"I feel… normal, I think. Not even worried about the Deorum anymore, like I usually am in the back of my mind," she explained.

Gesture considered her reply.

"I'm glad you're feeling okay now, though I'm not sure what to make of this apparent energy transfer."

Apathy proffered a theory.

"If I may suggest," she began, "the body we discovered had energy – a connection that was used to open a gateway to the heavens and summon the Deorum into Aradia here, no?"

The group gave their consensus.

"This process was interrupted before the transfer was complete, and we found the body an empty husk. That whoreson fink Dragoia has been hunting our dear Aradia as if his life depended on it, presumably to resume the ritual, which would mean that the required energy is in Aradia now."

"That's why they left the body behind. They don't need it now, since Aradia has all that's required!" Sariyah finished for her.

There were murmurings throughout the group, except Aradia who remained silent, anxious about this revelation.

Apathy gave a concurring motion.

"But if now, she does not feel connected to the Deorum in the slightest, perhaps that energy was transferred back to our friend the headless corpse there, and was promptly eliminated."

In joint realisation the room became silent for a full minute, each person considering the implications in their mind. The quiet made Aradia uneasy and she shuffled slightly closer to Sariyah and Scarlett for support.

Omen broke the silence.

"So… we win? Without a source of energy to make the rift, they can't summon anything, even if they had a hundred volunteers."

Gesture dismissed this optimistic theory.

"They may have more vessels; we cannot be sure. Besides, they are still an intricately connected organisation that must be destroyed, one way or another. I will inform my people of the developments and we shall continue the search for any holdings the cult has, so we may strike simultaneously and rid ourselves of this fanatical plague for good."

26 – A Taste of Blood

The search for Lockwood's base of operations progressed over multiple weeks, and the thought of a final invasion of the cult's holdings rapidly became distant in Aradia's mind. Each day transpired much the same as the previous one, yet each held its own distinct moments that she would treasure for as long as they remained in memory.

A substantial amount of her time had been spent training with Apathy, studying and internalising the forms and morals of Necromancy to better defend herself in case of attack. Her leisure time was predominantly spent with Scarlett, where she received an education on many aspects of popular culture that she had previously been conditioned to disdain.

Nothing can ever be entirely perfect, however, and she had wished in these weeks to be with Sariyah, Omen and Gesture far more than she'd been able. Gesture and Sariyah's position within the Adytum provided an obligation to work, and Omen's natural ability had become a vital means of transportation.

During one of her training sessions, the reality of the Lockwood case became far more apparent to Aradia.

"Miss Crypt, Aradia, may I have a moment?"

Gesture approached them across the garden, the others following quickly behind and gathering in a crescent around him.

"Certainly," Apathy nodded, taking a step back and allowing Aradia a moment to catch her breath.

Gesture took a moment to ensure he had all attention focused on him before he began.

"I know it has been a long couple of weeks, but the time has finally come. I am to deliver a speech similar to this with my second, Montanaro, to the Adytum forces later today, but I thought it better to tell you all beforehand, so that you have more time to prepare."

He removed his hands from his trouser pockets as he spoke, and gave a more formal, gesticulated address.

"We have located every single stronghold of the cult in the states, including the so-called Bastion in northern Louisiana, as Saeva Dragoia kindly informed us. Today our simultaneous invasion will begin, striking at all locations and subduing them, before surrounding the Bastion and capturing it last with a bolstered force."

Aradia felt nerves travel through her body, coupled with excitement at the fact that her parents would finally face justice for the harm they had caused her and so many others before.

"Mr Couture and Miss Crypt, I would request that you both accompany me to the Bastion to set up a perimeter and allow none to leave or enter its boundaries while our attacks elsewhere take place. Sariyah, you will take a force to dispatch one of the surrounding strongholds. Scarlett and Aradia are to remain here until this situation is dealt with."

Hearing this, Scarlett seemed to silently protest through body language alone and Aradia's mind wandered.

Maybe I would be safer staying here? But I want to help – to pay back my parents for what they've done!

Apathy moved behind her and, somewhat surprisingly, ran her fingers through Aradia's hair.

"If I may be so brazen, my sublime and elfin apprentice here is quite capable. I truly believe it would be better for her to gain experience by accompanying Sariyah on one of these little hit-and-run missions."

As she spoke, she ran her hands down to Aradia's shoulders and squeezed a little. Apathy's confidence in her ability was encouraging, but Aradia thought the physical attention slightly disconcerting – especially from one as un-tactile as Apathy. What was her game?

Sighing, Gesture pondered the matter for a moment.

"I suppose if it is a markedly less dangerous location, and if Sariyah can keep her safe, then I'll allow it."

Aradia grinned and looked to Sariyah who returned it. The thrill of her first proper assignment, and the enjoyment she would receive from becoming a thorn in her parent's side, filled her immediately. She kept her countenance modest, however, sympathetic for Scarlett's dejection at being forced to remain home.

The roaring of tyres on the road thundered in Aradia's ears. Sariyah was attacking the journey at an almost unnecessary speed, escorting three transit vans that held the small paramilitary force that would aid them in capturing the stronghold they were headed to. Aradia reckoned the adrenaline and nervous energy was fuelling Sariyah's need for haste.

"I know we're about to go into more danger together, and I'm sure it will be fine but… thank you for staying with me all this time," Aradia expressed her gratitude.

Sariyah smiled, glancing away from the road for a second.

"Of course. I could never let anything happen to you."

"I really mean it. You've cared for me, nurtured me, taught me." In slight embarrassment she lowered her voice. "It's more than I can say for my own mother."

A break in the conversation formed for a few agonizingly sweet seconds and Sariyah gave Aradia's hand a gentle squeeze, honest emotion plain on her face.

"Even if we're separated, you'll never be out of thought, and always in my heart." Sariyah had a slight quiver in her voice before she refocused her attention on driving. Aradia smiled. The warmth of a mother's love and nurture provided a stability that she grasped onto. The feeling was new.

After a further hour of travel, they arrived at their location outside the Kisatchie National forest that the Bastion was reportedly located within. Parking a safe distance away, Sariyah led them on foot up to a small treeline that stood to the right side of the road and hid them from sight.

As the band of twenty Mage soldiers prepared themselves, stretching and adhering to Sariyah's every command, Aradia caught a glimpse of their target. To call it a stronghold seemed to her an exaggeration. The image she had created in her mind was sorely lacking from what lay before her.

The one street hamlet seemed practically abandoned except for the occasional resident crossing from one house to another. The options for properties to enter were limited to five. In the centre of the street, acting as the focal point to which all the houses were drawn, was a church – not as decrepit as the one Aradia first encountered, yet still lacking in care. She was certain that the interior would lack no such grandeur.

"Now, upon the call to church, we will attack, catching them all out in the street unawares. This way we can be sure that every one of these worshippers is apprehended or otherwise," Sariyah explained. She had a commanding authority to her address that Aradia hadn't witnessed before. The group affirmed.

Aradia knelt at Sariyah's side, the adrenaline beginning to fill her. Her magic was charging in her stomach, eager to be put to use through the skills she'd learnt with Apathy.

The church bells rang sharp and clear into the crisp November air and Aradia's heart skipped a beat as she counted each person to exit a house and begin heading toward the church. As she did so, a slight tickling made her involuntarily twitch her neck. She discovered the source to be Virbius, poking his head out of her jacket collar.

Thirty-two I count. We'll be alright, won't we Virbius? Only slightly outnumbered.

As soon as the door of the final house had shut, Sariyah ordered the assault to begin. Each soldier burst forward with speed and Aradia just managed to keep the pace, falling to the back of the group.

Startled and enraged faces turned toward them. A handful began to flee, while those remaining readied themselves for combat.

As the two groups collided, the cries and blasts of combat consumed the hamlet and Aradia's ears rang. Stumbling to the side against a low garden wall, the reality of battle rapidly became apparent to her. The combat was intense and hot between Sariyah and enemy Sorcerers. White hot beams of energy fired from the palms of each Mage. The combination made Aradia sweat, and she could see heatwaves simmering off the tarmac.

As terror sought to overthrow her emotions, her natural instinct was to take cover – to hide in safety and wait out the chaos. She was underprepared and ill advised. What was Apathy thinking sending her into this? The screams of death and injury pierced her to the core, and a sickening feeling began to take hold – a coldness. Her magic latched on to each death, making her aware of the exact energy signature that had passed into the next world.

She leapt behind the curtain wall and curled into a protective position, hugging her knees. Yet, as she did so, she felt disappointment and shame in her soul.

Her thoughts raced. Somehow, they were not her own. She felt a degree of encouragement from a far off, yet connected source.

A Necromancer embraces death, it is our tool, our ordnance. Do not let it consume you, use it Aradia. Use it!

The final line repeated endlessly in her head. Aradia let out a roar and the weakness the death had brought became her strength and utility. A fresh wave of courage and adrenaline seized her and she burst from her hiding place, shadows streaking down her arms and wrapping around her hands in rapid motion.

The battle progressed before her and multiple bodies were strewn across the road. Blood surrounded their remains in nauseating pools. They were mostly worshippers, Aradia noted with morbid positivity.

One such body had a Mage soldier stooped over it, his jacket spattered with blood. His dislodged helmet was failing in its duty to protect him, and a worshipper dressed in everyday attire was raising a fist to strike him.

Reacting entirely from instinct, Aradia extended her arm, allowing her magic to pulse the shadows outward to latch onto the assailant. With a heave she wrenched her arm back, drawing him in, shadows retracting, before delivering a swift punch to the sternum and forcing him backwards onto the ground.

The noise that escaped Aradia's mouth was almost a laugh of surprise, shocked at her achievement. She took a step back to avoid the man grabbing for her ankles. If there was one thing Apathy had taught her, it was that a Necromancer should always remain standing, unless making a feint.

As the worshipper began to stir from the sudden attack, Aradia's shadows practically bubbled, eager to respond to her command. She focused her magic and they embraced solidity to form thick, near impenetrable, plates around her knuckles, urging her to make her next move. Acknowledging the idea as an appropriate course of action she quickly dropped her stance and delivered a vicious blow to the man's forehead as he attempted to sit up. His head snapped back hard into the tarmac and he lay still.

"Aradia!" Sariyah's voice called shrilly in alarm, but moments too late as a crackling burst of yellow energy caught Aradia in her side and launched her several metres backward into the front garden she had previously hidden in. She rolled to a standstill on the soft grass, stopping just before the concrete slabs at the front door.

Her jacket had absorbed the deadly burning heat of the blast, but she groaned in pain from the blunt force. She attempted to rise to her feet, only managing one knee.

"A newbie like me!" a young voice laughed unnervingly. "Boy, this'll be fun."

Turning her head, she saw a girl only a little older than herself, with short brown unkempt hair. In her eyes was the unforgettable thirst and lust of murder.

Rapidly, Aradia twisted her body, launching a torrent of shadows that caught the girl unawares, causing her to let out a short scream of pain as they impacted with her shoulder. Aradia rose to her feet, confidence and impassioned anger rising, but before she could launch her second assault the girl responded. Disks of bright yellow energy formed in her palms and she launched one to each limb, trapping Aradia's feet and hands in place where they were, leaving her body open and exposed.

The girl strode toward her.

"Hmm, for that one I'm going to beat you bloody. And when I'm done, I'll drag your body to my master and I'll be rewarded handsomely."

"Try me," Aradia snarled.

"No need," she shrugged. With a vindictive smirk she launched a blast of energy, point blank to Aradia's chest, that sent her hurtling through the front door of the house and tumbling into the porch, her jacket bursting open to reveal the white cotton T-shirt beneath.

Aradia's magic swirled in her body, creating a disorienting feeling that prevented her from focusing to initiate any sort of counterattack.

The girl strode over to her.

"Such a naïve little thing. So unprepared for what we have in store for you."

Aradia struggled to make a response. The breath rushed out of her as the girl made a solid kick to her exposed stomach, causing her to curl up. Despite the futility of her situation and the pain rocketing through her body, Aradia remembered her promise to refuse surrender to anyone, no matter how steep the odds – and this was no different.

The girl raised her leg to deliver a second blow, but Aradia twisted and launched a ferocious barrage of shadows that burst from her palms and knocked the girl in the chin, catapulting her backward and slamming her against the foot of the stairs that stood behind her.

Rising to all fours and spitting onto the floorboards, Aradia didn't allow her adversary a moment's respite. She scrambled over and dived atop her, raining down a hailstorm of blows with shadow covered fists. With the technique of a boxer the girl covered her head, blocking with her forearms, and at the first opportunity locked her legs around Aradia's waist, flipping her over sideward and responding with her own struggled hooks.

In her opponent's eyes Aradia could see her own weary features. Blood from the girl's burst lip had splattered onto her. She felt her challenger's superior strength and she knew she would soon have to end this encounter lest she be beaten on grounds of endurance.

Seeking leverage, Aradia swung her leg back and drove a knee directly into the girl's hip and side, causing her to jerk back onto the hard edges of the stairs. She wasted no time in taking this advantage to dive atop her once more and gain the upper hand. The girl struggled and Aradia drew her arm back, the shadows responding to her subconscious need for survival and a desire to end the fight. They formed into a dagger of pure death energy.

Aradia brought the weapon down hard but the girl caught her wrist, the blade mere inches away from contact. Aradia grimaced and barred her teeth, growling and pouring her entire body weight into her drive downward. As she did so, the girl's resolve began to weaken and Aradia found immense pleasure in the look of fear that crept over her enemy's face – the acknowledgement of defeat.

A second later the girl's strength crumbled and failed, the knife of shadow plunged deep into her left shoulder and she screamed in agony. Aradia rose and stumbled backwards, panting, letting go of the knife which faded away into mist as she broke contact.

Tears filled her opponent's eyes and she began to cry, curling up and defensively cradling her fresh wound. The façade of aggression and brutality was utterly decimated.

Still recovering and unable to believe her victory, Aradia approached the girl. She tried to snap her mind out of its survivalist state, so she could make coherent decisions once more.

Calm... I won. She's beaten... I'm strong, now focus.

Aradia pondered the best course of action to take with her defeated assailant. She decided it best to simply knock her out and inform Sariyah of her location when the battle was done, so she could be taken in. Delivering her favoured knock-out blow with a shadow reinforced fist – rapidly becoming her signature – the girl's sobs were cut short and Aradia was left with the bloody, unconscious body of her first defeated adversary.

Outside there were calls of triumph and retreat, and Aradia rushed out of the house, clutching her aching body with one arm to view the battle's progress.

"Don't relent!" Sariyah called, weaving between the debris of buildings and the bodies of the fallen. About half the Mage force that had accompanied them to the site remained by her side. In retreat and attempting to get to any vehicles that remained intact were a handful of worshippers. Aradia grinned with relief at the overwhelming victory that had come out of the brutal fighting.

It was then that Sariyah saw a man out of the corner of her eye. Lean and in his late thirties, with dirty blonde hair, he wore an expensive suit, despite his rough shaven appearance. He was standing on the steps of the church. She could have sworn he wasn't there a moment ago.

He turned, observed the combat, and locked eyes with Sariyah. Then he vanished.

"Oh god," Aradia realised as she gazed at the empty space he had occupied. "Teleporter!"

No sooner had the words left her mouth than the man reappeared, multiple heavily armoured soldiers accompanying him. With them was a man clad head to toe in dragon scales with a cloak of the most royal Tyrian purple flowing behind him.

Sariyah moved to confront them, imminent defeat staring her in the face. Looking on in horror, Aradia rushed forward to join her friend.

"Sariyah, how kind of you to come along to this little battle as well as the girl. Two birds with one teleport!" Saeva sneered. He descended the church steps and strutted towards Sariyah. "Are we going to fight again, or are you going to save us all a great deal of time?"

Sariyah flexed her fingers behind her back. It created a wall of air that barred Aradia from coming any closer.

"You can't win, Saeva. Aradia doesn't have a connection to the Deorum anymore. She's of no use to you." Fear brought an edge to her voice, but she stood firm.

Her proclamation caused Saeva to hesitate for a moment.

"Even if I were to believe you, Lockwood would still like his daughter returned to him, and I will not accept letting both of you go again. There's no Omen Couture to rescue you this time."

Sariyah looked to the floor for a moment, her eyes brimming with tears, biting her lip. Then, with startling alacrity she spun, sweeping her leg around to release a wave of flames that engulfed the front of the church, taking all of her effort to do so.

"Go! Retreat! Full retreat!" she cried as the wall of flame began to part and Saeva stepped through.

Aradia charged forward, but was swept into the arms of a Mage soldier who rescued her from her ill-conceived action, following his orders to the letter.

"NO!" Aradia screamed, attempting to break free and reach out for Sariyah with her shadows, but her friend turned away from her in shame and defeat.

"I'm sorry," Sariyah mumbled.

Aradia wept in the arms of the soldier as she was taken back to the vans beside the road.

⚜

Sariyah faced Saeva and his forces alone.

"Well, how noble, but you realise you have sealed your own fate?" Saeva smiled, removing his mask, eyes glinting in the sunlight.

Sariyah observed those who now surrounded her – a seemingly endless amount of Saeva's personal guard and soldiers, along with a teleporter and Saeva himself. It wasn't worth entertaining the idea of a fight, for the outcome had been determined before she'd made a single move.

"Being silent with me, hmm?" Saeva continued. "I see how it is. Alright, that's fine, be childish."

Sariyah let out a long exhale and channelled her magic down to her feet. Quickly, she began to sink into the earth to tunnel to safety, but she was instantly ripped from the ground before she could sink below her ankles. Saeva's intuition and reactions were impossibly fast, and now his hand was wrapped around her throat and squeezing.

"Ah, ah… now let's not try and escape. We have so much to talk about."

Spluttering and gagging for air, Sariyah was restrained and the group adopted a connected formation for ease of teleportation. They vanished from the street in an instant, leaving only the evidence of destruction and conflict behind them.

27 – LOVE AND INTROSPECTION

———·∾∾·———

The view from the uppermost balcony of the mansion provided a spectacular view of the surrounding landscape, but Aradia couldn't care less for its beauty. Her mind stood alone and frozen; barely functioning past generic replies and basic biological processes. She was locked in a bottomless well of denial and self-doubt.

"Hey," Scarlett whispered gently, stepping onto the balcony beside her. Aradia gave no reply. A comet could have passed and she would have been ignorant to its glare.

"Hey!" Scarlett repeated, resting a hand on Aradia's shoulder and turning in to face her. "Ready to talk yet?"

Aradia gave an irresolute shrug, so Scarlett continued.

"Omen told me that the battle didn't go as planned; that Sariyah was taken. What happened?"

After a further moment of quiet, Aradia at last found words to fill the void.

"Dragoia, looking for me, and I couldn't help her," she said, deeply despondent.

"Against Dragoia! There was nothing you could have done. Sariyah knows that, I'm sure."

"Maybe, but… I don't know what to do without her," Aradia hung her head.

Struggling to find ways in which to improve Aradia's state of mind, Scarlett wrapped her in a warm embrace and lifted her head, giving as affectionate a smile as she could muster.

"We'll get her back, she'll be okay."

The two stood in silence for a few minutes more. Scarlett's warm nature providing some small relief and reassurance to Aradia, then she was alone with her thoughts again as Scarlett left momentarily to get drinks.

Staring at the afternoon sun, she drifted into a trance of earnest reflection, the world around her fading away like the stars of the morning.

What am I going to do? How am I going to fix this? You taught me about the power of this world, yet I'm powerless to change a thing; just a slave to the skill of others, ignored and trodden over. I was nothing before I met you, nothing that was worth treasuring or protecting at least. I was obsessed with prestige and perfection, all my futile actions to gain the respect of those who had socialized me to accept the abuse they dealt.

It was an existence not worth living – yet you saved me anyway. Taught me, cared for me, in a way foreign to any concept I knew before. I met the greatest people I've ever known through you. You swore to protect my life, my independence, even my naïveté and now… I don't know if I'm any different, though I should like to believe so. I know that you do, Sariyah. I won't let you down. I owe it to you to try, at least. I will rescue you, Sariyah, I swear it, or I'll die trying.

Her ruminations were brought to a close by Scarlett's return. She rested a tray of two incredibly pungent fruit smoothies on the balcony railing.

"Thought I would get something happy and summery. Might help a bit," she smiled, turning her head to the side a little and almost waiting for Aradia's approval.

Aradia turned to face her, a renewed determination seizing her.

"We're going to the Bastion; we have to rescue her."

Quickly dismissing the shocked expression from her face, Scarlett clasped her hands together. She could have lit a room with the enthusiasm she exuded.

"Oh yes! You really are amazing."

"I don't think so," Aradia sighed, the smallest of grateful smiles sneaking onto her face.

"You are!" Scarlett exclaimed, taking Aradia's hands in hers, then rapidly dropping them once she realised. "After everything you've been through, what you and others have told me, I know I could never experience so much and still have the bravery you do."

The smile grew.

"Thank you, really."

She looked at Scarlett, her pupils large and cheeks a little pink. Aradia took a moment to appreciate all that her friend had done for her over the last weeks to help her feel she belonged.

"I want to give Saeva some payback too… and I'll need you and Vartija if we're going to do this."

Scarlett stepped back and saluted.

"We are your humble soldier and medic!"

Aradia couldn't help but grin at Scarlett's preposterous ardour as she continued.

"I'll go get ready and convince Omen to let us go. You just focus on a plan, or get your game face on, or something… I don't know, but just don't worry that's all!"

Aradia watched as a highly flustered Scarlett skittered into the house. She turned her attention to the sky a final time. What Sariyah was having to endure she couldn't know, but she was confident that whatever it was, she would not have to suffer for long.

28 – ALONE AT LAST

Pain and intense strain were the only sensations Sariyah could retain a firm grip on as she hung lifelessly from a hook in the centre of the room. As far as she could remember, the two figures that stood conferring before her, dressed entirely in deep purple robes, had spent the last two hours evaluating the effectiveness of as many methods of inflicting excruciating pain on her as possible.

With the little sense she still possessed, she pondered the more humorous aspects of the experience. Through torture and plight, she found that somehow the mind finds a way to warp the experience into something positive, or at least mildly entertaining, to pass the time. Utilising this psychological phenomenon, Sariyah had determined that the woman before her preferred more physical methods of drawing her blood and cries, while her male counterpart was more interested in using techniques from the magical arts. Their differences in style proved fascinating in her irrational state of mind.

Sariyah jolted awake from her daydream as the chill bite of iced water threatened to consume her, and her tormentors observed her once more.

"No falling asleep, we're still on the clock for another ten minutes," one of them jeered.

The water provided her with a moment of lucidity. Sariyah lifted her head, attempting to see past the dripping hair that hung in front of her eyes.

The most glaring and obvious feature of the room in which she currently swayed back and forth was its intense, almost oppressive spectrum of red. The wood of the chair arms were made of mahogany, as were the counter tops that ran around the perimeter above cabinets full of books, glasses and bottles of alcohol. The furniture was 19th century and a shade of crimson or grey. Even the walls that surrounded her were red, adorned with a floral-patterned wallpaper defined by a deeper red hue.

Opposite where she was tied stood a grand stone fireplace centrally placed against a feature wall, its mantle housing various gothic statuettes. A portrait of a man Sariyah didn't recognise loomed over her, his blacked-out eyes watching blindly, ignorant of her suffering.

Sariyah's strength failed. The water had only provided her with temporary attentiveness and her neck lost the ability to continue supporting the weight of her head. Movement began anew around her and she could do nothing but stare blankly at the dark wooden floorboards and the blood that trickled downward, periodically dripping off her toes into the bucket that had been placed under her to preserve the floor. She found that a rather considerate touch.

As she let out a despairing sigh, hearing the two before her gathering their tools for the final ten minutes, the door practically burst from its hinges and Saeva roared, piercing the ears of all present.

"What are you doing you miscreant fools?!" he bellowed, striding into the room and barging between the two interrogators. "I did not permit this!"

Sariyah stared up past her eyebrows in an attempt to see what transpired. For the first time, Saeva was not wearing his signature scaled armour. Instead, he was dressed in a pristinely tailored black suit with a waistcoat and tie, the white shirt beneath gleaming in stark contrast. His stubble was neat and hair faultless. He had clearly put considerable effort into making himself presentable for some occasion.

"Master Dragoia, we were told to–"

"I don't care what you were told, now get out of my sight and do not return, lest you desire your eyes to be gouged from their sockets!" Dragoia shouted.

Convinced of his grave threat, the robed figures left promptly and nervously.

Saeva fixed the latch of the chamber door in place, his aggression quelled, and addressed the debilitated Sariyah in a gentle manner.

"I'm so sorry, my dear Sariyah. If I had known I would have come sooner, I assure you."

He carefully unlocked the metal cuffs that bound her wrists and fastened her to the ceiling hook, levering her cautiously downward and cradling her in his arms.

Lightly tumbling into his surprisingly warm embrace, the conscious part of her wished for nothing more than to escape this hell and run for the door, but she was too exhausted to make any attempt to do so.

Saeva knelt by a table to the side of one of the crimson sofas, Sariyah still supported in his arms. He took a small preprepared cloth and tenderly dabbed it across Sariyah's wounds, dressing and caring for them before laying her down on the sofa with a pillow to support her head. He knelt before her with a pitiful expression spread across his handsome features.

"We're alone at last, Sariyah. Safe… no distractions."

Sariyah's eyes fluttered slightly. She stared at Saeva, but remained silent, in a state of delirium.

"I'm here now, it's just the two of us. I had to save face before, in front of all of my soldiers. My insults were only partially sincere – you know how it is, being a leader."

The apparent honesty of his words wreaked havoc in Sariyah's addled mind. As she listened, she realised she should despise this man, but after her experience any degree of tender human contact felt like a heavenly gift.

"We can work on our relationship. I know I have much to atone for, as do you, but we can make it work this time. Let's get it right and forget all that went wrong. Forget your old family…"

As he spoke, he took Sariyah's hand in his own and gently squeezed. The warmth of his touch provided a sickening relief that she was powerless to suppress or prevent.

"They were toxic anyway… they hindered you, prevented you from blossoming into your full potential, but I saw to that. I took care of it – for *you*. You failed to see that at first, that's why I had to chase you around for so long."

His sincere demeanour cracked a little before he calmed himself once more.

"But… now I can show you why. We have all the time in the world."

Sariyah remained mute, simply absorbing the words and attempting to decipher meaning from them, be it deceit, honesty or otherwise.

Saeva's expression hardened as his phone vibrated in his inside pocket.

"Ah… just one… one moment dear."

He retrieved the source of his irritation and grunted as he read the screen before rising, straightening his suit and gazing down at Sariyah.

"I'm terribly sorry, I have a slight matter to attend to. It seems some incredibly ill-mannered intruders wish to ruin our happy reunion. We can pick this up later, once you're rested."

Her breaths steadily drawing longer with each exhale, Sariyah wasn't able to view Saeva exit the chamber as exhaustion overwhelmed her. Blackness consumed her vision and she passed out where she lay.

29 – CONFINED INVASION

S o, you're ready for this?" Omen questioned, a degree of uncertainty in his voice. "Because once I take us there it will be intense from the get-go, you know that. God… I can't believe you convinced me to enable this."

"I'm ready," Aradia affirmed, allowing herself a moment's composure as Omen fretted on the dangers of the destination.

Scarlett said the same and they all placed their hands in the centre of the group, overlapping so that everyone had a physical connection. In the brief moment of silence that followed, the nervous energy that filled Aradia and Scarlett alike involuntarily riled their magic. Shadows flowed over Aradia's hands in preparation and Scarlett's hair began to shine with brilliant white light. Vartija, for his part, remained entirely silent, still of body and mind. A soldier like him had seen innumerable battles. This was no different.

Omen looked to each member of the group and began to count down. "Three… two… one…"

Pandemonium consumed Aradia's surroundings. There were bustling soldiers in formation pacing the perimeter and distant explosions and cries of anguish scratching like a damaged recording as they teleported mid-action to the outskirts of the Bastion. Attempting to acclimatise and sharpen her focus, Aradia planted herself firmly on the ground and observed her new environment, blinking thoroughly to adjust for the contrast in light.

The Bastion resembled a perfectly normal, mid-sized town of northern Louisiana, apart from being unnaturally sheltered by miles of forest to preserve its anonymity. Within the streets ahead of her Aradia could make out the shapes of Adytum and Cultist forces locked in deadly conflict. Buildings crumbled and roads were ripped from the earth around them as they fought.

At a closer proximity was an organised base of operations. On the slim stretch of green that separated the Bastion from its protective treeline, compact and reinforced tents were placed strategically, systematically surrounding the entire town. Barricades and regular guard patrols ensured that none escaped, and the remaining army of the Adytum were also stationed here, preparing for the second wave of their attack, fifty paces from where Aradia now stood.

"The action is ahead of you. Please, please be careful. If you get into trouble, give me a call, I will find you," Omen instructed. "I need to get back in there and help Gesture and Apathy in the first wave assault. Good luck! Go get our girl back."

He tipped his hat and vanished.

Scarlett shot Aradia an expectant look, Vartija at her side, and Aradia realised that her recent strength in decision making meant she had inadvertently elected herself the de facto leader of their trio.

"Follow me. We should be stealthy and not get into any fights we don't have to," she dictated.

They sought to avoid any figures of authority from the Adytum and made their way into the Bastion through a side street, where the possibility of confrontation remained slim.

Despite their clandestine entry, the chaos and bedlam of war soon caught up with them. The remains of fallen Sorcerers and Mages decorated the street like a morbid mosaic, and the death strengthened Aradia's resolve and sharpened her vision. Its intense potency was unlike anything she had felt before.

For her part, Scarlett moved through the streets and crumbling buildings with the aid of slight natural agility and kept up as best as she was able. The blood, cries and war disoriented her greatly, but the strict parameters of their mission, and her dedication to following Aradia, gave her the focus and energy she needed to keep the rapid pace Aradia had set.

Turning sharply onto a street where the conflict had reached a pinnacle, Aradia had but moments to react as a sizzling beam of yellow energy hurtled past her. She was wrenched aside to safety by a shaft of light from Scarlett's hair that had extended outward, embracing solidity. It reeled her in and away from danger by Scarlett's silent command. The time to thank her friend sparse, Aradia immediately positioned herself behind a stationary vehicle for cover, readying her shadows for conflict. But before she could make any further move, Vartija vaulted across the hood of the car, simultaneously drawing his dual pistols. As he executed an acrobatic manoeuvre, he unloaded four shots into the chests of attacking worshippers, each one crumpling to the floor immobilised.

"He really is helpful to have around," Aradia gasped breathlessly, joining Scarlett's side as Vartija doubled back and returned to them.

"Uncle Don made sure to hire the best to protect me!" Scarlett exclaimed, raising her voice to be heard over the cries of war that echoed around them.

Without further delay, they continued their progress deep into the heart of the Bastion. The clangour of battle steadily became a faint disturbance, many streets behind them. Aradia felt confident that she and Scarlett were two of a few, if not the only, Adytum aligned Mages in this sector of the Bastion. They stopped at the end of an almost silent street to assess the situation.

"Where to from here?" Scarlett enquired, her tone hushed.

Aradia pondered the answer. She was unsure herself of which way to continue. In truth, she could hardly believe they had made it this far.

"Umm… I don't know. We need to find out where they keep prisoners."

As she spoke, Vartija nudged her shoulder, gesturing toward a building across the street. Following his direction, Aradia set eyes on a small café diner of some description, nestled between a three-story apartment building and a confectionary store. Faint sounds of music emanated from within, and she could make out figures through the dimmed windows.

"Interrogation… information," he suggested helpfully.

They crossed the street, avoiding detection. The worshippers were too preoccupied with the conflict at hand to notice anything out of the ordinary.

Standing before the faded turquoise, chipped door to the diner, Scarlett let out a prolonged and nervous exhale. Aradia tensed, almost growling under her breath, and Vartija remained silent, awaiting the command to enter.

Aradia called out and the doors burst inward, Vartija drawing his sword and forcing his way into the building. Aradia and Scarlett were quick to follow. All attention was turned toward them in an instant, but no one moved. Aradia counted ten worshippers, each sharing a bemused and bewildered look. It was as though they were shocked to a standstill by the arrogance of anyone brazen enough to venture so far into the Bastion without any kind of support. Both groups remained silent for a moment, assessing one another. The only sounds to be heard were far-off explosions and the upbeat music of the café's radio playing *King of Swords* by The Dear Hunter.

A mighty roar shattered the tension and the worshippers sprang into action, charging forward and preparing a variety of magical assaults. Avenues of attack and defence alike sprang to Aradia's mind and she found herself questioning her decisions thus far. She forced the concern to the back of her mind. Such regrets were far belated to consider now.

Confidently, Vartija sprang into action, meeting the worshippers head on. With unrivalled skill he began to dismantle his enemies with relative ease, twisting under physical attacks and utilising his blade to slice at the legs of those who dared venture too close.

Fully illuminated, Scarlett thrust her arm forward. The streaks of light that launched themselves from her voluminous hair, impossibly bright, attached themselves to Vartija, forming a protective barrier to shield him from an oncoming blast of energy. Purpose fulfilled, the lights retracted to the palm of Scarlett's hand, awaiting their next command.

As she upturned a table and fired a rapid succession of shadow blasts at her more distant enemies, Aradia acknowledged Scarlett's dedication to her discipline. Vitamancy was an almost entirely defensive craft, with very few avenues of attack, which Scarlett seemed not to want to explore.

The majority of opponents were gathered around Vartija, who was proving an admirable adversary, but towards the back of the open dining space Aradia spied one worshipper attempting to flee through the kitchen. Rising to a runner's crouch, she kicked off in pursuit of the escaping man, bursting through the double doors into a pristinely kept kitchen. As she crept close to a line of ovens, she couldn't discern any sign of the man she had chased. Assured of her ability and focused on her mission, she was fuelled by an almost arrogant fortitude.

"Where are you?" she asserted, attempting to sound intimidating. "Come out and face me!"

Met with silence Aradia let out a frustrated grunt and made to return to the dining room when the hard tile floor rushed up to meet her. The world flipped its axis as her head impacted against it. Instinctively raising her arms to protect herself, she became aware of a hand on her leg, pulling her down. A blurry figure filled her vision, something or someone straddling her and raising their arm. Despite her dazed state she managed to strike outwards, shadows lifting from the surface of her skin to strike the attacker across the chin and send them over backward.

Her mind clearing slightly, she scrambled away and blinked hard to rid her vision of the bright spots and blur that currently dominated it. Refocused, and ignoring the throbbing in the side of her head, Aradia saw her prey turned predator rising to his feet and turning to her with a flame in each hand. A Sorcerer.

Aradia dived behind the storage cabinets that made an island in the centre of the kitchen as a burst of flame engulfed the space she'd occupied. Heat seared past her face causing her to turn away to avoid its intense burn.

Instincts in turmoil, she extended her magic outward, lurching from her stomach to fingertips, attempting to sense the death created in the next room. Vartija's aptitude at ridding the earth of his foes was proving particularly useful when coupled with her ability to harness the energy released in death for her own gain. A wide grin spread across her face as she latched onto the energy. It filled her with strength and her shadows sharpened at her fingertips, forming claws of pure death.

The Sorcerer readied his second blast of flame, but his efforts proved futile as Aradia burst from cover and pounced, taking him unprepared and tackling him to the floor. Her claws carved deep wounds into his chest as she scraped and roared, the shadows tearing straight through her prey's clothing and drawing blood.

But before she could do any fatal damage, Aradia stopped herself, panting and pinning the Sorcerer to the floor underneath her, defeated and in pain.

The tumult of combat had ceased in the diner and Scarlett burst into the kitchen with Vartija. He stood over them, blood staining his armour and sword.

Aradia could smell the gore in the building and, despite the grotesquery, the macabre atmosphere strengthened her, and she almost enjoyed the feeling. Perhaps this was a natural part of her magical discipline.

After she had taken a moment to revel in these new experiences, she aggressively questioned the man before her.

"Where are the prisoners kept?"

Coughing and clutching at his wounded chest, the man spluttered in response.

"Why should I tell you?"

Rage consuming her, Aradia slashed at his leg with razor sharp shadows and he screamed.

"Where are prisoners kept?! And what are you people planning?"

Barring his teeth, grimacing, the man retained his resolve.

Vartija knelt beside them and drew his pistol, pressing the barrel to the Sorcerer's temple.

"Talk."

"I don't like hurting people if I can help it," Scarlett timidly piped up from behind Aradia. "But I know Vartija won't hesitate to kill you if you don't tell us, and there's a whole town of cultists we can get the information from."

After a moment's silence, with Vartija resting his finger on the trigger, the Sorcerer broke and confessed.

"Ugh… prisoners are kept in the courthouse, the biggest building at the north end of town. It's where everything important happens."

"What else are you are planning?" Aradia growled, raising her arm, her shadows forming a blade that jutted past her clenched fist as a threat.

The man began to laugh maniacally, then coughed with pain.

"It's probably already started!"

Scarlett pressed him for clarity, but no word or threat could disturb his mania. Using the butt of the pistol Vartija delivered a single, swift blow to the side of his head, knocking him out cold.

"What did he mean?" Scarlett asked nervously.

"I'm not sure…" Aradia mumbled.

Cautiously, they made their way outside, allowing Vartija to lead the way to ensure no one would surprise them. The door of the diner opened to reveal a thick wall of grey filling the street. Was it fog? Smoke?

They rushed into the street, surrounded on all sides by the mysterious fog that threatened to engulf and separate them if they strayed too far from one another. Aradia turned in all directions and spotted indistinct figures on rooftops, manipulating the air around them. They were causing the fog to grow denser and spread out through the Bastion.

The sounds of violence had all but ceased, but were replaced with desperate cries of isolation and fear; Adytum forces lost, confused and scattered. In the distance, at the far perimeter of the town, a shield of yellow energy shimmered and hummed with life, barring any reinforcements from entering. A significant portion of the invading force, along with their trio, were now trapped – blind in a foreign territory, with an enemy that knew the grounds expertly.

They had planned this.

30 – UNFETTERED BUT IMPRISONED

———— ∿ ————

Saeva had lied to her. A few hours later her impersonable torturer had returned – just one for this afternoon's session – an unforeseen advantage that Sariyah hadn't expected the universe to grant her, given the recent luck she had experienced. Nonetheless, the gift of rest that Saeva had granted her provided the perfect opportunity to spare herself a considerable amount of pain and humiliation.

The cloaked woman she had previously spent an extended period of time with lifted Sariyah harshly, without mercy or any sympathy for her long-term wounds. Arms stretched, she was hung once more from the hook in the centre of the room. Sariyah made no resistance, conserving every ounce of energy for what was to come.

The woman moved forward, positioning the bucket beneath Sariyah's feet in a matter of fact manner and rising directly in front of her.

"Ready for some more fun?" she sneered, her expression one of clear confidence and pomposity.

Sariyah neglected to answer, regulating her breathing and awaiting her slim window of opportunity.

"No words? We'll get you singing again, rest assured."

Her tormentor vulgarly snorted, turning her back on Sariyah to approach the table where her tools and weaponry lay.

With the flick of an internal switch Sariyah exerted every reserve of energy she had managed to accumulate during her rest and twisted her body, lifting her legs up and around the cloaked woman, trapping her neck between her thighs.

Sariyah let out a pained wheeze as she forced her legs closer together, putting increasing amounts of pressure onto her torturer's neck and windpipe, blocking her airflow.

The cultist flailed wildly, but was unable to emit any sound other than a strangled gagging. Sariyah held the pressure firmly, gritting her teeth from the exertion. She realised that she couldn't keep this up for much longer. The woman began to weaken, the slapping at Sariyah's legs lessening in strength with each blow until she barely resisted at all.

Pass out, pass out! Sariyah willed, as her efforts began to falter. From a deep-seated reserve, she harnessed all the magic she could muster and used it to strengthen the muscles in her legs for one brief moment before releasing, exhausted. The woman dropped to the floor in a crumpled heap, unconscious.

Breathing heavily, Sariyah hung, swaying back and forth over the body of her outwitted foe. She had to take a few minutes to compose herself and regain a morsel of vitality, but then let out a cry of intense effort and pain, curling inward, lifting her legs up. She relied almost entirely on her core strength, built up over years of training, until her feet rested flat against the ceiling beside the hook that the cuffs binding her wrists were attached to.

Painfully contorted and effort all but spent, Sariyah took a final moment's rest before pouring out the final dregs of her energy to channel her magic down and into the very fibres of the ceiling as if to tunnel. The plaster cracked and began to weaken the support around the hook. As it continued to splinter, she pulled with all her might, resisting the urge to scream as she did, cuffs digging into her wrists until weightless. All pressure released, she fell and impacted with the wooden floor, narrowly missing the metal bucket.

Sariyah groaned in pain, allowing herself a brief sob before rolling over to avoid any crumbling plaster from the ceiling from falling on her. The jagged metal hook now lay on the floor beside her, attached to the cuffs that still bound her. Multiple minutes passed before Sariyah managed to crawl toward the unconscious body of her tormentor to retrieve the key to her bonds and release herself.

Sariyah collapsed with her back against the sofa, attempting to stabilise herself and not reopen any wounds that Saeva had dressed. Still exhausted, she knew that in her current state she would never be able to recover to any significant degree. How would she ever escape unnoticed when she could hardly move and hadn't the faintest idea where she was? One thing was certain in her mind, which grew clearer by the minute – she would at least try. With considerable effort, she slowly and painfully rose to her feet to observe the room and search for her clothes and belongings.

31 – The Pitfalls of Hubris

It was difficult to see more than five metres in front of her as she moved through the streets of the Bastion. Aradia had been wandering with Scarlett and Vartija tailing behind for around ten minutes, yielding no progress in their search for the courthouse. Every street looked identical to the next, and the fog made the finer details of each structure around them almost impossible to discern unless they were directly in front of it.

Not only did the fog create a dissolution of bearing in her movement, it also carried with it a chill breeze that bit at any exposed skin and gave Aradia goosebumps down her arms despite them being covered. Beneath her clothes her shadows gathered around her torso to act as an underlayer in an effort to preserve warmth to the vital organs – though this came at the neglect of her fingers and ears that had already gone numb with the cold.

She turned sharply as she heard raised cries of anguish and combat, her sense of hearing heightened with the dampening of her other senses.

Noise means people fighting, and people fighting means at least some of them are on my side.

She decided to investigate the source as her best hope of finding any direction. Before investigating she turned to raise the query with Scarlett and Vartija, but all she was met with was further dense, impenetrable fog. Nerves spiking, she called out.

"Scarlett?" Then more desperately. "Scarlett!"

Anxiety bubbled within her at the lack of response. Isolated, shivering and afraid, she began to breath faster, her breath condensing in the air around her.

Where are they? Should I go back? Which way is that?

She wished for nothing more than to see Scarlett's rosy cheeks and Vartija's dark frame come running out of the fog to her, to rescue her, but no such salvation came. Blind and helpless she couldn't decipher where she had come from or which way would take her onward.

She stopped. Planting her feet firmly on the ground she let out a long exhale and attempted to refocus, assuring herself she would find her companions again soon. After a minute she decided that to retrace her steps would simply lead her to become more lost than she was already. She felt that the only appropriate course of action was to aid whoever was creating the ruckus beyond and seek their assistance in her next steps.

Tracing the sound to its source as best she could brought Aradia to an alleyway between an abandoned, partially destroyed corner shop and a block of terraced houses. Holding on to the corner bricks and peering into the smoggy darkness, Aradia could make out a small collection of figures, almost silhouetted. One was a woman, her arms spread wide, jagged tendrils lashing with a vicious alacrity at three opponents, carving them up as easily as a Thanksgiving turkey.

The sight would have horrified Aradia if she had not felt at rest in her soul. An ethereal force reassured her that the figure ahead was of no physical threat to her. Eagerly Aradia made her way into the alley, where she ran headlong into Apathy Crypt, almost toppling over with the force of the connection as Apathy caught her.

"You! What on earth are you doing here?" Apathy exclaimed. "I've sensed you have been in conflict for quite some time now."

"I'm here with Scarlett and Vartija!" Aradia blustered, relieved to be in the presence of a friendly face, despite Apathy's current scowl.

"I'm here to save Sariyah… so don't try and stop me."

Apathy tutted but didn't object, only questioned:

"And if you're caught?"

"They can't use me for their ritual, remember – nothing would happen," Aradia explained.

"If you were caught, they would realise that you are of no use to them and most likely torture you for the thrill of it," Apathy responded to her rhetorical question. "Arguably a worse fate, even if it would be an enlightening experience for you."

Aradia fell silent, unsure how to respond to Apathy's assumption, which was most probably correct.

"Regardless, it is good you are here," Apathy continued. "I was on the side of providing you with some valuable education in the art of clandestine military operations from the start. But now we're trapped, and we need to find whatever Mage is keeping this infernal shield in place, so we may swiftly force them to leave this mortal coil and win the battle."

Aradia nodded in agreement.

"Before our forces were dispersed, Consul Gesture ordered a battalion to deal with the Sorcerers sustaining this chilling fog. That leaves our focus solely on the former issue."

Recalling the information taken from the recent interrogation Aradia informed her, "If one person is keeping up this shield they're probably in the courthouse in the north end of town. That's where everything important takes place."

Without questioning her source of information, Apathy nodded and set out from the alley, Aradia quick at her heels as they strode into the streets once more.

Scouring the streets became significantly more effective with the more experienced Apathy at the lead, her shadows bursting forth from her long coat to part the fog slightly and reveal their path forward with greater clarity. Yet despite this improved searching ability, it still yielded no results as the streets became a maze. It was almost as if they had been designed to look identical, bar certain landmarks.

Apathy halted, crouching behind a public mailbox at a street corner. Aradia knelt at her side and squinted into the distance.

Across the street, a small group of worshippers dressed in blood stained purple attire were making their way deeper into the Bastion. Apart from the head of the group, each was wounded in some way or another; some limping, others clutching open wounds.

"Wounded from battle," Apathy whispered, voicing her thoughts. "Even if they don't lead us to this courthouse you speak of, being guided to their sick and wounded to dispose of them would be a rather useful endeavour."

Remaining at a safe distance, the two tailed the collection of wounded cultists to a central square and split off, concealing themselves in the shadows, watching as the cultists entered a doctor's surgery of some kind that stood on the square.

Apathy clicked her neck and rose to move toward the surgery, licking her lips as if to prepare for slaughter, but Aradia reached out, pulling her gently back into cover.

"What?!" Apathy frowned.

Having spied the object of her desire, Aradia pointed across the square through a small public park, beyond which stood a building significantly grander and larger than those that stood around it. While its finer details were hard to make out from this distance, the fog in this sector was less dense further into the Bastion, and Aradia could make out grand steps leading through a colonnade towards an entryway that clearly wished to be noticed and celebrated.

It must be the courthouse.

Apathy grumbled under her breath about priorities ruining her fun as they altered their path and travelled silently across the grass of the park toward the imposing structure.

Favouring a more covert entry to audaciously charging through the front entrance, Apathy located a side passage and a door that already stood ajar. They slipped inside and Aradia closed the door behind her.

Inside the courthouse, what immediately struck Aradia was the total repletion of purple that consumed the corridor where they stood. Just like the church that had heralded her path into the world of magic, the walls were decorated with deep indigo panels and opaque windows of a lighter, lavender hue. The quiet that descended upon them in this vacant corridor was eerie and unnerving. As they traversed it, Aradia noted the stark comparison between mortal exteriors and magical interiors. The juxtaposition of these two worlds continued to stagger her, even after all she had seen over the last month.

Before long, they arrived at the entry chamber that the main entrance would inevitably have led them into. This focal point, from which branched all the corridors of the building, had a staggeringly high ceiling – the entire space resembling a Greek or Roman temple. An internal semi-engaged colonnade made up the perimeter of the space, with a large circular mosaic in the centre of the room where a cult statue might have been placed.

Desks for a reception area lined the left-hand side of the hall by the entrance, and across the smooth marble floor from them, a large number of cultists gathered, talking amongst themselves, awaiting orders from a higher power. Aradia ducked behind one of the empty reception desks, Apathy crouching beside her.

One group of worshippers were gathered around the central mosaic. The light from the surrounding windows illuminated it perfectly. Above the mosaic, a section of the ceiling was domed, and from the centre hung a chandelier of intricate design, clearly added to increase the grandeur and ceremonial appearance of the chamber. Brilliantly gleaming silver and glistening filigree gave it the appearance of a source of light. Aradia thought it should belong in the palace of a ruler, rather than the headquarters of a group of insane religious fanatics. She also noted that the structural integrity of the feature seemed dubious. The thinning concrete of the dome looked fragile compared to the obvious weight of the chandelier.

I guess not all Mages are smarter than mortals, she thought.

"We'll have to split up," Apathy whispered to her. "Ridding ourselves of the Mage keeping the shield up ought to be the top priority… but it is clear you are here to rescue Sariyah and I cannot dissuade you from that quest."

Her usual cold demeanour softened slightly in light of the situation. It was one of the few heartfelt comments Aradia had heard Apathy give.

"Good luck, I wish you the best in rescuing our Sariyah."

Aradia gently hugged Apathy, savouring the moment before she would have to render herself alone and vulnerable once more. Initially protesting, then simply allowing the embrace, the hint of a smile crept at the corners of Apathy's mouth.

Before they could depart, there was movement in the chamber and Aradia reacted sharply, immediately seeking further cover for them. Cultists swarmed as a new arrival entered from a side corridor, breathless and afraid. Aradia listened keenly to his ranting.

"There's an unstoppable assassin and a young girl wreaking havoc in the security room. We need support over there!" he gasped, flustered and sweating. "And more forces are needed up top. One of the Adytum commanders is fighting his way towards the command centre with a few soldiers!"

Thankful that Scarlett had safely found her way to the courthouse with Vartija brought great relief to Aradia, though she worried about the forces that could imminently converge upon them.

The worshippers scattered, heading in different directions, some following the man who called for reinforcements and others heading for the elevators at the back of the chamber. Only a handful remained, on guard to detect any hostile activity.

"I'll take care of these lambs. Take to your heels, dear," Apathy said with a callous smile. She leapt from cover and strode towards the startled cultists.

Apathy's maniacal laugh echoed in Aradia's ears as she launched herself forward, sprinting into an adjoining corridor as combat erupted in the main chamber.

Roaming the amaranthine halls, Aradia quickly came to realise that she hadn't the faintest idea where or what she was looking for, and that she could quite possibly be travelling in the opposite direction to the cells. Slowing to a halt and examining her surroundings more carefully for any signage that could aid her, she continued to mull over the situation, recalling the values of her parents.

Prisoners are kept in cells. If the cells were here then, surely, they would be on the lower levels. Suitably separating the elevated and the undesirable is key to a society like this.

Decision made, she renewed her search for a stairwell that would take her into the lower levels, below ground. Making her way into the west wing of the convoluted maze of a building, Aradia happened upon a set of stairs that would lead her to her destination.

As she opened the door she paused, her attention purloined by a glance and a passing thought. To the side of the stairwell was an extended corridor with various rooms branching off. An informative plaque above each door bore a name and title, presumably of those who were beyond it. Stepping into this space, Aradia carefully examined each name, recognising none other than Saeva Dragoia above the most opulent egress.

Perhaps these are the personal quarters of the most high-ranking cultists? Aradia pondered. *Dragoia is obsessed with Sariyah. Would he keep her captive in his own bedroom? Wouldn't hurt to check…*

Cautiously she tried the handle. It was locked. Her initial thought was to use brute force to blow the door inward and take any occupants by surprise, exerting a degree of dominance when announcing her presence. But there was a risk that Saeva himself could be in the room, so she favoured a more surreptitious method of gaining entry.

Silently praying that none other than Sariyah would be inside, Aradia called upon Virbius who slithered out from under her sleeve, stretching forward and disappearing into the crack of the door. Aradia consciously directed her pet, attempting to dislodge the latch that kept the door firmly sealed. After significant, fine detailed movement, a satisfying click sounded and she smiled, slowly twisting the handle to enter the room.

Aradia opened the door the slightest amount possible, heart thundering in her chest. The room was silent. She moved further into the room and allowed the door to click shut behind her.

The intense carmine of the living space was stunning to the eye, in contrast to the purple that consumed its exterior. To her consternation, an overturned bloody bucket and handcuffs lay bare in the centre of the dark wooden floor. The unconscious body of a woman in robes lay beside them. Aradia took a step forward, approaching gradually and cautiously.

"Aradia?"

A familiar voice called out and Aradia spun around. Sariyah practically fell upon her, almost knocking her down with the weight of the embrace. Hope restored and anxiety subdued, Aradia wrapped her arms around Sariyah and the two fell to their knees, each unwilling to release the other. Tears filled Aradia's eyes.

"I'm sorry. I'm so sorry I couldn't help," she wept, her head resting on Sariyah's shoulder.

Similarly emotional, Sariyah expressed her gratitude, absolving Aradia of any responsibility in the circumstances of her capture.

"Thank you, it's okay… we're together again."

The two sustained their loving embrace for a further minute before Sariyah broke off, wiping a tear from Aradia's eye and smiling at her.

"God, I should be saying what are you doing here, it isn't safe… but I'm just glad that you are, I could never get out alone."

Aradia smiled, her heart whole once more. But the illusion of safety was instantly shattered when a bitterly smooth voice fatally impaled her confidence.

"What a happy reunion."

Saeva Dragoia smiled cruelly, leaning against the doorframe in full armour minus his helmet. In his eyes raged a sadism that chilled Aradia to the bone.

"It is truly quite adorable, but I'll have to put Sariyah back to bed now. She needs her rest. Then perhaps I could do with finding a new hook for my ceiling and hanging *you* from it, girl." He snarled at Aradia. "That ought to teach you for meddling in adult personal relationships."

Sariyah uneasily rose to her feet and stepped in front of Aradia.

"Stay back, Saeva…"

Aradia could hear the fatigue in her command and knew it was an entirely empty warning.

Disregarding Sariyah, Saeva moved into the room and stood by the roaring fireplace.

"Are we really going to fight? *Again?* Sariyah, you need to rest. You can barely stand as it is, and that whoreson girl wouldn't last a minute in a fight against me."

Taking Sariyah's hand in her own, Aradia stepped forward and took a deep breath. She released it and her anxiety along with it. She figured she had already come too far to simply surrender now.

No, she decided, *I will not let this man come between me and Sariyah ever again.*

Aradia flung her arms forward with all her might, channelling her magic through her body and careering her shadows outwards in massive pulse. They impacted harshly with her unsuspecting enemy, knocking him into the fireplace and causing the flames to fan outward.

Seizing this opportunity, Sariyah flexed her fingers and fanned the flames, to further disorient and enrage Saeva. Aradia grabbed hold of her and hustled her out of the room and down the corridor.

Hearing Saeva's infuriated growls as he climbed out the fireplace gave Aradia goosebumps as she moved as fast as she could with a wounded Sariyah, back down the corridors, wishing to be into an open space, or at least somewhere large enough to hide.

Their grace period expired rapidly and bursts of ferocious blue flame scorched the air behind them as Saeva took chase, attempting by any means to slow their escape. With the corridors narrowing and the distance between shortening, Aradia made a jerk movement and sidestepped into a chamber vacant of life and slammed the door shut behind them. Her mind raced as she desperately searched for anything to create a barricade and began to strain as she pushed a large cabinet toward the door, Sariyah aiding her from behind.

The door rattled in its frame. Saeva attempted to force his way in by means of physical strength, but Aradia pushed back hard against the cabinet and the barricade held strong. After a series of crashes against the heavy-set door, all fell silent. Breathing heavily, Aradia looked around to Sariyah for an explanation, but was cut short before she could raise a query. Wood splintered and Aradia screamed in shock as a cold hand burst through and grabbed hold of her clothing. Saeva's upper body strained through the splintered gap and he managed to wrap one hand around her throat and begin to squeeze, growling like an antagonized hunting dog.

Sariyah fell back a step and cried out in pain as she thrust her own hand forward, snapping her palm up and releasing a powerful blast of air that sent Saeva staggering and freed Aradia from his vice.

Gasping for air and eyes wide with fear, Aradia took Sariyah's hand once more and using an adjoining door, moved into the next room. Behind them, Saeva continued to smash at the door, his rage so potent that the focus needed to use his magic efficiently was wholly absent.

They were now in a regular living space of some kind. Aradia moved toward the exit, but as she did so Sariyah sagged, dropping to her knees with a wheeze.

"Come on we need to go!" she exclaimed, turning back.

Sariyah only groaned in response, attempting to rise onto legs burning with lactic acid and using muscles devoid of energy.

Saeva had broken through and was now entering the second chamber. Aradia dropped to the floor, dragging Sariyah to cover behind a sofa at the far end of the room. She held her breath for fear of detection.

"Where are you hiding?" Saeva's voice boomed. He began flipping tables and toppling chairs.

Aradia gulped, attempting to extinguish the terror that was causing her legs to shake. Saeva was rapidly losing sane, emotional control. She had no desire to experience the pain he might cause her on a regular day, let alone in his current state.

Quiet descended on the room and Aradia cautiously peered around the side of her cover. There was nothing but a destroyed room. Saeva was nowhere to be seen. Optimistically thinking that he had abandoned his search of the chamber, Aradia leant further out to investigate and felt an iron grip seize her from above. Before she had time to respond, she found herself flying through the air to crash against the wall in the corridor. Sariyah followed, rolling to a moaning stop beside her. Aradia battled the fatal plague of weariness, rising to all fours, and helped Sariyah's exhausted body to her feet.

Running once more, it was obvious that Sariyah was entirely spent. She fell multiple times as her legs failed her, and Aradia practically dragged her along the floor, draining a considerable amount of her energy in the process.

Hope resided in the main chamber she had previously entered with Apathy. As they entered the space, she saw that it lay unguarded. But that hope was immediately extinguished as a sudden, extreme gust of wind swept Aradia off her feet and launched her forward, sliding across the polished floor to the centre of the room.

She rose to her knees, spitting and gasping for breath. She raised her head to see Saeva with Sariyah in his clutches, hanging limply.

Shadows covering her hands, Aradia stood for a final confrontation, even if her efforts would ultimately prove futile. Saeva saw her resolve and allowed Sariyah to slump to the ground.

"I'll give you a fair shot at it," Saeva snarled, half laughing. "You have the first hit!"

He jutted his chin forward and stood entirely open to attack. Was he simply goading her into an elaborate counterattack? Perhaps his unyielding arrogance would truly allow her a free strike.

Aradia paused, considering her options. She stood in the centre of the mosaic pattern of the hall and released a torrent of shadows. Much to Saeva's surprise, Aradia stepped back and latched her shadows onto Sariyah's arm, dragging her smoothly across the floor to her side.

Saeva gave a casual shrug.

"On your error be it."

He began to stride toward them, blue flames ignited in his hands, a malevolent smirk across his now unsettled, unkempt features.

With death rapidly approaching, Aradia turned her attention to the domed section of the ceiling and planted herself firmly at a safe distance ready to strike. Saeva neared, stepping into the mosaic pattern, mere metres away. Sitting up, Sariyah released her final reserves of energy, roaring and throwing every ounce of strength into blasts of air and bursts of bright orange flame to stall Saeva's progress and bring him momentarily to a standstill.

Simultaneously, Aradia commanded her shadows outward. They snaked their way up to the ceiling, stretching to their greatest extent, and began to hack with razor sharpness at the chandelier attachment she noted earlier. Saeva took a firm step forward, overcoming Sariyah's savage barrage, and Aradia began to panic, twisting, twirling and slicing her shadows at the metal, attempting to weaken the already precarious support just enough to cause collapse.

Swinging his arms wide Saeva burst out from Sariyah's assault and she collapsed, spent and exhausted. He took a moment to catch his breath.

"Admirable... but not enough."

He chuckled slightly as the dust settled around him. Aradia cried out as she swung a final desperate shadow and sliced clean through the chandelier's supports. With only a second to react Saeva turned his attention to the ceiling, but was crushed under the explosive force of the chandelier, glass shattering and metal warping.

Aradia clasped her hands to her ears and turned her back briefly on the splintering glass. She turned to see Saeva struggling, pinned under the intense weight of the metal framework. He flailed and gasped, attempting to move his arms, but his efforts to escape were dilatory.

The entire dome structure began to crumble, and concrete debris tumbled, impacting with the pristine marble floor and exploding outward into smaller chunks of rubble. Each slab that fell compromised the structure around it, until the entire roof had caved in, mounting an immeasurable weight onto the chandelier, with Saeva Dragoia beneath the chaos.

Aradia couldn't remove her eyes from the mountain of marble, concrete and wrangled metal before her. Next to her, Sariyah sat and stared in disbelief. The two sat for a full minute in silence, attempting to process the events and the realisation of victory, before Aradia rose to her feet, helping Sariyah to do the same, and supporting her weight.

"We uhh…" she began, still in partial shock. "We need to get to the command centre, up top. People are fighting there and there is a shield around the Bastion barring entry to our reinforcements."

Sariyah nodded.

"Where's Gesture?"

"I don't know, but they said one commander had made their way to the command room. We need to find Vartija and Scarlett too. She might be able to help you with your injuries."

Sariyah gave the grave of Saeva Dragoia one final look, acknowledging the history between the two of them, before joining Aradia in limping towards the elevators at the back of the hall.

32 – Tribulation and Revelation

The elevator doors parted and Aradia swallowed nervously at the sight that greeted them. Before her lay an extended corridor. A wide array of jewellery and skilful works of art were on display down the entire length, which led toward a grand set of double doors at the far end. The splendour and wealth were severely marred by countless bodies strewn across the carpeted floor – Adytum and Cultist forces alike. A battle of significant proportions had taken place here. It took all the mental strength Aradia could muster not to gag due to the putrid smell.

As she exited the elevator, Sariyah stumbled behind her, almost collapsing. Aradia caught her.

"Set me down…" she grimaced, sighing and attempting to quell the fresh pain that seized her. Aradia gently brought her to rest, leaning on a nearby cabinet against the wall, away from the bodies.

"Are you okay?" Aradia asked, concerned; love evident in her eyes.

Sariyah nodded.

"Yeah, I'll be okay, just… can't go on; need to rest."

"Alright. If Scarlett comes by, she can help you. Try not to move."

A sudden series of crashes and the sound of vicious combat interrupted and startled Aradia as she spoke. The source of the disturbance lay beyond the double doors ahead.

"I have to help them in there."

As she spoke, Aradia surprised herself with the courage she was exhibiting. She decided to harness that, to bolster it perhaps, and decrease the likelihood that second thoughts would arise.

"I understand, go… kick some ass."

Sariyah managed a smile, squeezing Aradia's hand tightly before letting go like a mother whose child was leaving home. She closed her eyes in rest.

Rising to her feet and beginning to approach the doors ahead of her, Aradia knew it would be easy to simply ensure Sariyah's safety and leave the war to those with experience. But she was a part of something larger than herself now, and no thought provided her with more pleasure than that of exacting revenge.

Allowing herself a final breath before the action, Aradia opened the doors onto a room consumed with the bitter rivalry of opposing leadership. It was the chaos of battle between two veterans. The command centre, as the worshippers called it, consisted of a chamber constructed remarkably similarly to its sibling on the first floor, but on a more compact scale. Columns lined the walls and two doors into further rooms sat between them at either side. At the far end of the chamber, facing the doors by which she had entered, was a desk that spanned a large majority of the space between the walls. A man sat behind it, eyes closed, looking as if he were in a trance of some kind. Beside him, standing as ostentatiously guileful as the day they had parted, was Cecilia Lockwood, wearing a light blue full-length dress that mimicked her heartless cerulean eyes.

To her side, Apathy was backed into a corner, practically encircled by cultist soldiers with a unique insignia on their shoulders. They were poised, awaiting the Necromancer's next move, which could prove to be her last.

In the very centre of the room, fighting to determine the tide of the larger war, was Donovan Gesture, hair slick with sweat and dressed in blue padded leather, and her own father, Vincent Lockwood.

Unsure how to respond, Aradia stared on as Gesture launched an incursion at Lockwood that was rapidly deflected and countered. Her father caught Gesture in the stomach with a sharp blow and managed to twist him into a headlock, rendering him immobilised.

"So, we are *finally* reunited dear daughter!" he scorned sarcastically. "At last we may finalise your *transformation* and initiation. I shan't be long ridding us of these *irritations.*"

Aradia retained her steely countenance and snapped back for the first time to her father.

"You won't take me without a fight! Your plans are useless anyway, since I'm not even connected to the Deorum anymore."

A hint of surprise flashed across Lockwood's face, but only briefly, instantly replaced by vexation.

"*Stupid girl!* What would you know of such powers? You *dare* attempt to make me look the fool through deceit?"

"I'm serious," Aradia concealed her growing stammer. "I've learnt a lot in the last month and you can't use me anymore or ever again."

Lockwood hesitated.

"You're bluffing…" but his brief dithering provided the perfect opportunity for Gesture to resume the fight. He jerked and spun himself free, launching an upward strike that sent Lockwood staggering. Repositioning and not faltering for a second, Gesture exploited the moment of weakness to its fullest, grounding his stance, inhaling deeply and thrusting an arm forward. With a crackling intensity, blue lightning fired out from his fingers, arcing through the air and striking Lockwood in the chest so fast Aradia barely had time to register it. A belated boom followed the flash a second later.

While all eyes fixed on the newly ignited conflict, Apathy let forth a torrent of shadows which split into multiple tendrils, striking or impaling her nearby opponents, and chaos resumed in the chamber.

In wake of the events around her, Aradia locked eyes with her mother who thus far hadn't responded to a single occurrence since she had entered – only impassively observed. With a cry of ferocious energy, Aradia charged, shadows flowing out onto her fists as she did so. Finally, she would deliver the just desserts her mother was owed – for her own innocence, for all of her fallen siblings before her. Then the entire world crumbled before her.

"Aradia, don't!" Donovan called, but to no avail. Aradia froze where she stood before her mother. Both were silent, holding an unbreakable eye contact. Understanding the psychic trance the two were now engaged in, and as he watched Lockwood rise to his feet, Donovan vowed to end this conflict then free Aradia from her confinement if she could not manage the feat alone.

The two rivals shared a moment of intense, burning silence, each awaiting the other's action. Donovan made the first attack, throwing his arms back and utilising his magic to propel himself forward. Rocketing toward Lockwood, he brought round a fist crackling with lightning for a square blow, but his savage attack was countered. Lockwood slid back and raised his hand, catching the punch in a disc of yellow energy, sparks flying as the two connected.

Lockwood pushed off, firing in response a thinly concentrated, deadly beam of energy that narrowly missed Donovan's head going over his shoulder. Pre-empting a second attack, Donovan spun, striking Lockwood with the back of his hand and moving back to create distance between them to disrupt his enemy's flow.

Growling in anger, Lockwood ducked low, sending a flat disk of energy that lodged under Donovan's left foot, causing it to sink into the ground to his knee, forcing the other leg to buckle unexpectedly. Donovan made a motion to repel Lockwood, who approached with confidence, but his defence was cut short as a chain of sizzling yellow fastened around his wrist and anchored to the ground behind him, leaving only one arm unencumbered.

A final blast came hurtling towards Donovan that he caught in an open palm, absorbing the attack, protecting himself with the use of wild electricity once more. An incredible thundering echoed around the room as a result. Constant deflections built the rage in Lockwood as he strode forward.

Another chain bound Donovan's remaining limb and gripped him by the throat. Lockwood spat as he raved.

"Why won't you just die?!"

His hands lit with the same intense yellow and began to burn. Grunting in pain, Donovan scowled and gritted his teeth, straining against the bonds that held him in place, eyes beginning to crackle with their own sparks of power.

The pain sharpened, but it only served to augment the growing strength and variety in Donovan's counters. Eyes scintillating, twin streaks of lightning shot forward and electrified his adversary, peeling the skin in arcs across both cheeks and catapulting him across the floor.

With a roar and sudden strength fuelling him, Donovan forcefully brought his arms together, shattering the bonds that held them and lifting his leg from the cavern Lockwood had created. Before he could advance, however, the doors to the sides of the chamber burst open, and a small battalion of cultist reinforcements poured in from both angles.

Breathing heavily and refocusing her efforts, Apathy turned to face the new onslaught, heavily outnumbered, while Donovan jerked back, reached over his shoulder and released a jagged torrent of lightning from his fingertips toward the crowd of worshippers. Each bolt found its mark, electrifying those at the front of the group before relaying to others further back with a domino effect. Those who avoided the agony of lightning were almost equally stunned by the sonic boom that followed the attack.

The light faded and Donovan exhaled, energy rapidly draining from him with the use of his abilities. The remaining reinforcements surrounded him and Apathy. Both now backed into the centre of the room.

"Up for a little more?" Donovan asked, while inwardly questioning his ability to continue for any prolonged period.

"Always. If you die, I'll simply use the release to bolster my own attacks and conclude this business in your absence," Apathy stated plainly, masking her own state of weariness.

Donovan raised his arms ready for the resumption of conflict.

"How pleasant…"

A great burst of flame disrupted the group around them, diverting their attention to the entrance of the chamber.

"Let's at least make it a fair fight," Sariyah called, vitality restored and revitalised. Scarlett was beside her, hair alight, and Vartija with guns drawn.

Donovan stared at his beloved niece, primed, confident and with a grin of astronomical proportions across her face. He would have questioned and chastised her presence, had he not been so thankful for it.

Armed engagement resumed. Vartija fired multiple shots before drawing his sword and beginning a frenzied assault on his ill-prepared victims. Sariyah expertly partnered with Scarlett, trading off the shields and boosts she provided to send bursts of flame at any who neared, proving deadly when sufficiently motivated. Apathy positively cackled as the tide began to turn in their favour, shadows racing through the air and carving up her enemies with an almost harlequinade glee.

Lockwood rose once more, blood dripping from his chin and fury consuming his face. Donovan released an incredible surge of energy, lightning streaking from his hands and crackling across his entire body, launching him into the air. Flying above his enemy, he soared downward, grasping Lockwood by the collar and hauling him into the air to hover over the concluding battle below.

Struggling in Donovan's grasp, spittle flying, Lockwood began to hurl insults, but only a scream escaped his lips as Donovan channelled electricity through both their bodies, scorching Lockwood and causing his muscles to spasm uncontrollably. A few seconds passed and Lockwood fell limp, exhausted.

Donovan's pale blue eyes sparked with power and he let the fallen priest go, falling and falling until he slammed onto the hard floor, groaning then lying still. He gently descended and stood over the priest, his lightning beginning to burn out. He was near to exhaustion himself, having used his inherited talent for such a prolonged period. As Lockwood spat blood onto the floor before him, Donovan turned his attention to Aradia and her mother. They still stood like statues, locked into a psychic link that needed shattering, once and for all.

The world crumbled around Aradia and she fell, accelerating until she felt virtually weightless in a dark existence where nothing survived but her mind – and even that was beginning to become distorted in the darkness. A spec of dim light formed ahead of her, or below her – she found it impossible to tell – but it rapidly grew in size, coming closer and closer until she impacted with the ground.

Feeling no pain or damage to herself, Aradia sat up, perplexed and afraid. Surrounding her was a seemingly endless blank plain of wilted grass, but even that seemed to have no substance to it, only illusion. Recognising the phenomenon, Aradia called out, almost desperately.

"Where am I? What is this place?"

Her mother's voice pierced her previous confidence with brutality and Aradia spun around to face her. Cecilia stood ten paces away, dressed in the same flowing silk garments she had worn in her dreams.

"Why am I here? Tell me!" Aradia demanded, glowering with hatred.

An infuriating laugh echoed throughout the entirety of Aradia's current reality as her mother chided.

"Why, it's your own mind. The inner depths, or the astral plan as we psychics enjoy calling it."

Aradia stared in disbelief.

"I'm not sure what it is you are gawking at," Cecilia continued condescendingly. "I thought it rather obvious that I made this link with you. We've spent many a night together over the past few weeks. Until you became guarded, that is. I would have expected you to solve this particular puzzle by now, but you never were the most intelligent girl."

Indignation rising within her, Aradia growled.

"I'm a far better person now than I ever was under your poisonous influence."

That same vexing laugh.

"Are you sure? Even now, you're play acting. You think I don't know when you are putting on a brave face?"

Aradia began to feel meek before her.

"This, my dear, is all you have ever done. You reproduce the expected, *desired* behaviour others impose on you, because of your insatiable need to be liked and garner attention. You are no different with your new 'friends' than you were with me. It is an unfortunate truth I must dawn on you, that you are a rather pitiful creature in your habits; the useless, troubled daughter of a lineage corrupt and deceitful."

Her mother's words burnt holes in Aradia's spirit as her self-esteem ebbed away, and she could do little to prevent the rebuking.

"I know where I come from... the Aradians have a legacy written in legend!" she protested, her voice raised to mask her feelings.

"You truly believe that your family were always so hallowed? That your father was the one to break the mould and strike out? Heed me when I say the Aradians were corrupt for centuries in the shadows, worshipping the rightful gods rather than the betrayers. It was simply your father who brought his beliefs to the forefront and gathered a true following."

Aradia faltered.

"And you – you are hardly worthy to carry such a name, girl. You inherit so much, yet present so little. A mere Mage, hardly aware of the true potential you hold within. Even Vincent falters on that measure."

Without mercy she concluded her scathing affront.

Aradia shook tears from her eyes, the realisation of truth causing her to question her own motivations and purpose.

It can't be. It can't...

"Oh, but it is," Cecilia sneered.

"No!"

Aradia's anger reached a peak. Her self-esteem now stemmed from her own experiences, not that of her dysfunctional family. Sariyah's love and Scarlett's immortal words echoed within her.

"I won't be your plaything anymore. I don't care what you claim. I don't care what you think. Maybe my family were cruel, corrupt and forsaken… if that's the case, then may I be the one to redeem them. You won't deter me. I know who cares for me, who *knows* me. You never even took the time to try."

Displeasure consumed her mother's fair complexion and she began to walk toward Aradia domineeringly.

"Listen to me you wanton fiend. It has become clear to me that I didn't provide painful enough punishments for your insolence to inspire true obedience. If I had done so, perhaps we would not find ourselves in this situa–"

Her piqued address was harshly interrupted by a cry of anguish and Cecilia Lockwood crumpled to the floor. The field shifted and shimmered. Aradia stared in disbelief watching her mother twitch as if electrocuted. She began to hear familiar voices calling her name… Scarlett, Gesture.

Light flooded her vision and a splitting pain seized her mind. A hand grasped hers and she blinked away the pain, taking in her surroundings. She was back in the chamber, being pulled back to safety at the side of Gesture. Perplexed and disoriented, all seemed quiet as she adjusted to reality.

As the final dark spots faded from her vision Aradia saw the bodies that were strewn across the chamber, her friends beside her and her parents before her. Her father was wounded with blood-soaked features, but he was upright. Her mother was shaking off the residual effects of electric shock.

The silence was crippling and the heat between the two sides was tangible in the air.

Vincent uttered the first word.

"This fight was a worthy one… bravo Adytum *rats*, I grant you victory on this occasion. Take our soldier."

The man at the desk, who had not moved an inch since the conflict had started, remained with eyes closed, entirely unaware of the world around him.

Cecilia Lockwood had crept closer to the desk and flicked a switch underneath it. Vincent stepped back and took her hand.

"Now we must be leaving," Vincent said. "It is a shame you cannot follow the trail of a teleport or it would provide an interesting chase."

As he spoke, two figures appeared out of thin air behind him, one standing tall, the other bound and hunched.

Aradia grinned and a familiar voice rang out softly into the air with an unmistakable showman's flair.

33 – A Morbid Victory

Omen chuckled, releasing his captive who tumbled to the floor, hands and feet bound. Aradia could plainly read the exhaustion and humiliation on the man's face.

"I heed your call and present to you your thrall, dear Lockwoods. I do apologise for not being here sooner, I know it was imperative. But I first had to deal with my antagonistic relative."

He smiled gleefully as Vincent and Cecilia Lockwood spun around in shock to face him.

Anticipating their movements Omen swung his cane forward, striking Cecilia with the butt across the face, sending her staggering backward. Vincent attempted to charge but Omen simply evaded the indolent attack and released a short burst of power from the cane's head that sent Lockwood spiralling over the desk, falling to his knees before Gesture.

"Arrest me then!" he squirmed. "My followers will never disperse. They will always come for me!"

Pitifully observing the broken man, Gesture sighed heavily and gave a nod to Sariyah who swiftly covered Aradia's eyes and turned her away. Bemused as to the meaning of this, Aradia thought to raise a query until a sickening, deafening snap rang out, reverberating inside her mind and caused her stomach to churn.

She turned in time to witness the body of her father topple lifelessly to the floor, and Gesture step away solemnly.

"Nooo!"

A piercing scream filled the air.

"Heathens! Such savage and virulent vermin!" Cecilia screeched. A seething rage poured out of her in the form of an instinctual psychic attack that drilled into Aradia's head with intensity.

Impassioned fury overtaking her mother, the pain Aradia felt in her head ceased. It was replaced by gut-wrenching shock as Cecilia dived forward, grasping one of Vartija's fallen pistols. She fired a shot into Aradia's abdomen.

Aradia's ears rang and she felt nothing for a moment after the intense pain of lead piercing her skin through an opening in her jacket. She fell back and time slowed. The floor loomed but she was caught in Sariyah's arms and gently lowered to rest. A white hot pained seized her at the entry wound and blood began to pump at an alarming rate.

Dazed and in shock, Aradia stared on as her friends swarmed her mother in rage, only to be met with an empty space. In the confusion, the bound teleporter had managed to get a hand to her ankle and teleport them to safety elsewhere within the Bastion.

"Aradia, don't worry, it'll be okay, I've got you." Sariyah stammered, putting pressure on the wound. Aradia began to moan as the aching and burning increased.

"Get back!" Scarlett called, pushing through and dropping to her knees next to Aradia, terror across her face. "It won't last long, I can fix this."

Aradia sincerely hoped and depended on the accuracy of Scarlett's claim as she groaned and tears filled her eyes. She took rapid, shallow breaths.

Scarlett's hair began to glow once more, the light trickling downward and forming a sphere in her hand that she rapidly pressed into Aradia's fresh wound. The purity of the light mixed with the intense red of her blood.

An instant numbness descended upon her abdomen, silencing the majority of the pain. Scarlett appeared to have a look of immense concentration as Aradia began to calm slightly with the relief. All gathered around the two, keeping a safe distance while observing the process with keen concern. Scarlett's hands worked with an incredibly organised and practised skill, as if she were sewing a great tapestry.

After multiple minutes, the light began to fade, returning to her hair. Scarlett sat back, holding her breath in anticipation.

Aradia felt markedly relieved, with only a dull ache ailing her. She gazed down at the wound. Across her midriff was a small scar. It was still raw, but firmly closed. Apart from the blood that stained her clothing and the bullet in Scarlett's hand, all seemed to be regular and in order. Aradia nodded and exhaled, breathing normally.

"You're okay?" Scarlett enquired.

"I think so…" Aradia nodded, smiling slightly as she looked into Scarlett's watering eyes.

Scarlett laughed breathlessly.

"Oh… thank god. Oh, I did it!" Emotion overwhelmed her and she sobbed and leant forward, pressing her warm lips to Aradia's, closing her eyes.

Stunned and unsure how to react, Aradia simply allowed this to continue until Scarlett broke contact a second later and sheepishly sat back, blushing intensely.

"Well…" Omen began, breaking the tension. "This was an eventful five minutes."

Apathy hit him in the arm and he protested as each member of the group checked on Aradia's wellbeing. Gesture moved away with Vartija to break the trance of the Mage at the desk and arrest him.

Sariyah helped Aradia to her feet and stayed by her side as they watched the fog clear and the mighty shield disintegrating from the window behind the desk.

The impression left on Aradia's lips was a warm and pleasant one. The situation had never occurred to her as a possibility. Indeed, the concept had yet to even cross her mind. Yet, she knew that it felt incredible. She turned slightly, viewing Scarlett out of the corner of her eye. She was in the process of shyly cleaning herself up with a pack of wipes Omen had retrieved, cheeks still flushed red and Aradia smiled at the sight. The feeling within her was somehow different when she considered Scarlett. She wasn't entirely sure what it was, but Aradia knew she would very much like to find out.

Adytum forces began to trickle into the chamber, gathering fallen comrades and enemies alike and searching for survivors amongst the ruins of the courthouse. As Omen gathered everyone in the centre of the chamber, Aradia watched as her father's body was piled onto a stretcher and taken away. The sight provoked in her a degree of sadness, but she knew the pain he had caused to so many. She felt mostly indifferent to his passing, rather than revelling in the fulfilment of revenge, as she had previously anticipated.

"I think we all…" Omen began, indicating Scarlett and Aradia. "… and especially our intrepid and inspiring youngsters, deserve a good rest. If any who do not have further business here would like to accompany me…"

Scarlett took Omen's hand and looked up at him, Vartija following alongside. Omen looked to Aradia expectantly. Tentatively, Aradia took Scarlett's free hand and squeezed, nervously exchanging a smile before the familiar environment of Gesture Manor came into view in an instant.

34 – The Hearts of You and Me

C omfort, peace and a fresh drink. Those were the three things of most vital concern to Aradia at this moment in time. She had awakened to a remarkably, almost impossibly warm afternoon for November in New York State, and decided to take advantage of her good fortune with the weather. She sat alone on the rear terrace of Gesture Manor, staring at the sunlit sky in a plain T-shirt and shorts, with an empty glass in one hand. With the other she shielded her eyes from the sun as she gazed upward.

Her luxurious repose was briefly interrupted as Omen Couture and Apathy Crypt exited the main house and came up behind her. Omen on the right shoulder and Apathy the left.

"How's my second favourite Necromancer doing this fine afternoon?" Omen enquired, his regular jovial tone particularly elevated.

"Good," Aradia chuckled. "I thought you had both left already."

"My, my, you should know it's far more troublesome to rid yourself of me than that. We're simply taking a short holiday," Apathy smirked. "Though it appears you have beaten us to that goal already by the looks of you."

Aradia shrugged and turned to face them both.

Omen casually took Apathy's hand and addressed Aradia with sincerity.

"We just had to say before we left that we're really proud of you for what you accomplished and fought through the other day at the Bastion. Truly."

"Yes," Apathy agreed. "Your efforts were… admirable."

Touched, and finding it increasingly difficult not to blush at the compliments, Aradia hugged them both. Omen returned the warm embrace and Apathy allowed it.

"Thanks Omen, for being the most fun and awesome celebrity and person I've ever met; and Apathy, for teaching me everything I know about Necromancy and being ironically caring through your insensitivity."

Apathy rolled her eyes and gave a slight chortle.

"We shall see you soon, dear Aradia. Don't procrastinate while I'm away. I expect you to have improved your skills upon our next meeting."

Nodding insincerely, Aradia waved and watched as they vanished into thin air. For all the incredible reality of teleportation, its visual effects were greatly underwhelming.

Left alone once more, Aradia sat back and stretched. In the silence her mind began to wander. She reflected on the recent battle and tribulations she had faced. She thought about the fact that her mother's whereabouts were entirely unknown. But then she stopped herself.

Enough stress, enough turmoil. Even if there are still questions to be answered, they can wait a day at least. Let's just focus on the good in store for the future, and the good of the present. Though… there is one question outstanding in terms of…

Exiting onto the garden path toward the barn, Scarlett hurried past, auburn hair flowing.

"Scarlett!" she called, leaping from her seat and chasing her down, stopping in the centre of the path.

Scarlett turned to face her. The faultless white, lightweight dress she wore only accentuated her radiance to Aradia, and complemented the streaks in her hair. She held herself as though she had been accosted by Aradia, and seemed embarrassed and awkward.

"Y… yeah?" she stammered.

Attempting to broach the subject of her heart's desire, Aradia stumbled slightly with her words.

"Can we… talk about it? You know. We'll have to eventually… get things straight."

Scarlett nodded in agreement quickly, trying to avoid Aradia's gaze.

"I'm sorry… I just really like you," Scarlett blustered. "I think you're so amazing for being as you are after all you've been through, and I just feel right when I spend time with you. I have done since we met. Back there, I think I just let my emotions get the better of me…"

Her tone was almost despondent, and Aradia barely stifled a giggle at hearing the words ring true. Forcing herself to take a more serious tone, she gently lifted Scarlett's head to look at her.

"Well, make sure it doesn't happen like that again."

Scarlett nodded, downcast.

Unable to contain her glee, Aradia laughed.

"If you're going to kiss me, I want it to last longer!"

As she spoke, she wrapped her arms around Scarlett, pulling her close and kissing her softly, holding the embrace.

As they kissed, Aradia felt all the warmth of a summer sun course through her. The almost lightning connection of their lips excited her in a way she had never felt before.

After a significant time, Aradia at last broke away, smiling widely, Scarlett staring in disbelief, cheeks flushed as red as her hair.

"You're mean," she protested. "Trickster!"

Aradia shrugged and they hugged tightly.

"Guilty."

As they parted, Aradia could practically feel Scarlett's love in the air, it was so potent, and the excitement between them for a future was unbreakable. The feeling was entirely foreign to Aradia, but more welcome than any she could have possibly imagined.

Aradia spent the rest of that day enjoying it to its fullest, exploring the full grounds of the manor with Scarlett, playing chess with Gesture before he left on an important call, and finally searching out Sariyah as the sun began to set in the sky. She eventually located her on the same balcony she had looked out from when Sariyah had been captured. She had conflicted feelings over this particular part of the house.

"Heya," Aradia smiled, joining Sariyah's side, looking at the orange glow in the distant sky. "How are things?"

Sariyah returned the smile and explained solemnly.

"Well, the Adytum is running wild. Gesture is dealing with the fallout of the siege of the Bastion – mostly a success – but they don't have the first clue as to where your mother fled, only theories. They think she may have gone to the cult cells that are spread across Europe, as we've all but eradicated them here in America."

Aradia nodded, listening intently before interjecting.

"But how are *you* holding up?"

With a slight chuckle Sariyah answered the actual question.

"Ah, I'm recovering. Happy to be off duty for a little while to rest."

"That's good!" Aradia exclaimed. She was confused as to why she detected a hint of sadness and fear in Sariyah's intonation.

"Yeah it is… but they cleared out the rubble from the courthouse. Saeva's body was gone. He's escaped somewhere. I'm not sure how I feel about that," she explained gravely.

Truth uncovered, Aradia gently linked her arm with Sariyah's.

"We beat him before and we can do it again – and we'll be even more experienced each time he comes. When we defeat him again, we'll make sure he is definitely… *definitely* dead."

She attempted to lighten the mood and lift Sariyah's spirits, despite the fact that the possibility that Saeva was alive somewhere unsettled her greatly. Her efforts seemed to bear fruit.

"You're amazing, you know that?" Sariyah encouraged. "You've really matured so much from the girl I lifted off that altar and put to bed in my spare bedroom!"

Aradia couldn't help but agree.

"I feel like a much better person being away from the fatal influence I was under before… though there was something my mother said. I'm not so sure…"

Sariyah raised an eyebrow.

"I'm easily led. I fit to the group. I have an undying need to be liked and a desire for attention…"

Sariyah waved her hand dismissively, then gave Aradia's shoulders a gentle shake.

"Nonsense. Everyone can be a little bit like that. But you're strong and very introspective, you'll figure it out, I know it."

The two stood in silence for a few minutes, the cold rapidly encroaching as the sun began to disappear behind the treeline ahead of them. Aradia felt nothing but security beside her companion.

After a short while, Sariyah struck up conversation once more.

"Do you know where you'll be staying for the future? Even if you don't act like it, you're only a teenager!"

"I'm… not sure. I hadn't actually thought about it yet," Aradia mumbled in response.

"Well," Sariyah proposed, "I was thinking of getting a little place near here in a nice quiet old town. You could come and stay with me if you want, have your own room and live like a relatively normal magical shadow-wielding girl, aside from the adventures."

A wide grin broke out across Aradia's face.

"I'd like that a lot!"

Sariyah wrapped a tender arm around her, pulling her close.

Standing with Sariyah, wrapped in her embrace, watching the shimmering twilight, Aradia felt an urge within her. It was the desire to tell Sariyah what she had been meaning to for quite some time, but had never found the place, time or courage to do so. At Sariyah's side she felt nothing but the brilliant, unconditional care a mother provides; the kind of love she had always read about, but never experienced in her own life. She deliberated over the thought for several silent, internally agonizing minutes, before finally working up the courage.

"Jessica?" she began. The use of her seldom-heard real name, startled her friend. "I feel so much more with you than I ever have from anyone before. Nobody cared for me or protected me from danger like you have… and I always feel safe with you even when we're in peril."

Jessica listened without interrupting, her head slightly angled, taking in the heartfelt endearment.

"And I know," she continued. "That no matter what strife we may go through, wherever we may be… that we can always find a home in the hearts of you and me."

She felt her voice quiver slightly, and she finally spoke the words she had never found the reason or truth to tell another before.

"I love you. Thank you, for everything."

A sincere smile and watering eyes encapsulated the gratitude and emotion Jessica felt from the declaration. Her reply came with total confidence.

"I love you too, Sophie. I love you too."

Dramatis Personae

Sophie Lockwood: Cultivated innocence and pomposity to its fullest. While authoritarian in her views, an inward strength aids her resistance to the wicked influence around her.

Aradia Vastate: True nature revealed, she tries her utmost to be a moral person after her experiences, but still holds doubt over the genuineness of her intentions. She is yet to realise her full potential.

Sariyah Pierce: An eager young officer recently returned from extended personal leave, the reasons for which are shrouded in mystery. Her affection for those she cares for is boundless, and beneath her inherent skill lies a true insecurity.

Donovan Gesture: Head Consul of the southern Adytum, and steadfast in his physique and manner. He has significant backing from most members of the Adytum and is the favoured successor to the Imperator. Yet, family commitments and trauma dissuade him from accepting such a position.

Apathy Crypt: A peculiar blend of Machiavellian deceitfulness and insensitive candour, her intentions with regard to her new apprentice seem somewhat dubious. However, with a troubled history, solace and emotion is found in the presence of her long-term partner.

Omen Couture: Flamboyant and charmingly eccentric, he remains one of only seven teleporters still alive. His intentions are assuredly pure in every action, and he is one of the only people to hold celebrity status in the mortal world as well as the magical.

Scarlett Fable: Young and endearingly positive, with mostly pacifist views, she wishes to unlock the secrets of Vitamancy to become the Adytum's most treasured and skilled battlefield medic.

Vartija: Professional bodyguard and assassin, hired for an annual fee from a magical black-market agency. He has expert knowledge in a myriad of combat and survival techniques. The composition of his seemingly impenetrable and irremovable armour is entirely unknown.

Allier Montanaro: The second Consul of the southern Adytum, and closest friend of Donovan Gesture, his mistrust of the current authority could not be more apparent in his actions. Harbouring secret sympathies, it is only conjecture to accuse him of treason, though perhaps it is not entirely false.

Chesil Orotund: Current Imperator of the southern Adytum and successor to the revered Emmaline Gesture. While not entirely incompetent in his abilities, most consider him to be a malignant narcissist, gaslighting his way into the upper echelons of magical society.

Neurrira **and Amona Latebras:** Well respected tailors that have mostly left their magical days behind them. Despite her kind and sage-like demeanour, Amona holds grave secrets of the past and a history of adventure deep within.

Saeva Dragoia: The suave and capricious higherup within the cult, and obsessive ex-lover of Sariyah. With alarmingly murderous tendencies when denied his desires, he is easy on the eye, but is truly jaded with malice in his soul.

Cecilia Lockwood: Cruel and vindictive, she raises her children with the fear of punishment being a primary motivator, and with the express purpose of either inducting them into the cult, or preparing them for future sacrifice. One of the most powerful psychics that history has recorded, she remains at the top of the Adytum's most wanted list.

Vincent Lockwood: Equally callous, though less personally involved than his wife, he is marked by years of scheming and holds the hallmarks of an expert extremist speaker. While he concealed his true abilities for years, he pales in comparison to the potential his bloodline provides, and has passed this to his daughter.

CHARACTER THEMES PLAYLIST

The songs that helped inspire each character:

Aradia Vastate
Tah Dah! – Dirt Poor Robins

Sariyah Pierce
Psychotica – Bootleg Rascal

Apathy Crypt
Devil's Flesh & Bones – Eliza Rickman

Donavan Gesture
Leave Me Alone – IDKHow

Saeva Dragoia
Maker of My Sorrow – Eliza Rickman

Omen Couture
Friend Like Me – Aladdin Original Broadway Cast

Scarlett Fable
Riches and Wonders – Eliza Rickman

SARIYAH'S MIX

All music mentioned in the series plus some assorted others, for use as a soundtrack.

Printed in Great Britain
by Amazon